A LESSON IN MURDER

Detective Reyes nodded at Sandra, appreciative of the fact she was such a fountain of information. Then he turned back to Maya. "Who is your client?"

"I don't have to tell you that," Maya said.

Reyes gave her a withering look.

"But I will," Maya said. "My daughter. She wanted me to find out who was responsible for the site because she was afraid all the anger and finger-pointing was just going to get worse."

"And you called nine-one-one?" Reyes asked Maya.

"Yes, right after I found the body."

"She wrote a suicide note. It's pinned to her sweater. She explains everything, how the guilt became too much for her," Sandra piped in excitedly. "I can only imagine how she must have felt after seeing the consequences of her vicious website."

"I don't think she felt guilty about anything," Maya remarked.

Reyes looked at her curiously. "Why not?"

"Because I don't think this was a suicide."

"What? But the note . . . ," Sandra said.

Maya shrugged. "We don't know for sure she wrote it."

Books by Lee Hollis

Hayley Powell Mysteries

DEATH OF A KITCHEN DIVA
DEATH OF A COUNTRY FRIED REDNECK
DEATH OF A COUPON CLIPPER
DEATH OF A CHOCOHOLIC
DEATH OF A CHRISTMAS CATERER
DEATH OF A CUPCAKE QUEEN
DEATH OF A BACON HEIRESS
DEATH OF A PUMPKIN CARVER
DEATH OF A LOBSTER LOVER
DEATH OF A COOKBOOK AUTHOR
DEATH OF A WEDDING CAKE BAKER
DEATH OF A BLUEBERRY TART
DEATH OF A WICKED WITCH

Collections

EGGNOG MURDER
(with Leslie Meier and Barbara Ross)
YULE LOG MURDER
(with Leslie Meier and Barbara Ross)
HAUNTED HOUSE MURDER
(with Leslie Meier and Barbara Ross)
CHRISTMAS CARD MURDER
(with Leslie Meier and Peggy Ehrhart)

Poppy Harmon Mysteries

POPPY HARMON INVESTIGATES
POPPY HARMON AND THE HUNG JURY

Maya & Sandra Mysteries

MURDER AT THE PTA
MURDER AT THE BAKE SALE

Published by Kensington Publishing Corp.

Murder at the PTA

Lee Hollis

KENSINGTON BOOKS
www.kensingtonbooks.com

KENSINGTON BOOKS are published by

Kensington Publishing Corp.
119 West 40th Street
New York, NY 10018

All Kensington titles, imprints, and distributed lines are available at special quantity discounts for bulk purchases for sales promotion, premiums, fund-raising, educational, or institutional use.

Special book excerpts or customized printings can also be created to fit specific needs. For details, write or phone the office of the Kensington Sales Manager: Attn.: Sales Department. Kensington Publishing Corp., 119 West 40th Street, New York, NY 10018. Phone: 1-800-221-2647.

Kensington and the K logo Reg. U.S. Pat. & TM Off.

First Kensington Books Mass Market Paperback Printing: October 2020
ISBN-13: 978-1-4967-2448-9
ISBN-10: 1-4967-2448-8

ISBN-13: 978-1-4967-1987-4 (ebook)
ISBN-10: 1-4967-1987-5 (ebook)

10 9 8 7 6 5 4 3 2

Printed in the United States of America

CHAPTER ONE

Sandra Wallage stood behind the podium on top of a wooden box so her five-foot-three frame could be seen above the microphone into which she was about to speak to the auditorium full of parents. This was her first major address since being elected as president of the parent-teacher association. She had been working on her speech all week, crossing out paragraphs, rewriting whole chunks, obsessing over every word that she planned to utter in order to avoid any unnecessary conflict or controversy, which wasn't easy when it came to the South Portland High School PTA.

There was also her innate fear of public speaking that took hold way back in high school, when she was named valedictorian of her class and was tasked with speaking on behalf of the entire student body. She opened her mouth to start her speech and burped.

Loudly.

Right into the microphone.

Damn that plate of nachos she had devoured with her girlfriends, in their caps and gowns, an hour earlier at the Mexican restaurant down the street from their school.

Everyone in the audience burst into uproarious laughter. Students, teachers, parents, everyone. It was her most humiliating moment up to that point in her young adolescent life. After they had all managed to calm down, Sandra was able to mutter her way through her speech, ignoring the titters from her fellow students, and, yes, even a few insensitive adults, and then as she stepped down off the stage, she vowed then and there that she would never put her fragile self-esteem at risk like that ever again.

But now, all these years later, public speaking should have been second nature to her. She was the wife of a United States senator representing the great state of Maine. She had attended hundreds of luncheons and fund-raisers where she was almost always expected to say at least a few words. But she found that it never got any easier for her. She had tried every trick in the book, even picturing the whole audience in their underwear to calm her nerves and make the ordeal a little bit easier, as her son once casually suggested. But that never really worked either. Nothing ever worked. She felt nauseous every time she was asked to step in front of a microphone.

And yet here she was, one more time, standing in front of two hundred people, all ready to hang on her every word, and all she could think about was the run in her stocking. She had noticed it right before the school principal, the dashing John Hicks, had introduced her. She couldn't help but glance down at it now, the small almost imperceptible imperfection. She always worked so hard to be the perfect wife, the perfect mother, the perfect PTA president, and for the most part, she certainly looked the part. Her freshly pressed designer white skirt suit from Nordstrom, her elegant matching Salvatore Ferragamo bow pump shoes, her impeccable coiffured blond hair, everything, all of it was working.

Except for that ignoble, irritating run in her stocking.

Sandra took a deep breath.

Just because you always expect to be perfect doesn't mean everybody else does.

She smiled out at the audience.

You can do this.

"Good afternoon. Thank you, Principal Hicks, for that warm and gracious introduction. Parents, teachers, students, welcome to our first PTA meeting of the fall semester at South Portland High School!"

The applause gave her the opportunity to glance down at the stack of index cards she was holding in her hands.

There was a lot to cover.

Parent involvement.

Budget approval.

Fund-raising ideas.

She then commenced to plow through them all, covering every topic on her agenda, telling herself to slow down as she raced to get through to the end.

She stumbled a couple of times, tripping over a word here, a word there, looking up, red-faced, only to be met with friendly, understanding smiles. That relaxed her a bit. Then, down went her head again, eyes fixed on her index cards until she was holding the last one in her hand.

"So in conclusion, let's all work together to make this year at SoPo High the best one yet!"

The auditorium erupted in applause.

That was it.

She was almost done.

Just a five-minute question and answer session and then she would be home free.

The first question was an easy one about the new football uniforms.

"I'm happy to report the uniforms have been ordered and will arrive before the homecoming game in October," Sandra reported, smiling.

Next, a breathlessly excited mother shot her hand up in the air with an inquiry about the fall musical. "I heard they might do *Hello, Dolly!* Is that true? I love that musical, and although I'm biased, I think my daughter, Jana, would be the perfect Dolly Levi!"

Sandra caught a few eye rolls from the other parents.

She had to suppress a smile.

"I'm not sure our director, the ridiculously talented Georgina Callis, has selected which musical the theater department will be staging this fall, but please keep checking the school's web page for updates."

Sandra resisted the urge to check her watch.

She was eager to get out of there but didn't want to let on that she was in too much of a rush to wrap things up. She wanted to give the parents all the time they needed.

A father stood and asked if there was going to be a spring trip to Paris for the French class after what happened last year with the temporary detainment of one student for attempting to draw a mustache on *Mona Lisa* at the Louvre with a magic marker.

"That was an isolated incident, so I see no reason why this year's class should be punished. . . ."

Suddenly Sandra heard a bunch of cell phone alerts ringing from all over the auditorium. She hadn't seen this many phones going off since she and her husband were at their son's Little League game way back in 2010 when word went out all over the world that a SEAL team had nailed Bin Laden. Whatever the news was, it sounded awfully important.

There was a lot of urgent whispering and murmurs as people looked down at their phones. Sandra was now dying of curiosity and wanted to step off the stage and fish her own phone out of her bag to see what had everyone buzzing.

"If there are no more questions . . ."

A woman, with bright red hair and a color-print blouse that was so loud it practically screamed, solemnly stood from her chair with her hand raised.

"Yes, I have one."

Sandra waited expectantly as the woman took a deep breath and glanced down at her phone, which she clutched in her right hand. "Would you like to address the latest headline on Dirty Laundry?"

Sandra sighed.

She was quite familiar with Dirty Laundry, a gossipy website that had popped up recently, solely focused on salacious scandals relating to people involved with SoPo High—students, teachers, coaches, even parents. It was a no-holds-barred trash bin full of rumors and innuendos, none of it backed up with any meaningful evidence. And despite the school's best efforts to unmask the identity of the site's creator, so far they had had zero luck.

Sandra didn't want to give this putrid site any more oxygen, but as she gazed across the auditorium at the shocked faces of the parents in attendance, she couldn't help but finally ask, "What are they saying *now*?"

The redhead with the ugly blouse cleared her throat,

swaying from side to side uncomfortably as she gathered up her courage to speak. "If you don't mind me just reading the headline . . . ?"

Sandra nodded.

Permission granted.

" 'New PTA President's Senator Husband Uses Taxpayer Money to Hush Up Blockbuster Sex Scandal.' "

Sandra grabbed both edges of the podium with her hands to keep from falling.

The words were like a gut punch.

The whispers and murmurs stopped.

Two hundred people stared at her, waiting for her reaction.

She opened her mouth to speak.

But nothing came out.

She had absolutely no idea how to respond.

She just felt her face flush with embarrassment. Her knees were so wobbly she wasn't sure if she would even be able to walk out of there.

"I . . . I . . . ," Sandra stammered.

Finally, knowing it was a lost cause, she leaned down into the microphone, and through deafening scratchy feedback, managed to get out, "I'm sorry. . . . Excuse me. . . ."

She fled to the wings of the theater and out a side door as she heard the principal, John Hicks, speaking into the microphone she had just deserted. "Thank you all for coming . . ."

CHAPTER TWO

Sandra stumbled out of the building and directly into the large, sprawling high school parking lot. It was dusk with limited visibility as the sun dipped and disappeared in the west. She squinted at the rows and rows of cars parked all around her and couldn't immediately spot her silver Audi A6 sedan. Sandra frantically rummaged through her purse for her car keys, finally managing to extract them and press down on the remote to unlock her car. She heard a chirp just a few rows away and followed the sound till she mercifully saw the flashing red lights on her Audi as she pressed down on the remote again a few more times with her thumb.

Her head was still spinning from the shock of the lurid Dirty Laundry headline, and she felt dizzy, but she fought to remain calm in order to get herself home and out of public view. She was a U.S. senator's wife. It was critical she maintain her dignity and not collapse to the ground, weeping uncontrollably. It was exactly what she wanted to do at the moment, but alas, that was just not an option.

As she reached for the car door handle, she suddenly stopped. Behind her, she heard shouting. She spun around to see the assistant principal, Maisie Portman, having a loud argument with another woman. Maisie was small in stature, a real spitfire, and her round freckled face always seemed to be on the verge of anger no matter what the topic she happened to be discussing at the time. Her abundance of black curls always seemed to be bobbing up and down as she spoke. If anything, Maisie was a loyal soldier to her boss, Principal Hicks, which was why Sandra was surprised Maisie wasn't inside the school at the moment, by his side, ready to jump to his defense if need be.

No, she was outside, yelling at a woman Sandra didn't recognize. Perhaps she did know her, but it was almost completely dark now with the sun already below the horizon, so it was a miracle Sandra could even make out Maisie. Sandra watched the two women going at it for a few seconds, not quite sure if she should make her presence known, but then the unidentified woman violently shoved Maisie up against the side of a parked van, and her hands wrapped around Maisie's throat. Maisie struggled to push the woman away, but she was too tiny; the woman was about a foot and a half taller than she was.

Sandra rushed forward. "Stop it! Let her go!"

The instant the woman heard Sandra, she released her grip on Maisie. Maisie, embarrassed, glanced over at Sandra, who was fast approaching them, and quickly exchanged a look with her assailant. Maisie stepped forward, in front of the other woman, and her mouth broke into a friendly smile.

"Good evening, Mrs. Wallage. So nice to see you," Maisie said in a calm, reassuring tone.

"Is everything all right, Maisie?" Sandra asked, suspiciously eyeing the woman behind Maisie, who was trying to slink away and disappear into the darkness.

"Oh, yes, everything's fine. No problem at all. We just got into a heated discussion about something silly really, nothing important."

Sandra stepped closer toward them, trying to get a good look at the woman. "Hello, I'm Sandra Wallage."

"Nice to meet you," the woman muttered. "I better go. I'll see you later, Maisie."

And then she scurried away without introducing herself.

"Who was that?" Sandra asked, turning back to Maisie.

"You don't know her. I better get back inside in case John needs me," Maisie said, running off, her black curls bobbing.

Sandra considered chasing after her in order to find out exactly why that woman had her hands around Maisie's throat, but then she caught sight of dozens of parents pouring out of the school and into the parking lot. The PTA meeting had officially been adjourned, and she was about to be surrounded by curious busybodies all eager to hear what she had to say about the latest Dirty Laundry claim.

Sandra dashed back to her car, jumped in, and roared away. When she was safely off school property, she pulled into a vacant lot next to a closed warehouse where she could have some privacy and shifted the gear into park. She grabbed her phone off the passenger seat and scrolled down the Dirty Laundry article about her husband's alleged sexual harassment scandal. As she suspected, it was short on facts and long on gossipy innuendo and unsubstantiated speculation. Still, the fact that the mere suggestion was out there was not good. She decided it was time to call her husband, who she knew was in Washington, DC, probably in the senate chamber at the moment.

After a few rings, she heard a man answer gruffly. "Yes?"

It wasn't Stephen.

It was his young aide Preston Lambert.

Sandra couldn't stand the kid. He was smug, overly ambitious, and as her kids liked to call him, "A real slimeball." But for some reason, he was indispensable to Stephen, who refused to fire him despite his off-putting and cloying personality. What Sandra hated about him the most, however, was just how irritatingly patronizing he was to her.

"Hi, Preston, it's Sandra. I need to speak to Stephen right away."

"Well, hello, Mrs. Wallage. It's so nice to hear your sweet, friendly voice this evening."

Liar.

He knew damn well Sandra wasn't sweet or friendly when it came to him.

She hated him.

"It's an emergency," Sandra said coldly.

"What kind of emergency?" Preston gasped, playing along.

"I'd really rather discuss it with Stephen, if that's all right with you."

"Of course. I understand," he said.

She could picture him sneering on the other end of the line.

"The only problem is," Preston drawled, trying his damnedest to be sympathetic and understanding but failing miserably. "He's down the hall just a few seconds away from being interviewed by CNN on the floor vote."

"I don't care, Preston. I need to speak to him right now. Put him on," Sandra demanded.

"Oops, there he goes. He's on live right now with Anderson Cooper. You don't want me to interrupt him while he's talking to Anderson Cooper, do you?"

Sandra sighed. "How long is it going to take?"

"Shouldn't be more than five minutes. They have to cut to a commercial at some point, right? Just hold on. We'll wait together."

Preston let a few moments go by before attempting a little small talk. "How are the boys?"

"They're fine," Sandra said, refusing to offer any more.

"Stephen showed me pictures. I can't believe how much they've grown! They're young men now!"

"Yes," Sandra said through gritted teeth.

Preston finally got the message and stopped trying to engage her in a conversation. After a few more minutes of awkward silence, Preston said cheerily, "He just wrapped up. Sit tight. I'll put him on."

Sandra waited just a few seconds before she heard the laconic, soothing voice of her husband, Stephen.

"Hey, honey, what's up?"

"Have you heard about what Dirty Laundry is saying about you?"

"Wait . . . hold up. Dirty what?"

"Dirty Laundry . . . I told you about it when you were home a couple of weekends ago. It's that awful site that targets people connected to the high school, putting out clickbait by drumming up scandals and headlines, some true, some fake."

"Right. I remember. So what are they saying?"

Sandra clicked over to the site and read her husband the headline.

There was a long silence.

"Are you still there?" Sandra asked.

He let loose with a hearty laugh. "You've got to be kidding me . . ."

"No, I'm not. It says so right here in front of me."

"That's the most ridiculous thing I've ever heard. There is not a shred of truth to it."

Sandra believed him.

She *had* to believe him.

Otherwise, then where would she be?

"It came out while I was delivering my welcome speech as the new PTA president. It really threw me. I didn't know what to say, so I got out of there. I'm sure Principal Hicks is furious with me for bailing, but I just had to talk to you and get your reaction."

"And you got it. Don't sweat it, babe. Even if the mainstream media somehow picks it up, once people figure out it's all lies, they'll move on to something else. It won't even last a full news cycle."

"Well, is there some sort of recourse we can take? Get whomever posted it to take it down?"

"Don't waste your energy," Stephen said. "Like you said, most of what pops up on that site is fake news, so I don't expect too many people to take it seriously, okay?"

"Okay," Sandra said.

"Now, I have to get back inside. They're about to take a vote," Stephen said. "Stop worrying, Sandra."

"I will," Sandra promised.

"No, you won't. I know you. This is nothing, believe me."

"I love you," Sandra whispered.

"I love you too, sweetheart. I'll call you to say good night when I get back to my apartment later."

And then he hung up.

Sandra felt better.

That's what Stephen was so good at.

Making people feel better.

Which was why he was a two-term senator who sailed to victory in his last election by a whopping twenty-two points.

Sandra pushed the gear of her Audi into drive and drove home to her upscale residential neighborhood and her nineteenth-century New England–style colonial house that she and Stephen had recently restored to its original glory. As she rounded the corner, she instinctively slammed on the brakes, screeching to a stop in the middle of the road. Just ahead, camped out on her front lawn, was a swarm of reporters and cameras and harsh lights and a long line of news vans parked all the way down the street. And one thing was crystal clear in her mind. They were all waiting for her.

CHAPTER THREE

Sandra took a deep breath and continued driving down the street, taking a sharp right turn into her driveway. The throng of reporters surged forward, trampling her front lawn and surrounding her car. She reached up and pressed the button to open the garage, but the door didn't open. She tried again. And then again. Nothing. The door remained firmly closed. The battery in the remote had been giving her trouble the last few weeks. She knew she should've gotten the battery changed. But she kept putting it off, and now the damn thing was kaput. She was going to have to get out of the car and fight her way into the house through the front door.

She grabbed her purse and mentally prepared herself for the ordeal of pushing and shoving her way past the cluster of reporters who would jostle around her to get some kind of statement.

Do not engage with them.

She said it to herself a few more times until she was ready.

And then, she pushed open the door and stepped out of the car. She kept her head down as the reporters descended upon her, excitedly shouting questions.

"What do you have to say about your husband using taxpayer money to squash a sexual harassment claim against him?"

"Do you know your husband's accuser?"

"Is there more than one woman? Do you have a number? Three? Six? More than a dozen?"

"Were you aware of this claim against your husband?"

"Mrs. Wallage, have you filed for divorce?"

She got knocked in the head with a microphone. One overly aggressive female reporter grabbed a fistful of her white suit jacket and tugged on it, trying to slow her down as she struggled to make it to her front door. Sandra yanked free and kept pushing forward, and then, with the enormity of it all overcoming her, she felt tears welling up in her eyes.

Don't cry.

For heaven's sake, don't cry.

She raised an arm to cover her face, not to protect herself from the flashing lights and prying camera lenses, but to hide the fact that tears were now streaming down her cheeks.

She wasn't going to make it.

The front door still seemed miles away, and the reporters, who didn't seem to care that they were on private property, kept blocking her path, shouting insulting question after insulting question.

She was ready to collapse on the lawn and curl up in a

ball when the female reporter who had so rudely grabbed her screamed. Everyone stopped for a moment to look at her. She was soaking wet, her hair matted and her clothes drenched.

Nobody knew what had just happened.

And then, Sandra caught sight of a yellow blur sailing through the air, nailing a reporter from the local NBC affiliate right in the head and exploding, splashing him with water.

A cameraman from FOX News got it next as a purple balloon shot out of nowhere and blasted him in the chest, soaking him.

Everyone looked toward the Wallage house and could clearly see two shadowy figures in a second-floor window hurling water bombs down at the reporters.

There was pandemonium as the news crews rushed to protect their expensive equipment. During the chaos, Sandra, sensing an opportunity, bolted for the house. A few reporters chased after her, but she outran them and managed to get inside and slam the door, double locking it behind her.

She dropped her bag on a side table and trudged upstairs to find her two sons, Jack and Ryan, in the bathroom reloading by filling balloons with water from the faucet.

"I suppose as a good mother, I should punish you for scaring those poor reporters outside," she said, smiling.

"Okay, how about we only get two helpings of dessert tonight at dinner?" Ryan helpfully suggested.

"Tough, but fair," Jack agreed.

Sandra nodded. "Yes. You need to learn a lesson."

She stared at her two handsome sons proudly. Jack was the oldest at sixteen, big and brawny with a high-wattage smile and endless charisma. He was only a junior but already the star quarterback of SoPo High's football team. He was outgoing, popular, and a decent student. He could've been better if he pushed himself more, but because he was so important to his coach and to his team, many of the teachers tended to give him a lot of leeway. Sandra was especially proud that her son was brave enough to tell her he was gay about a year ago. She and Stephen had worried at first that he might have a difficult time at school, but to her relief and surprise, nobody even blinked, and his announcement seemed to just make him even more popular with his peers. Ryan, on the other hand, at fifteen, was more quiet and withdrawn. He was leaner than his athletic brother and a foot shorter. He was a talented artist, sometimes moody and unpredictable, whip-smart, on the honor roll, and could be found most nights writing songs and poetry in his room about his search for true love with the amazing woman he had yet to meet. A true hipster at heart. The brothers couldn't be more opposite if they tried, and she could safely say she loved them both equally. Stephen adored his sons too, naming them Jack and Ryan because he had always been an avid fan of Tom Clancy novels since college.

The boys fought a lot, disagreeing on just about everything, but Sandra knew that in a pinch, they would always have each other's backs. And it touched her that evening that they had banded together in order to protect their mother.

"Thank you," Sandra whispered to the boys.

"No worries. We're just getting started," Jack said, grinning, as he ambled out of the bathroom back into his bedroom. He crossed to the window and let loose with a red balloon and waited for it to hit its target.

The boys suddenly erupted in laughter.

"Oh man, look at that camera guy running for his truck!"

Sandra walked over and shut the window. "I think they've suffered enough."

"What's for dinner? I'm starving," Jack said.

"Turkey meat loaf," Sandra said. She had made it the previous evening because of her speech and just needed to pop it in the oven to warm it up.

"Can we eat soon? I have plans later," Ryan said.

"On a school night?" Sandra asked incredulously.

"I'm not going anywhere. I'm just Skyping with someone," Ryan said.

"He's got a new girl," Jack teased. "You can bet he's already written a song about her."

"Do I know her?" Sandra asked, suddenly curious.

"No, I don't think so," Ryan said, looking away.

"What's her name?"

Ryan paused.

"He won't tell me either," Jack said.

"I just don't want you all to make a big deal about it. It probably won't last, so I'd rather not talk about it yet," Ryan said. "So can we just drop the twenty questions?"

Sandra threw her hands up in surrender. "Fine. I'll mind my own business and go heat up the meat loaf."

She started to walk out of the bedroom but then turned back around. "By the way . . . I spoke to your father."

The boys looked at her expectantly.

"You can ignore what that Dirty Laundry site is claiming. Your father told me the story has no basis in fact. It's all lies."

"We know, Mom," Jack said.

"I just wanted to make it clear," Sandra said.

"Got it," Ryan said.

As she left Jack's bedroom and headed back down the stairs, Sandra knew the boys wouldn't be sucked in by a ridiculous rumor. They loved their dad and trusted him and would always give him the benefit of the doubt.

She just wished she could do the same.

Later, as her sons scarfed down the meat loaf and two helpings of a homemade peanut butter pie she had bought at a bake sale the previous weekend, the boys recounted the highlights of their day, as was dinner tradition: Jack's makeup test for failing a bio exam, Ryan's new creative writing teacher who was encouraging him to start a novel, the upcoming football schedule, Ryan's intention to try out for the fall musical. They successfully managed to ignore the pandemonium outside.

At one point, Sandra got up and closed the blinds so she didn't have to look at a gaggle of nosy reporters staring at them while they ate. She always worked hard to keep up a sense of normalcy. Once they were done and clearing the plates from the table, Ryan excused himself to dash upstairs for his call with his new girlfriend. Jack hung around to help his mother load the dishwasher. They were just about done when Jack received a text on his phone. Sandra noticed his worried face as he stared at it.

"What's wrong?" she asked.

"I just got a text from Dale. He heard Kevin Metcalf was just rushed to the hospital in an ambulance," Jack said quietly.

"What for?"

Jack frantically texted back his friend who had delivered the news. He instantly got a reply. "He doesn't know."

Kevin was a close friend of Jack's, a running back on the team, and the first of his teammates to publicly support him for coming out. So he was held in high regard by the whole Wallage family.

"Mom, we have to go . . . ," Jack pleaded.

Sandra didn't even let him finish. She called upstairs to Ryan to hold down the fort, marched to the foyer, and grabbed her bag off the side table. Despite the challenge of maneuvering their way through the circus on their front lawn, they were going to the hospital.

CHAPTER FOUR

Sandra and Jack spotted Joel Metcalf in the waiting area as they emerged from the elevator on the second floor of the South Portland hospital. He looked pale and stricken as he sat slumped over in a chair, a cup of coffee in his hand, staring straight ahead as if in a trance. He was a tall man, well over six feet, lanky build, head shaven, and he sported a brown goatee punctuated with specks of gray. Sitting next to Joel, with a hand around his shoulder, was Coach Vinnie Cooper, about a foot shorter, with a buzz cut, stout and bulky with a big belly, and wearing a nylon jacket with the high school team's insignia.

As Sandra and Jack approached, Joel's eyes flickered toward them, and he attempted a smile, but he just couldn't get there.

Joel stood up to greet them. "I'm glad you're here."

Sandra hugged him. "How is he?"

Joel shrugged. "I don't know. They're still working on him."

Joel fought hard not to cry. The usually tough, sturdy, resilient construction worker was on the verge of a breakdown.

Sandra nodded to Coach Cooper, who remained seated and offered her a grim nod. She turned back to Joel. "Was he at home when it happened?"

Joel shook his head. "No. He was at school. In the locker room. Luckily Coach Cooper was still in his office doing paperwork at the time. He found him passed out on the floor as he was leaving for the day and called the ambulance."

Jack finally stepped forward and stood next to his mother. "What is it? What's wrong with him?"

Joel stared down at the floor and shrugged, unable to answer.

Coach Cooper stood up and patted Joel on the back. "They suspect it might be a drug overdose."

Sandra's eyes widened. *"Drugs?"*

Coach Cooper nodded solemnly. "They found opioids in his backpack."

"Oh dear God . . ." Sandra whispered.

Joel's eyes welled up with tears. He was losing the battle to stay strong and stoic.

Sandra grabbed his hand.

"I . . . I had no idea he was taking drugs . . . ," Joel stammered. "I never saw any evidence of it. . . . But I should have seen the signs . . . don't know . . . with Stacy gone and me working all the time . . . I try to be a good father, but maybe I'm just not around enough to keep an eye on him. . . ."

Sandra squeezed Joel's hand. "Do not beat yourself up. This is not your fault. Don't you watch the news? This is a national epidemic."

"I've been trying to tell him the same thing," Coach Cooper said quietly, clasping Joel's shoulder with his pudgy hand in a show of support.

"Listen, I'd appreciate it if you and Jack kept mum about all this. I don't want it getting out that Kevin was mixed up with drugs. He's been struggling a lot lately, especially since his mom died, and . . . well, he's been applying to colleges, and I really don't want this destroying his reputation," Joel said in a desperate tone.

"Of course," Sandra said.

Jack nodded in agreement, not quite knowing what to say.

Sandra noticed the coffee cup Joel clutched in his right hand. "It looks like you need a refill. Let us go get you one."

Joel stared down at his empty cup. "Thank you. I could use the caffeine. It's going to be a long night."

Sandra glanced over at Coach Cooper. "Coach?"

He shook his head. "I'm good, thank you. I should be getting home. You hang in there, buddy. It's all going to be fine."

Coach Cooper grabbed Joel in a bear hug and held him in his grasp as Joel dissolved into tears. Sandra felt awkward watching this raw moment between the two men, so she gently took Jack by the arm and led him down the hallway toward the cafeteria.

As they walked, Sandra turned to her son. "Did you know Kevin was taking opioids?"

Jack vigorously shook his head. "No. I didn't have a clue!"

"You guys are close. Have you noticed any changes in his behavior lately?"

"Yeah, he's been really depressed for a while now."

"Do you think it has to do with his mother's passing last year?"

"No . . . I mean, maybe a little, but I think a lot of it has to do with Tara Jackson dumping him last semester."

"Who's Tara Jackson?"

"Just one of the hottest girls at school. Everyone calls her Beyoncé because she looks exactly like her and always sings lead in the show choir. Kevin was, like, totally in love with her, and they dated for a few months, but then she got bored and moved on. Kevin was so devastated."

"Enough to take opioids?"

Jack shrugged. "I don't know. Maybe . . ."

They rounded the corner into the cafeteria, where Sandra bought two cups of coffee, one for Joel and one for herself, and a candy bar and bottled water for Jack. As they checked out, Sandra noticed Cathy Langford, a nurse in blue scrubs and a tan knitted sweater to keep herself warm, sitting at a table by herself reading something on her iPad. Sandra had gone to high school with Cathy, and although they would run into each other occasionally at school events, since Ryan and Cathy's daughter, Amelia, were in the same class, they weren't particularly close. Still, Sandra thought it would be rude if she didn't at least say hello.

Jack was ahead of her, munching on his Twix bar, and was already ambling back down the hall toward the waiting area when Sandra stopped at Cathy's table.

"How are you, Cathy?"

She looked up from her iPad, surprised. "Sandra,

what are you doing here? Don't tell me it's one of your boys . . . ?"

"No, they're both fine," she said, pausing to consider just how she should respond. "I'm just here to see a friend."

She wasn't about to break her promise to Joel, but she suspected Cathy would find out about Kevin Metcalf soon enough. It just wasn't going to come from her.

"I'm sorry I missed your welcome speech at the PTA meeting tonight. I've been here working a double shift," Cathy said, sighing.

"You didn't miss much," Sandra said.

Cathy smiled tightly as if she knew Sandra was lying and was already fully aware of how her first meeting as PTA president had ended in disaster.

Sandra casually glanced at Cathy's iPad, which she had just set down on the table, and saw the blaring logo of the Dirty Laundry site on the screen along with the top headline about Senator Wallage and his alleged sexual harassment scandal.

Cathy immediately noticed her faux pas and hastily clicked out of the site and went back to her home screen. She scooped the device up off the table and clutched it to her chest.

There was an awkward moment, as neither woman knew what to say.

Finally, Cathy could no longer take the tension. "Well, I promise I will make the next meeting."

"I'll see you there then," Sandra said with a forced smile before heading out the door and scurrying down the hall to catch up with her son, her high heels clicking loudly on the linoleum floor of the hospital.

Sandra had a sinking feeling the Dirty Laundry site

wasn't going anywhere, and given more time, the latest story would just gain traction and hundreds perhaps thousands of more clicks. And despite the fact that the scandal about her husband was a complete fabrication, the fallout from it was only going to get worse.

CHAPTER FIVE

Maya Kendrick sat behind the wheel of her Chevy Volt, which was parked across the street from an opulent two-story house in a quiet residential neighborhood just outside Portland. The lights were on inside the house, and she could see him every so often pass by a window, in the kitchen popping open a cold bottle of beer, settling down in the living room to watch a football game. He didn't appear to be going anywhere, and that was bad news for Maya. She had been staking out Cyrus Farrow's house while his wife was out of town, patiently waiting for her subject to make a move, any move, to meet his mistress who lived across town.

Jessica Farrow, Cyrus's long-suffering wife, was Maya's client and had recently hired Maya to find proof of her husband's infidelity so she could use it against him when she officially filed for divorce in the coming weeks.

But Cyrus had been a good boy, at least this week, just going to and from work at a downtown Portland bank. It seemed implausible that he wouldn't go at some point to meet Maggie MacDonald, one of the wispy young tellers fresh out of college who he had jumped to hire after meeting her and her size D cups. Maya was starting to suspect that Cyrus somehow knew she was following him and watching him, and so he was purposefully behaving like a loyal and loving husband.

Jessica was scheduled to be out of town only until the end of the week, and if she returned and Maya still had no pictures of Cyrus with his secret girlfriend, she fully expected to be fired.

Maya saw movement inside the house. Cyrus was standing up with his cell phone clamped to his ear. Maya put down her half-eaten roast beef sub.

Maya's sixteen-year-old daughter, Vanessa, who was sitting next to her, in the passenger's seat, looked up from her iPad. "Is he on the move?"

"He's talking to someone on the phone."

"Do you think it's Maggie?"

"I'm not sure. I can't exactly afford to hire some brainiac IT guy to help me tap his phone."

Vanessa chuckled and went back to her iPad.

"How's the studying going?" Maya asked, glancing over at her daughter.

Vanessa shrugged. "Okay, I guess. I hate chemistry. I'm never going to use it in life, so what's the point?"

"You don't know that. Keep at it."

"I'm so going to fail this test tomorrow."

"Positive thoughts."

Maya watched Cyrus through the house's big bay windows pace back and forth, looking like he was cajoling someone on the other end of his phone.

It could just be Jessica calling from Chicago, where she was on a business trip. Or, if luck was on her side, it might be Maggie wanting to see him. After a few minutes, Cyrus ended the call and just stood in the middle of the living room, staring into space as the football game, which was in its final minutes, played out on the giant wall screen behind him.

Finally, he sat back down on the couch to finish watching the game.

Maya sighed loudly.

"Not going anywhere?" Vanessa asked.

"Doesn't look like it," Maya said, frowning.

She felt bad dragging her daughter out on a school night to join her on a stakeout. It screamed of bad parenting. But Maya's partner in her private detective agency, Frances Turner, was nearly eight months pregnant and was so big she was about to burst. In the last two months, Frances had had to scale back dramatically on her workload, leaving Maya to pick up the slack. They couldn't afford to turn down any clients, so Maya had taken it all on, working fourteen- to fifteen-hour days to cover all their active cases. And this night, after leaving Vanessa home one too many times alone, she insisted they have some mother-daughter bonding time, even if that meant sitting together in her Chevy Volt, spying on a cheating husband.

Maya was incredibly proud of her daughter, who was very social and funny and playful, like her father, but also tough and no-nonsense, like her mother, who had been hardened by her years in law enforcement before she quit and started her own PI firm.

Raising Vanessa had been easy and joyful, that is up until she reached the point where she started gushing with her friends about boys. There had been one who came sniffing around recently, trying to get Vanessa's attention. He was a badass rocker dude type with a lot of tattoos. Maya had taken an instant dislike to him and, after investigating him a little, found out he had been arrested twice for shoplifting. She managed to put the kibosh on that one. But boys were like ants, once you squashed one, there were bound to be more around.

"Did you hear from Frances? How did her ultrasound go today?" Vanessa asked, bored with staring at numbers and symbols on her iPad.

"Everything looks good apparently. She sounded very upbeat."

"Good. How long will she be out on maternity leave?"

"We haven't talked about it, but I assume at least a couple of months."

Vanessa nodded and quietly gazed out the window.

"What?" Maya asked.

"Nothing."

"Come on, what?"

"That means you'll be working weekends for the foreseeable future."

"Unfortunately yes. We can't afford to lose any cases. Why?"

Vanessa shrugged.

She didn't have to answer.

Maya knew exactly what her daughter was hinting at.

"We'll go see him the minute I get a break. I promise."

She was talking about her ex-husband, Maya's father, Max, who at the moment was serving five to ten years in the state penitentiary. Max Kendrick had been a police captain in the Portland division before getting caught up in a widespread corruption scandal. He was indicted on Vanessa's thirteenth birthday and convicted on his and Maya's fifteenth wedding anniversary. Max always had good timing.

Maya took Vanessa to see him as much as she could, but it was an hour-and-a-half drive each way to the prison, and it took another hour to be processed and admitted, and then they could visit with him for only thirty minutes, forty-five if they were lucky. It was exhausting, and Maya found it difficult to put on a happy face and pretend everything was peachy keen when they were with him. Since his incarceration, Maya's life had become topsy-turvy. She had resigned from the force to avoid the judgment and angry faces of her fellow cops, started her own business with Frances, and kept the bills paid and food on the table after their nest egg had been wiped out by legal fees. She was working to make the best of a very bad situation, and she knew her daughter was hanging her hopes on the myriad of appeals that had been filed on behalf of her father, appeals that Maya knew in her gut would be turned down because the cold, hard fact was her ex-husband was guilty of every crime and rightfully convicted. He just needed to keep his head down and serve his time. But she couldn't exactly say that to her daughter, who even as she saw him in an orange jumpsuit and with his wrists handcuffed, still held him up on a pedestal.

"Mom, he's leaving!" Vanessa cried.

Maya whipped around to see Cyrus, struggling to put on his coat, halfway to his car, which was parked in the driveway.

She started the Chevy Volt, thankful her choice of ve-

hicle was one that made zero noise, and pulled out behind
Cyrus as he drove off down the street.

"You think he's going to see Maggie?" Vanessa asked.

"Fingers crossed."

Maya silently prayed that was exactly where he was
going because if she got the evidence Jessica Farrow so
desperately craved, then her wealthy client would surely
cut a nice check for a job well done by early next week.

Vanessa was now caught up in tailing Cyrus and set
her iPad down on her lap. When they reached a stoplight,
Maya noticed what was on her screen.

"You are not reading your chemistry notes, Vanessa!"

Vanessa looked down guiltily at her screen and then
grabbed the iPad and hid it from her mother's view. "I'm
sorry."

She had been scrolling through the Dirty Laundry
website.

"I told you I don't like you reading that filth."

"I know, but everyone at school is texting about the
latest headline. It's so juicy!"

Maya didn't want to ask but couldn't deny she was just
a little bit curious. Luckily her daughter was a gossip,
again like her father, so she knew she wouldn't have to
wait long to find out.

"The new PTA president, the wife of that senator, was
in the middle of her welcome speech when the news hit
that her husband is embroiled in some kind of sexual harassment hush-money scandal."

"What's her name again?"

"Sandra Wallage."

"That's right," Maya said.

"I met her once when she came to a football game. Her
son Jack is on the team. I was sitting next to her on the

bleachers with some of my friends. This was way be-fore . . ." Vanessa's voice trailed off.

"Way before what?"

Vanessa had no desire to elaborate any further. "Nothing. Anyway, she seemed like a very nice lady."

"Well, I remember her from way back when we were in high school together, and she didn't seem so nice then."

"Really?"

"Yes, the Sandra I remember was very stuck-up and cliquish, and she was like the mean-girl boss to a bunch of other girls . . . you know . . . the queen bee, if that's what you still call them."

"Not really, but I get the picture."

"Get back to studying for your chemistry test."

Vanessa sighed and clicked out of the Dirty Laundry site.

And Maya breathed a sigh of relief as she followed Cyrus off the highway and into the town of Scarborough, where the pretty, buxom bank teller Maggie MacDonald resided.

CHAPTER SIX

The following evening, Frances Turner pretended to be stunned when six of her girlfriends, not including Maya and her daughter, Vanessa, stood eagerly in the living room to yell "Surprise!" when she entered Maya's modest single-level home in a slightly run-down working-class neighborhood still a few years away from gentrification.

Frances was a trained police officer and licensed private investigator. It was her job to know what to expect and what she might walk into at all times. Maya had tried keeping the secret, sneaking around, planning all the baby-shower details, and Frances at least attempted to stay in the dark, but there were just too many obvious clues. Like the adorable stuffed elephant with the price tag still on it that she had spotted in Maya's closet one night while hanging up her coat when she stopped by to discuss a case; the unusual number of texts she noticed that kept popping up on Maya's cell phone at the office from a few girlfriends Frances went to high school with as well as a couple of women who worked with her in the police department back in the day; and then, the most suspicious of all signs, Maya pressuring her into coming over for dinner on this particular night, the same night of the week that Maya always stayed home to watch her hero and role model Mariska Hargitay collar the dangerous sex fiends marauding New York on a new episode of *Law & Order: Special Victims Unit.* Why was she so insistent that Frances come over on this night, the one night France's BFF, Abby, had off from work? It didn't take a detective, and yes, Frances was one, to solve this mystery.

Maya could see Frances trying her best to act genuinely shocked and overjoyed as the women rushed at her with hugs and kisses on the cheek as Frances marveled at the large pile of exquisitely wrapped baby gifts that were on Maya's coffee table.

"You got me. I sure did not see this coming . . . ," Frances lied, shaking her head, clutching her heart, perhaps overdoing it just a smidge.

Vanessa arrived from the kitchen, handing the expectant mother-to-be a virgin cocktail, a Shirley Temple, before escorting her over to the couch, where she sat down and took center stage to gab with her girlfriends and bring everyone up to speed on her progress.

"I just want this little bugger out of me already. I'm tired of carrying him around," Frances joked.

"He doesn't look so little from here," a zaftig, wide-eyed African American woman with gorgeous red nails said with a smile, raising her half-empty wineglass. "And we've all seen his daddy!"

"Yes, if he's as big as his father, I'm terrified he's going to rip me apart when I finally give birth!" Frances wailed.

"You'll be fine. That's what the drugs are for," Maya said, laughing.

Vanessa scooted back to the kitchen to check on the hors d'oeuvres she had baking in the oven. She had volunteered to help Maya throw the party because she was fond of her aunt Frances, even though she wasn't really her aunt. Plus it gave her a night off from her mother hounding her about her schoolwork.

After about an hour of gossip, Frances began opening her gifts, most of which were wrapped in blue paper, since Frances already knew she was having a boy. There was a polished gold first-year frame for monthly pictures; an adorable long-sleeve romper that read on the front *Ladies, I Have Arrived*; a package of drool bibs in assorted colors; some teething toys; and, most practically, in addition to the stuffed elephant, a baby diaper tote bag from Maya. Even though Frances despised being the center of attention, and on more than one occasion had scoffed at the idea of anyone throwing her a baby shower, Maya knew the gifts from her friends would be a lifesaver since neither parent of the soon-to-be-born boy was pulling down a big income to be in any kind of position to buy a lot of baby supplies. They would both be grateful for this very generous head start.

Maya plowed her way through the middle of the party, scooping up the discarded wrapping paper and ribbons and clearing the area so they could chat and laugh some more. Althea, the one with the fiery red nails, was in the middle of a story about going into labor while at a movie theater watching an Avengers movie that was so loud, no one around her could hear her screaming with labor pains, when the doorbell rang.

Maya scanned the roomful of guests. Everyone on the guest list was present and accounted for, so she couldn't imagine who it might be. She excused herself to open the door.

It was Frances's baby daddy, Vinnie Cooper, the football coach at SoPo High.

He grinned knowingly. "Hey, Maya. I hope we're not interrupting anything!"

Vinnie wasn't alone. Behind him was a muscled, bronzed man with an impossibly handsome face and radiant smile that threatened to melt hearts. He was a couple inches taller than Vinnie, not too tall, Maya's perfect type of man, if she had one.

Vinnie stepped aside so the man was directly in front of Maya. "This is my bro Mateo, Mateo Reyes."

"Nice to meet you, Mateo," Maya said, offering her hand.

"Likewise," he said, taking it and squeezing it ever so slightly, enough to send a shiver up Maya's spine.

"He's a detective too, works homicide," Vinnie boasted.

"I'd like to go private someday, like you," Mateo said, still slaying her with that sexy smile.

"Well, there is a lot to be said for the steady paycheck you get at the department." Maya laughed before ushering them both inside.

She knew Frances had told Vinnie about the shower, and she strongly suspected Frances had encouraged him to crash it because if there was one thing Frances detested, it was frilly, giggly, girly affairs, where she feared she might get bored quickly. But Maya still couldn't figure out why Vinnie would bother to enlist the aid of his handsome friend Mateo. What guy would ever want to drag a good buddy to a baby shower?

The women's lively conversation quickly halted at the sight of the two men ambling into the living room. All eyes were glued to Mateo, who nodded bashfully at the women staring at him.

Althea picked up the *Ladies . . . I Have Arrived* romper and quipped, "I'll say he has!"

There was raucous laughter from the women, who made room for the two men to sit down and join the party. Vinnie excitedly started to pore over all the gifts.

Maya leaned down to Vinnie. "Can I get you something to drink, Vinnie?"

"How about a Maker's Mark with a splash of ginger ale?"

He noticed Frances eyeing him warily. "What? I'm not the one who's pregnant!"

There was more laughter from the women.

"Mateo?" Maya asked.

"Just some water, thank you," he answered with a wink.

Maya's knees nearly buckled, but she kept her balance and hurried to the kitchen. On her way, she noticed Frances signaling Vinnie to help her stand up, since her giant belly made it difficult for her to do it on her own. Within moments, Frances had made her way to the kitchen, where Maya was pouring whiskey over a glass of ice.

"He's cute, isn't he?" Frances whispered.

"Who?"

"You know who. Mateo."

Maya pretended to glance back into the living room and notice him for the first time. "I suppose so, yes."

"Come on, I saw the look on your face when you let him in. You think he's gorgeous!"

"What is he doing here? Did you tell Vinnie to show up and crash your baby shower just in case you hated it and wanted to go home?"

Frances shrugged and smiled. "Maybe."

"You're terrible."

"Well, I told you not to throw me one, and I knew you were lying through your teeth when you promised me you wouldn't."

"I spent a lot on that diaper tote bag, so damn it, you're going to be grateful and enjoy it!"

"I love it. And I'm very happy you didn't listen to me. I got a great haul, and I'm psyched to see all the girls."

"You're welcome. Now, you didn't answer my question."

"I know . . . ," Frances said with a sly smile.

The reality hit Maya like a splash of cold water. "Tell me you didn't."

"I may have," Frances said, picking up a chicken empanada, which was cooling on a tray on top of the stove, and stuffing it into her mouth.

"This is a *fix-up*?" Maya groaned.

"Why not? Look at him. He's beautiful; he has a successful career, a car, his own home; and, get ready for the kicker, he's actually *single*!"

"No, I am not going to let you do this."

"Come on, Maya, you have to dip your toe back in the pool at some point. Otherwise, sooner or later you'll forget how to swim."

"How many times have we been in the office, or out working a case, or at a bar having a cocktail, and I've told you in no uncertain terms I am not looking to date anyone right now?"

"And I respected your wishes, but that was before I got the idea of putting you and Mateo together. You two are a perfect match."

"And how many times have I said I would never date, let alone marry, anyone in law enforcement ever again?"

"You've got to get over that."

"My police-captain husband is in prison for corruption! I really think you should cut me some slack!"

"Ex-husband," Frances reminded her as she grabbed a glass from the cupboard, filled it with water, and handed it to Frances. "Now go serve your guests some drinks and wipe that gloomy look off your face. You're the hostess of this shindig, and you are going to go out there and give the performance of a lifetime!"

"What happened to just be yourself?" Maya asked.

"I'm not taking any chances," Frances said.

Maya stared daggers at her and then whipped around and marched back to the living room, carrying the whiskey and water.

CHAPTER SEVEN

As Sandra pulled into her driveway at dusk the next day, she was relieved to find that the swarm of reporters who had been camped out on her lawn and sidewalk, along with their big trucks and vans, had all finally packed up and gone. Thankfully the erupting scandal had receded a bit, at least for now, especially after Stephen had issued a full-throated and passionate denial that any taxpayer money had been used in any kind of nondisclosure agreement with a mistress. Stephen said in no uncertain terms that he was a faithful husband to his wife and was outright aghast that anyone would suggest otherwise. But Sandra had no illusions that there were dozens of dogged, determined reporters out there painstakingly searching for concrete evidence that would prove Senator Stephen Wallage was a liar.

She couldn't think about that now. She was too busy

putting out her own fires. The late-afternoon meeting with Principal Hicks had lasted two hours, and although it was awkward and uncomfortable discussing her personal life, she had assured Hicks that the salacious headlines on the Dirty Laundry website were absolutely false. She was ready to put the baseless accusations behind her and move on planning for the school year.

Hicks seemed mostly appeased by Sandra's persuasive presentation, and he took the opportunity to stress to her after she had finished that she had his full support. But still, Sandra noticed he was a little more reserved than usual, and there were worry lines on his face that she hadn't noticed before. She didn't blame him at all, because more often than not, eventually the stories posted on the site were proven to be true.

She got out of her car and walked toward the front door of the house. Sandra hadn't even thought about what to make the boys for dinner. She was so eager to get home from her meeting that she drove right past the grocery store. Maybe she would just order them all Chinese food or have a pizza delivered. As she entered the foyer, she stopped suddenly. The familiar smell of a rich marinara sauce wafted in from the kitchen.

She knew it was her husband's signature turkey meatballs, a recipe his Italian grandmother on his mother's side had taught him to make when he was a boy.

Stephen was home from DC.

She marched into the kitchen to see her husband and two sons crowded around the counter and stove, making dinner. Stephen was stirring a bubbling pot of sauce on one of the front burners with a wooden spoon. His sleeves were rolled up; his pale blue Brooks Brothers dress shirt sported a few tomato stains. He didn't like wearing aprons, so she always had to take his shirt to the dry cleaner's after he took it upon himself to cook a meal. Jack was busy tossing a salad in a large wooden bowl, while Ryan ripped open a package of organic spaghetti to dump into a boiling pot of water on one of the back burners.

"What are you doing here?" Sandra asked, a little flummoxed.

Stephen looked up, eyes twinkling, then he wiped his hands on a towel and sauntered over to his wife, enveloping her in a bear hug. "I caught a late-afternoon flight home at the last minute. They're always overbooked on Fridays, but I got lucky today with a cancellation."

"I wasn't expecting you—" Sandra said.

Still hugging her, he leaned down and kissed her softly on the lips. "I know. I wanted to surprise you."

His body felt warm. She could smell garlic on his breath from taste-testing his homemade sauce.

"He's here for the whole weekend," Ryan said, beaming.

Sandra gently pulled out of his hug. "I thought there was a fund-raiser in Georgetown you couldn't miss on Sunday . . ."

"I got out of it," he said, winking at the boys.

"He'll be able to come to my game tomorrow," Jack said as he popped a grape tomato from the salad into his mouth.

This was certainly a rare occurrence, having Stephen home for a full weekend. She could see how happy the boys were, and so she kept mum and didn't press him for any more details as to why all of a sudden he felt the need to be at home with his family. She didn't have to, because she knew full well what he was doing there. With all those nasty rumors flying around, it was important to show the world that he was a staunch family man, willing to put his fast-track career in the United States Senate on hold in order to spend quality time with his wife and two teenage sons. It was a calculated and necessary move, and Sandra didn't blame him for it. As a politician's wife, she had long come to accept the importance of optics.

After going to her bedroom to change out of her business suit into more casual attire, she descended the stairs just as Stephen and the boys were sitting down at the dining room table to enjoy their Italian feast. Before they had finished their salads, Stephen was putting down his fork to make an announcement.

He adopted a grave face and serious tone. "I want to get this out of the way so we can have a fun weekend together, okay?"

The boys nodded, both gnawing on large hunks of buttery garlic bread.

Sandra braced herself.

She knew what was coming.

"What they are saying on that muckraking, libelous website—what's it called again?"

"Dirty Laundry," Ryan answered.

Another calculated move, Sandra thought. Of course Stephen knew the name of the site. He had probably pored over the article multiple times in order to strategize a response.

"Right. Dirty Laundry. I want to assure all of you that there is not one word of truth to it. What they're claiming is categorically false. It never happened. I was not having an affair, and there was no hush money. *Ever*. Take my word for it."

"You don't have to do this, Dad. We believe you," Jack said.

Ryan nodded in agreement. He couldn't talk because he was busy chewing, his mouth full of garlic bread.

"Actually I do have to do this, Jack. Because someone is out there questioning my honor, and that's not okay with me. And I couldn't stand the fact that my family might take any of that trash seriously."

But the boys didn't seem to care. They knew in their hearts their father would never do anything so dumb. But as Jack and Ryan continued to reassure Stephen that they loved him and had his back, Sandra quite noticeably refrained from comment.

Mercifully the topic quickly changed to Jack's upcoming football game against a fierce rival team the next day and Ryan's audition for the fall musical, which he felt went pretty well. He would know if he snagged the lead on Monday and was feeling nervous. But Sandra was confident he would be cast because he was the most talented actor in the entire school. Yes, there was a little motherly bias in her opinion, but the kid was good.

Sandra offered to clean up, since Stephen and the boys had cooked, so they retreated to the living room to watch a horror movie on Netflix. It gave Sandra the opportunity to decompress from the day and be left alone with her thoughts. After loading the dishwasher and wiping down the stovetop with some surface cleaner and a rag, she disappeared upstairs, where she quickly brushed her teeth, undressed, and crawled into bed. It was only a few minutes after ten o'clock, but the movie was in the midst of its harrowing climax and would be over soon, and Stephen would be coming up to bed.

She heard the suspenseful score swell and assumed the end credits were rolling. The TV was shut off, and she faintly heard Stephen saying good night to the boys as he came up the stairs. She could hear him coming, so she closed her eyes and pretended to be asleep. He quietly walked into the room and headed into the master bath, closing the door. She knew his routine. He would be in there for ten minutes. She buried her head deep into the pillow.

When he finally emerged, probably shirtless and in his silk pajama bottoms, he knelt down and kissed her forehead, waiting to see if she would respond.

She didn't.

He circled around to the other side of the bed and climbed in, slipping under the covers and wrapping his strong arm around her waist, pulling her closer to him.

"You still awake?" he whispered in her ear.

She moaned and shifted her body, hoping that would be enough to discourage him.

He started nuzzling the back of her neck.

He was not about to give up.

She didn't have a choice.

Sandra opened her eyes and turned around to face him. He had the look of an expectant puppy hoping if it was good it might get a bone or a chew toy.

"I'm not there yet," Sandra said.

The color drained from his face, and he nodded. "I understand."

He backed away from her, moving slowly, closer to the edge of his own side of the bed.

"I didn't do it, Sandra. I want you to know that," he muttered.

"Yes, Stephen, you've made that quite clear to me and the boys tonight, but you must realize how difficult it is for me to so readily accept your adamant denial."

"I know . . . ," he said, a twinge of guilt in his voice.

She could have left it at that, but she wasn't feeling generous. "Since it's happened before . . ."

She waited for his response. As a politician, he was an expert at putting out an appropriate response.

But this time, he had nothing. After a few moments, she could hear him turn over so they were now facing away from each other, back to back.

"Good night, honey," he said quietly.

"Good night, Stephen."

CHAPTER EIGHT

The numbers were just not adding up. After investing in a monthly budget app for her phone, Maya thought she would finally be able to get a handle on her mounting bills, but the math didn't lie. She slumped over, frustrated, at her kitchen table, staring at the final number. She was going to be more than two hundred dollars short this month.

It had been a struggle ever since Frances announced she was pregnant. Maya was working double time to make up for Frances's frequent absences, but they were still splitting the money the agency took in, fifty-fifty. Maya simply could not imagine suggesting that she take a bigger cut from their monthly haul for doing more work because she knew Frances was having a tough time financially too. Frances's insurance covered only a percentage of her medical bills, plus she had invested a lot of money in a series of Lamaze classes to help prepare her for the childbirth.

So Maya had decided to just keep her mouth shut and continue carrying the burden of running their detective agency and handling the majority of their caseload. She didn't tell Frances that they had already lost three top-paying clients to bigger firms because they wanted faster results, or that the office rent check had bounced and she had to do some fast-talking to avoid an eviction notice. The landlord was eager to boot them out because then he could raise the rent for a business that was more flushed with cash. It took a lot of cajoling and pleading for him to give Maya an extra week, but eventually he begrudgingly agreed.

Maya decided to crunch the numbers again. Maybe in her haste, she had typed a few wrong digits that might have thrown everything off. She carefully went through the list of bills—mortgage, health insurance, utilities, credit cards (at least the ones that hadn't been canceled yet), groceries, car payment. When she got to the end, scratching off the reserve cash she had listed under miscellaneous expenses in order to squeeze out a few more dollars to balance the budget with, she realized her instinct had been right. She had added up the numbers wrong. She wasn't two hundred dollars short. She was two hundred and seventy-six dollars short.

Maya dropped her head down on the table. With the way things were going, she had no clue how she was going to be able to keep the business afloat until after Frances returned from maternity leave. And at this point, she still didn't know how much time Frances was planning on taking. Two months? Three months? Four? She felt like she was drowning in quicksand with no fallen tree branch in sight to grab hold of in order to pull herself out.

She was so wrapped up in her own internal drama, she didn't hear Vanessa stroll into the kitchen and open the fridge to get some water. They had long cut out buying the bottled stuff because it had gotten way too expensive, but Frances had given them a water pitcher filter for Christmas last year, and it had luckily saved a lot of money.

Vanessa took a glass down from the cupboard and poured from the pitcher. "You look stressed, Mom."

"No, I'm not," Maya lied.

Vanessa sat down next to her mother with her glass of water and eyed the budget on Maya's phone app.

"Yikes, that's not good. Two hundred and seventy-six dollars short?"

"It's nothing for you to worry about."

"I can help out more, you know."

"Yes, I know. You're a very capable young woman, and I'm immensely proud of you. But you need to focus on school. I don't want you working for me all the time. God forbid your grades start to slip and then you don't get into a good college."

"Wow, talk about going from zero to sixty. Suddenly I've been rejected by all the Ivy League colleges?"

"I'm just saying I'm the adult here. It's my responsibility to keep a roof over our heads, and it's your job to enjoy your high school years and prepare for college without having to worry about the electric bill."

"But winter's on the way, and you know we don't have a wood burner, so that bill is going to like triple what it is now by December."

"Again, not your problem."

"I can work and still get good grades. I'll just drop out of the fall musical."

"I didn't know you were even auditioning for the fall musical," Maya said, sitting up in her chair, surprised.

Vanessa nodded, slightly embarrassed. "Some girls dared me after they heard me singing in the locker room shower. I kind of did it on a lark. I honestly didn't expect anything to come of it, but the theater director, Ms. Callis, says I'll get something."

"Well, that's great."

Vanessa shrugged. "It probably won't be a big part, maybe the chorus. It's no big deal. I don't have to do it."

"You're not bowing out. We'll be fine."

Maya noticed her daughter's skeptical look. She took Vanessa's hand and squeezed it. "Really. Okay?"

"Okay," Vanessa said.

Maya could tell her daughter was relieved because this was something she really wanted to do despite her lackadaisical attitude that she was showing off to her mom.

Vanessa's phone buzzed, and she excitedly peered at the screen. A smile crept across her lips as she frantically typed a reply.

"Who is that? Lucy?"

Vanessa shook her head.

"Emily?"

"Nope."

Studying her daughter's euphoric face, the answer finally came to her. "A boy?"

This time she got no reaction, which was basically a confirmation.

"What's his name?" Maya sighed.

Vanessa finished sending her text and stuffed the phone into her back pocket. "I'm not ready to tell you."

"What do you mean you're not ready? I'm your mother."

"There's no way I'm telling you his name yet. I know you. You'll go all private eye on me and do this huge extensive background check on him and everybody he knows, and pretty soon you'll know more about him than I do at this point."

"I'd like to deny I would do something like that, but you're probably right. Okay, you don't have to tell me . . . yet. But if it gets serious, we need to talk about it."

"We're not having sex, Mom," Vanessa said matter-of-factly.

Maya sighed with relief. "Good. But if it progresses to the point where you're thinking about it, we need to have the talk."

"We've already had the talk," Vanessa said, rolling her eyes.

"We have?"

"Yes, like three times."

"Really?"

"Yes, I pretty much know everything, and what I don't know, I can find on the internet."

"I'm happy you haven't gone all the way, but can you at least tell me how far you *have* gone? Kissing? Heavy petting?"

"I'm not doing this," Vanessa cried as she jumped up from the table and bolted out of the room.

Maya couldn't help it. Her mind was racing. Who was he? Did she know him or his family? If she knew just his name, she could easily google him. Maybe she could swipe Vanessa's phone when she was asleep and find out some information from all their back-and-forth texts.

No, Maya said to herself. She couldn't do that, as much as she really wanted to, because she had to trust her daughter. But that didn't mean she couldn't hazard a few guesses as to the identity of this mystery boy. It was a hell of a lot more interesting than worrying about her monthly budget.

CHAPTER NINE

Sandra knew everyone in the stands was watching them. It was her first public appearance with her husband since the tawdry scandal about Stephen had been blasted across the Dirty Laundry website. They sat about halfway up the bleachers, smack-dab in the middle, where she felt trapped and claustrophobic, but she had to keep smiling.

For the sake of her family.

Stephen was right.

It was best for them to present a united front and not let anyone believe that what the site was saying had any serious effect on them.

Stephen had his arm draped around Sandra's shoulder, and whenever one of his constituents stopped to say hello, he'd gently pull her in closer to him in an effort to prove they were just as happy and loving as they had always been.

It struck Sandra as insincere and quite frankly artificial, but she knew it was vitally important for Stephen to act as if nothing was wrong.

She couldn't help but wonder if his trip up from Washington, DC, was more about damage control than about missing his family. She hated herself for making judgments about her husband and his motives. However, she had spent years playing the role of the loyal politician's wife, always upbeat and smiling, but underneath the surface she had become hardened and jaded to that unattainable public image.

Everyone in the bleachers jumped up and cheered as the home team wrested control of the ball. It was the fourth quarter. They were behind by seven points now after the opposing team had taken advantage of a fumble and scored an unexpected touchdown. The pressure was on for a win, since they had lost the last two games. Sandra couldn't imagine what was going on in her son Jack's head. He was the first-string quarterback. The team's fortunes seemed to rise and fall on his shoulders. She watched him conferring with his team and Coach Cooper in a huddle.

There were just a few seconds left on the clock.

Stephen clapped his hands and shouted, "Come on, boys, you can do it! Woo-hoo!"

Sandra looked at him. Was he showing off for the crowd, trying to be the engaged, supportive father who came to every game to cheer his oldest son on, even though this was the first one he had attended all season?

She scolded herself for being so cynical.

She noticed Ryan sitting on the opposite side of Stephen. He appeared distracted, staring over at the left side of the bleachers, down a few rows. Sandra followed his gaze but couldn't see what he found so interesting. She did notice a statuesque woman with beautiful brown skin and gorgeous curly black hair sitting with a pregnant friend and a very pretty young girl, probably fifteen or sixteen, who bore a striking resemblance to the tall woman and was probably her daughter. Sandra stared at the gorgeous, confident woman. She looked so familiar. Had they gone to high school together? Before she could place her, the team broke from their huddle and was back on the field.

She leaned across Stephen and spoke to Ryan. "What are you looking at so intently?"

Embarrassed, Ryan just shrugged. "Nothing."

He quickly averted his eyes back to the game.

Stephen continued shouting words of encouragement to the team, clapping his hands.

Sandra stood up with the rest of the football fans in the bleachers as the cheerleaders, a mix of boys and girls, finished up a rallying cry complete with cartwheels.

She felt a wave of sadness when she noticed Joel Metcalf wasn't down in the front row on the end like he usually was. He never missed a game, but of course didn't make it today given his son's situation.

The clock resumed, counting down the last few seconds, and the center lineman bent over and snapped the ball to Jack, who grabbed it and backed up to pass to the wide receiver as the offensive line kept the opposing players at bay. The receiver was wide-open, arms outstretched, and all Jack had to do was throw the ball, but he just stood there, stunned for a moment before slamming the ball to the ground and leaping on top of a player who had broken through the defense.

They punched and kicked each other, rolling around on the field as the rest of the players from both teams piled on, shouting and fighting. The referee blew his whistle, and the coaches sprinted out onto the field to break up the brawl.

Once the boys were dragged off each other and escorted back to their respective sides of the field, the red-faced referee officially ejected Jack from the game to a cacophony of boos from the irate home crowd, who, despite what they had seen with their own eyes, believed the fight was the fault of the visiting team and certainly not theirs.

Stephen yelled at the referee, who appeared slightly shaken when he looked to the crowd and spotted a U.S. senator berating him. Sandra watched as Jack stalked off the field, yanked his helmet from his head, and hurled it to the ground, where he promptly kicked it with his cleat. The helmet sailed through the air, nearly beaning a male cheerleader who had to duck out of the way.

The game resumed and the opposing team, which now had possession of the ball, managed to run out the clock and won the game by seven points. As Sandra glared at her benched son, who sat alone in his grass-stained football uniform, his head buried in his hands, she was sure of one thing. He had started that fight for some reason, and it had cost his team the game.

CHAPTER TEN

"I would like for you to explain to me why I shouldn't bounce you off the team for the remainder of the season," Principal Hicks said, sitting behind his desk with his arms folded, a stern look on his face.

Jack, sitting in a chair opposite him, stared down at his Nike Air Force sneakers and just shrugged.

"Principal Hicks asked you a question, Jack." Sandra sighed, nudging her son's arm.

"I don't know," he muttered, keeping his eyes fixed on the floor.

Sandra had warned her son that it was in his best interest to apologize for starting the brawl that had led to his ejection from the game and just take his punishment like a man. Jack had spent the Saturday evening after the game and all day Sunday pouting in his room. And now, Monday morning in the principal's office, he was still acting remote and uncommunicative.

Sandra gave Principal Hicks an apologetic look, not sure what was wrong with her usually socially adept and carefree son.

Hicks unfolded his arms and slapped his hands down on his desk. "Okay, if you are not going to help me out here, I'm just going to have to make a decision on my own."

There was a knock at the door.

Hicks, annoyed, called out. "Yes?"

The door opened, and Coach Vinnie Cooper popped his head into the office. "Sorry to interrupt. I was hoping you might let me say a few words."

"By all means, Coach, come in," Hicks said, waving him in. "I would love it if you could offer us a little insight as to what happened on Saturday."

"As a matter of fact, I can," Coach Cooper said, slipping in and closing the door behind him. "Morning, Mrs. Wallage."

"Good morning, Coach," Sandra said, smiling.

Coach Cooper stepped around to the other side of Jack, who still sat slumped over in his chair, a sullen look on his face. "Jack . . ."

"Coach . . . ," Jack mumbled, wishing he was anywhere else.

Sandra could not believe her son was acting like this. It was so out of character, and she couldn't imagine what was bothering him so much that he would pick a fight during a football game.

She didn't have to wait long to get her answer.

Coach Cooper cleared his throat. "I spoke to some of Jack's teammates yesterday, and they told me that the linebacker from Yarmouth who Jack went after on the field had made a crack about Kevin Metcalf. . . ."

There was a long pause.

Hicks leaned forward. "Is that true, Jack?"

Jack didn't respond at first. He just shifted in his seat uncomfortably and then gave a small, almost imperceptible nod.

Sandra touched his arm. "Why didn't you say anything?"

Jack just offered another obstinate shrug.

But Sandra was not about to drop the matter. "Jack . . . ?"

Realizing he was outnumbered by three adults now, Jack knew he couldn't avoid participating in the interrogation any longer and huffed, "I just didn't want to make a big deal out of it, okay?"

"Apparently the kid was making fun of Kevin's recent struggles with addiction. Jack was just defending his teammate," Coach Cooper said, reaching down and squeezing Jack's shoulder in a show of support.

Sandra never thought she could love her sons any more than she already did, but in this moment, with this revelation, her heart swelled a tiny bit more. But she knew her feelings were not going to get him off the hook with the high school principal. She wanted to hug him and tell him how proud she was of him for sticking up for his friend, but she refrained and kept her tough-disciplinarian-mother face on in order to show a united front with Principal Hicks.

At least until they were safely out of the office.

"So I was thinking detention for a week, a letter of

apology to the Yarmouth player, and he's back on the field for Saturday's away game at Thornton Academy," Coach Cooper said, in an attempt to curb what he feared might be a harsher punishment.

Hicks considered the proposal and then outright rejected it. "I have a zero-tolerance policy for violence no matter what the reason."

Coach Cooper stepped forward. "I understand that, John, but—"

Hicks stopped him in his tracks. "I'm not going to cut Jack some slack just because he's your star player. That wouldn't be fair to my other students. One-week suspension, a letter of apology, and he's benched for the next three games."

Coach Cooper opened his mouth to argue, but Sandra cut him off. "I think that's absolutely fair. Don't you, Jack?"

Another sullen shrug from the peanut gallery.

Coach Cooper frowned. He had obviously been prepared to put up more of a fight, but there was no way he could win with the kid's mother taking the principal's side, so he just gave up and retreated from the office after a cursory nod.

"Thank you," Sandra said, standing up and shaking Hicks's hand.

"I'll see you at the next PTA meeting, Sandra," Hicks said, circling around his desk to show them to the door. "Try to keep that temper in check, okay, Jack?"

Jack never made eye contact. He gave the principal a half wave and scooted out the door ahead of his mother. She gave Hicks another apologetic smile and then raced to catch up with him.

After Hicks closed the door to his office, Sandra turned and ran smack into Maisie Portman, the assistant principal. Sandra hadn't seen her since the night of the PTA meeting when she saw Maisie squabbling with that mysterious woman in the high school parking lot.

"How did it go?" Maisie asked, tied up in knots. "Hicks has been on such a law-and-order kick lately I was afraid Jack might get expelled."

"Not too bad. One-week suspension and a three-game ban," Sandra said, relieved.

"*Three* games? That's outrageous! The team needs Jack if we're going to have any chance at a state championship trophy! Would you like me to talk to him? Maybe I can work on him to get a reduced sentence."

"I appreciate it, Maisie, but honestly, Jack needs this punishment. What he did was wrong, and if we let it slide, he might develop some kind of hotshot attitude where he starts to think he's above the rules," Sandra said.

"You're a hell of a lot better mother than I ever would be," Maisie said, laughing.

"Oh, come on, I think you'd be great."

"That's because you barely know me. My mother had to do an intervention to rescue my houseplants because I kept forgetting to water them," Maisie said.

"I guess I'll have to find another home for that Chinese elm bonsai tree I was going to give you for your next birthday!"

Maisie howled. "Only if it comes in plastic. See you at the next PTA meeting!"

"Will do! I better go find my son before he tackles somebody else!" Sandra called out as she scurried off down the hall. She caught up with Jack, who was at his locker, cleaning it out and throwing his books and supplies into a backpack.

"Just because you're going to be home this week, don't think it's a school vacation where you can play video games and watch movies on your iPad," Sandra warned.

"I know . . . ," Jack groaned.

"And there will be physical labor involved as well. The lawn is in desperate need of a mowing and the hedges could use a trim."

"If Dad was here . . ."

"If Dad was here *what*?"

"Nothing," Jack whispered, slamming his locker shut.

"No, tell me, Jack, what?"

Jack turned to face her. "If Dad was here, he would go a whole lot easier on me."

Sandra pursed her lips. She had expected this kind of reaction. Stephen was always the good cop, and she was always the bad cop. They had grown comfortable in their respective parental roles, but that didn't make her job any easier. "You're right. He probably would. But he's not here. He took the red eye back to DC last night, and he no longer has a say, so I'm afraid you're stuck with me. Got it?"

Jack slung the backpack over his shoulder and moodily stared at the floor. "Yeah . . ."

"Good," Sandra said. "One more thing."

Jack sighed dramatically. "What?"

"I don't necessarily approve of your methods, but I'm awfully proud of you for standing up for Kevin."

She gave him a peck on the check.

At first he was mortified and spun his head around to make sure none of his peers had seen him get a kiss from his mother. But luckily the halls were empty with the whole student body safely tucked away in the classrooms, so he didn't have to make a full-blown scene.

Instead, he just feigned annoyance and whined, "Mom!"

CHAPTER ELEVEN

On their way home, Sandra made the snap decision to turn right instead of left at the intersection, heading in the opposite direction of their house. Jack sat up in his seat and looked around.

"Where are we going?"

"You'll see," Sandra said, gripping the wheel, with a steely look of determination.

When she turned onto a quiet road dotted with a few houses, Jack figured out their destination and a smile crept across his face.

"Thank you . . . ," he whispered.

Sandra looked at him and nodded, then turned back, keeping her eyes on the road until they pulled up to a modest single-level house in desperate need of a fresh coat of paint, a yard that hadn't been mowed in weeks, if not months, and a red rusted Mustang parked out front that hadn't seen too many more better days than the house.

Jack eagerly flung open the passenger's side door and jumped out. He ran across the overgrown grass to the front door and rapped on it with his clenched fist. Sandra got out, and by the time she could catch up and join him, the door had slowly creaked opened and Joel Metcalf stood there. His perturbed expression melted away at the sight of Jack.

"Sorry we didn't call first," Jack said.

"Don't be silly," Joel scoffed. "Kevin will be so happy you're here."

He enveloped Jack in a brief bear hug and then stepped aside and ushered him into the house. "He's in the living room watching TV."

Jack scooted inside as Joel gave Sandra a half-hearted smile. "Looks like we both have kids at home for the foreseeable future."

"You already heard?" Sandra asked, surprised.

"News travels fast in these parts."

"Yes, but we literally just left the school. You should be working as a reporter for the *Portland Press Herald*."

"My politics are too conservative for them," Joel laughed. "Come on in, I'll put a pot of coffee on."

As Sandra entered the house and headed to the kitchen, she had to pass the living room, where she spotted Jack sitting on the couch with his buddy Kevin. The boys were already engaged in an intense conversation. Kevin looked rail-thin, drawn, and tired. He had on a pair of grungy gray sweatpants and a wrinkled black T-shirt with the number 83 on it, which was the same number as his football jersey.

"How are you, Kevin?" Sandra asked.

He turned and stared at her with a blank expression, almost as if he had no idea who she was. After blinking a few times, he registered a slight hint of recognition. "Fine, thanks, Mrs. W."

Joel herded Sandra into the kitchen before she had a chance to say anything else and pulled out a chair for her at the small rickety table. He then moved to the coffeemaker and began pouring a bag of grounds into the top. "It's been rough going. He got home from the hospital, and I'm supposed to put him in a rehab program, but we have some insurance issues, and it's not as easy as people think. So basically I've been the one helping him get detoxed."

"On your own? Joel, that's crazy. You need professional help," Sandra said, concerned.

"If you know of anybody who works for free, be sure to let me know," he growled before catching himself and softening his tone. "It's just hard."

Sandra stood up and walked over and placed a hand on his shoulder. "If there is anything I can do . . ."

He turned to face her, his eyes moist with tears. "I hate to ask . . ."

She knew what was coming.

She had heard it many times before.

"Stephen . . . ," she whispered.

Joel nodded. "Yes. People will listen to him. Maybe he can cut through some of the red tape and get us some state aid or something, just speed up the process so Kevin doesn't fall too far backward."

"He flew back to DC last night, but I will call him and see what he can do. I promise."

"I appreciate it," Joel said, eyes lowered, embarrassed.

"Do you have any idea when Kevin might be well enough to go back to school?"

Joel shrugged. "I honestly think the boy would be better off if he never did go back. I swear, Sandra, if I wasn't a high school dropout, I'd homeschool him myself."

"I really don't think that's the answer. Kevin would miss out socially. He has lots of friends; look at Jack—"

"Yes, Jack's a good kid, but have you heard what those other snot-nosed bastards in his class are saying about him?"

"It wasn't one of his classmates. It was just some dumb player from the visiting team."

"I'm not talking about what happened at the game on Saturday. Have you seen this?" Joel asked as he scooped up a laptop from the counter and set it down in front of Sandra on the kitchen table.

Sandra stared at the screen. It was the Dirty Laundry website and the latest headline. Just above the salacious allegations about Stephen's sexual harassment scandal was a teasing story about Kevin Metcalf's losing battle with drug addiction.

"Go on, read it," Joel barked. "They're saying he's practically dead and buried already!"

Sandra read the first few sentences but could not go on any further. She closed the computer. "You shouldn't be reading this filth, Joel. We both know there is not a shred of truth to anything this person writes."

Joel's fury grew. His face turned a deep red, his eyes were blazing, and the veins on his neck began to pop out. His finger shook as he raised it and pointed it at her. "I swear to you, Sandra, if I find out who is behind this despicable site, whether it's one person or a dozen . . . I will hunt them down, and, I swear to God, I will wrap my hands around every last neck responsible and squeeze as hard as I can . . . until I hear the last gasps of air come out of their big, lying mouths . . ."

"Joel, please . . . ," Sandra whispered urgently, not wanting to hear any more.

She shuddered to think he was capable of such violence, but in her gut, she knew he was dead serious.

CHAPTER TWELVE

Maya took the check from her client Jessica Farrow, who sat across from her in a hard-back chair, a satisfied smile on her face. Maya glanced down at the number of zeroes in the amount scribbled on the check and tried hard not to break out into a wide grin.

"Thank you," Maya said gratefully.

All of the bills were now going to get paid this month.

"It was a job well done. That photographic evidence you captured of Cyrus sucking face with that silicone-infused dimwit he's been boffing on the side just secured me the house on the cape in the divorce settlement."

Whatever makes you happy, Maya thought to herself. She folded her hands and rested them on the desk and decided to drive home her usual sales pitch. "If you ever find yourself in need of our services again . . ."

Jessica Farrow stood up and extended her hand. "I will be sure to keep you in mind. I have many wealthy girl-friends, most of whom are also married to horny cheating husbands, so I'll be sure to keep your number on hand."

"I certainly appreciate it, Mrs. Farrow," Maya said, jumping up from her chair and shaking her hand.

"Jessica, please. I thought about going back to my maiden name after the divorce papers are signed, but then I thought, the name Farrow also gets me a good table at most of the finer restaurants in the Old Port."

"Wise thinking."

"Are you married, Maya?"

"Yes, I mean, well, no, not anymore—"

It was such a simple question, why did she always fumble it so badly?

"One of the smart ones, I see," Jessica said with a wink.

Maya wasn't too sure about that. She could barely cover her electric bill, and Jessica Farrow was about to secure the deed to a sprawling mansion situated next to the Kennedy compound in Cape Cod.

Jessica turned to leave, when there was a quick knock on the door. It flew open and Vanessa stood in the door-way.

"Oh, sorry, I didn't know you were with a client," Vanessa said sheepishly.

"Why aren't you in school?" Maya asked.

"It's almost four thirty. School was over an hour ago," Vanessa sighed.

Maya checked her watch. "Oh. I guess I lost track of time. Don't you have theater rehearsal or something?"

"Not until six. I told you that this morning."

"That's right," Maya smiled apologetically. "I remember now."

"Is this your daughter?" Jessica asked, taking a step toward Vanessa, who still hovered in the doorway, not sure if she should come in.

"Yes, this is Vanessa," Maya said.

"She's gorgeous," Jessica exclaimed.

Maya and Vanessa both spoke at the same time. "Thank you."

"I have to run. Thanks again, Maya. I'll be in touch," Jessica said, breezing past Vanessa, down the hall, the clicking of her high heels fading as she rounded the corner toward the elevator.

Vanessa waited until she was completely gone before slipping into the office and closing the door behind her. "Did she give you a check?"

Maya held it up in front of her. "Five grand."

"Awesome!" Vanessa said. "Now I won't have to study at night by candlelight. I can actually use a lamp with a light bulb and electricity and everything."

"Don't be flippant," Maya scolded. "What are you doing here?"

"Can't a loving daughter just pop by her mother's office to say hello after a long day of learning at school?"

"Of course. But you're not that kind of loving daughter. You would only swing by here if you needed something."

"That hurt," Vanessa said, putting on a fake pout.

"It was meant to," Maya said matter-of-factly. "So what do you need?"

Vanessa contemplated pretending some more that her motive for this unexpected visit was pure, but she quickly gave up on that and came clean. "I need a favor."

"I'm listening . . ."

"This Dirty Laundry site is getting way out of hand. It's literally tearing my school apart."

"I'm very aware of that. But it's only thriving because every student is clicking on the site constantly to read the latest gossipy headline. If everybody at your school boycotted it, the site would lose oxygen and finally wither away and die. It's a very simple solution."

"Well, we both know that's *never* going to happen. People can't help themselves. They're too curious to know what story the site is going to break next."

"Including you," Maya said.

"Yes, including me. All my friends, they check it out three, sometimes four times a day. I have to keep up."

"What can *I* do?"

Vanessa took a deep breath and then planted both of her hands down on her mother's desk. "I want you to investigate the site and find out who's behind it."

"You want to hire me?"

"Yes. Well, obviously I can't pay you anything."

"Obviously."

"But you're a really good detective, and if anybody can finger who is hurting people at the school and causing so much pain, it's you."

"I appreciate the flattery, but you know I don't have the time to do it."

"What are you talking about? You just wrapped up your only case. You made five grand."

"Yes, and that five grand will pay for all the bills I didn't pay in September and all the ones pouring in now for October. I also have November to worry about now. I need to focus on finding a paying client with real, honest-to-goodness money."

"Can't you multitask? You've always been so good at that."

"Vanessa, I can't . . ."

"I know it's been tough with Frances gone so much, and I'm willing to drop out of the musical and come work at the office every day and night after school to help out if that's what it takes."

"You really want me to do this?"

"Yes, I do. I believe in you, and what this person who runs the site is doing is wrong, and I really want to expose him or her."

"How did I raise such a conscientious daughter?"

"It was mostly Dad," Vanessa joked.

"I'm not even going to touch that one."

"It was a joke. Everyone knows Dad's in prison. I honestly think he would find that funny. I get my dark humor from him."

Maya leaned forward in her chair and tapped her fingers on the desk, thinking.

Vanessa folded her arms. "If you're really worried about the money, you can take your retainer fee from my college fund."

"What college fund?"

Vanessa sat upright. "I don't have a college fund?"

Maya cracked a smile. "Your father isn't the only one with a sly sense of humor."

Vanessa laughed. "So you'll do it?"

"I'll do it," Maya sighed. "But if a paying client comes along, that case takes priority. Deal?"

"Deal," Vanessa quickly agreed.

Maya couldn't believe she had just been hired by a new client.

Her own daughter.

CHAPTER THIRTEEN

This was Maya's first time back in the precinct where she once worked since the day she had handed in her letter of resignation to the acting captain, cleaned out her locker, and marched out the door, ignoring the mix of sympathetic and judgmental looks from her fellow officers. It had been a painful time, an exceedingly stressful period in her life. She had thought she had finally managed to purge all the broiling emotions that she had felt during those final days as a police officer—her feelings of failure, of complicity in her husband's crimes by turning a blind eye to all the signs. But to her surprise, they still lingered and came bubbling to the surface every so often, especially now as she entered the building.

Her mind replayed that awful scene, that fateful day when she was sitting at her desk, typing up a report on her computer, and federal agents flashing their FBI badges

stormed into the precinct and placed her boss and husband, Captain Max Kendrick, under arrest. She would
never forget the look on his face as they carted him away,
an uneasy combination of shame and defiance. He stared
straight ahead, not making eye contact with anyone, not
even his wife, who called out to him, who at the time was
naively confident that this had to be some terrible mistake.

But of course it wasn't. And after she was confronted
with the evidence and had to accept that her life as she
knew it was officially over, there had to be major changes,
the first of which was quitting. She could never carry out
her duties as a police officer with the shadow of her husband's crimes following her everywhere. And so her dream
of becoming Portland, Maine's first female chief of police had come to a swift and bitter end.

"Looking for me?"

Maya spun around.

It was Detective Mateo Reyes.

Frances's fix-up.

The really hot one.

"No," Maya said, perhaps a bit too quickly.

He looked slightly wounded but covered with a smile.
"Aw, I was sure you realized you had made a huge mistake by not giving me a chance to take you to dinner
sometime and so you came here to ask me out."

"Sorry," Maya said, although there was a small part of
her that wondered if she should take a chance and do just
that.

But she was on a mission and didn't have time to in-
dulge in a rom-com scene with Frances's friend, despite
the fact that he was so startlingly good-looking and, on
the surface, perfectly charming.

"Okay, heartbreaker, how can I help you?" Mateo asked.

"I'm looking for Oscar Dunford."

"I see. So you prefer the bookish computer-geek type?"

"I don't have a type. I just need to talk to him."

She didn't have time to play games. Maya knew she was probably coming off as cold and distant to this guy, and she felt bad about that, but if she let her guard down, then she just might probably relent and agree to go out on a date with him. And she had no intention of even going there.

At least not right now.

"Is he still in the same office?" Maya asked.

Mateo nodded. "Yup. Day and night. The guy never leaves this place. I'm guessing it's due to a lack of a rewarding social life."

Maya cracked a half smile, and then turned on her heel and headed down the hall.

"Nice seeing you again, Maya," Mateo called out after her. "I'm just going to stand here now and pretend I'm not dying inside from yet another rejection."

Cute.

But not cute enough to get her to turn around and keep the conversation going. She walked all the way down the hall to the last office on the left, otherwise known as the cybercrimes unit. It wasn't a real unit, just in name only. The South Portland Police Department could hardly afford to fund a whole unit dedicated to solving cybercrimes. They basically had one guy who was good with computers.

Oscar Dunford was more of an IT guy than a cop, but they gave him a badge because his services proved invaluable when it came to investigating computer-related cases. He was an unabashed nerd and spent his free time role-playing in some avatar fantasy adventure that Maya didn't even pretend to understand. But they had become fast friends from the day he showed up for his first day at work and got Maya's decades-old desktop computer running smoothly again after it froze up on her with just a few quick clicks.

As she rounded the corner, she spotted Oscar standing by a communal coffee station, holding a cup of steaming coffee in one hand while wiping off some he had just spilled on his shirt with the other. His face was red, and he looked as if he was silently cursing himself for being so clumsy.

"Check the fridge for some club soda. That should get the stain out," Maya offered.

The tension in Oscar's face melted away at the sight of Maya.

"Maya! Have you come back to rescue me from my dreary existence, like Richard Gere in his white military uniform, who marches in and scoops factory worker Debra Winger up in his arms and carries her off to live happily ever after?"

"Is that a movie you're talking about?"

"*An Officer and a Gentleman*, 1982."

"That's like ten years before you were even born."

"Big film buff, especially the classics."

"Well, I appreciate you making *me* the hero and *you* the love interest. That's very enlightened of you."

"I'm very giving that way."

"I need a favor."

"You know I am hopelessly in love with you and willing to do anything to curry favor with you on the off chance you might someday go out on a date with me."

"You too? What is with you guys? Hasn't the Me Too movement taught you anything?"

"Well, since you are no longer an employee here, technically you can't accuse me of sexual harassment in the workplace."

He dropped the soiled napkin in the trash bin and then moved to the small refrigerator and opened it. "We're out of club soda. I guess I'm going to have to live with the stain. At least it will now match most of my other shirts at home."

He shuffled off down the hall to his small, cramped office. Maya followed him and sat across from him as he settled back down at his desk. He took a sip from his paper cup of hot coffee and burned his lip. Maya suppressed a smile. She really did have an affection for him, especially his gawky demeanor and lovesick-puppy personality.

"There is a website out there hurting a lot of people. Do you think you can trace the IP address?" Maya asked.

"In my sleep."

"I'll need it as fast as possible."

"I can stay late tonight if you bring me dinner."

"I'm serving my kid leftover lasagna from last night. You okay with that?"

"I have a craving for takeout from Saeng Thai House."

Maya sighed. "Crab rangoon and crispy pad thai?"

"You remember! See, we belong together."

She stood up. "Thanks, Oscar. I'll be back later."

"It will be our first date."

"Sure," Maya said, laughing.

"So how far do you usually go on a first date?"

"No kiss, but maybe after you give me the IP address,

I'll scoop you up in my arms and carry you to your car so you can at least pretend you're Debra Winger."

"Deal!"

He was around five feet four and a 135 pounds. Maya figured she could carry Oscar around, so it was a relatively easy concession to make, and it would be a good story for Oscar to tell his buddies with whom he played all those fantasy-adventure games.

And for that very small price, she would know the name of the mean-spirited mastermind behind the Dirty Laundry site.

CHAPTER FOURTEEN

"Step down?" Sandra whispered frantically as she stared into the frightened eyes of Assistant Principal Maisie Portman in the hallway outside the administrative offices at the high school.

Maisie shifted uncomfortably, upset over having been tasked with this delicate assignment of requesting Sandra's resignation as PTA president.

"But I've barely even started," Sandra argued, still stunned by what she had just heard.

"I know, and if it was up to me, I wouldn't even be standing here asking you to do this, but as you know, this is not up to me. I'm just following his orders."

"On what grounds does Mr. Hicks have for wanting me to quit?"

"I think we're both fully aware of the reason," Maisie muttered.

"The Dirty Laundry piece? Oh, come on, Maisie, there is not one shred of truth to those ridiculous rumors, and everyone knows it. I already spoke to him about this, and he said not to worry."

"Yes, but that was before John met with the school board. They're scared by any whiff of scandal, and with all the publicity about your . . . predicament . . . swirling around, they . . . I mean, he just thinks it might be a good idea for someone else to take over temporarily . . . just until all that nasty business blows over."

"But if we give in now, it will only embolden the person behind the Dirty Laundry website to keep printing lies about the teachers and students and administrators. Who knows, Maisie? *You* could be next."

If Maisie had been wearing pearls, she would have clutched them at that moment. She vigorously shook her head, aghast. "But I haven't done anything. . . ."

"Neither have *I*," Sandra said evenly.

"I appreciate your point, and I agree wholeheartedly that it's simply not fair. But I'm sorry, Sandra, my hands are tied. This is what Johnny wants."

"Johnny?"

Maisie cleared her throat. "I mean Mr. Hicks."

"Whatever happened to 'innocent until proven guilty'?"

"Unfortunately this is a classroom, not a courtroom," Maisie said.

Sandra pondered this for a few moments, considered her options, and then smiled at Maisie. "You're right."

Maisie breathed a sigh of relief. "Thank you. I think it's for the best."

"Hicks is a principal, not a judge. He can't force me to do anything. I'm not resigning. If he wants me gone, he's going to have to force a school board vote to have me removed, and believe me, if you think I'm above making a stink in the press, you're dead wrong. How about this for a headline? 'U.S. Senator's Wife Fired from PTA Over Unsubstantiated Rumors by Skittish Principal and Scared School Board!'"

Maisie blanched and her mouth dropped open.

"And I'm not just talking about Dirty Laundry, I'm talking about the *Washington Post*. Now, if you will excuse me, I have a PTA meeting to run."

Sandra marched down the hall toward the high school auditorium, leaving a defeated Maisie in her wake. She felt bad for Maisie. After all, she was just the messenger, but Sandra was in no way going to be bullied by Principal Hicks and punished for a false story. Even if the rumors about Stephen's scandal had been true, it had nothing to do with her. In her mind, it was outright misogynistic for Hicks to go after her, of all people. The *wife*! She had actually liked Hicks in the beginning, but now his true colors were showing, and she was not going to be a victim of his and the school board's rash, self-serving decision-making.

As Sandra rounded the corner, she stopped dead in her tracks. Down the hall, Ryan had a pretty girl pushed up against the locker. Ryan's head blocked the girl's face, but they were both pelvis to pelvis and their lips were locked tightly together as they swapped spit and groped each other. His hands were firmly planted on her butt, and Sandra let out an audible gasp. Luckily they didn't hear her because the sudden shouting from the auditorium easily drowned it out.

Ryan and his girlfriend ignored the commotion, never even bothering to come up for air, but Sandra knew that whatever conflict was unfolding in the auditorium had to do with her PTA meeting, and, as president, she needed to be there. She would just have to deal with her son's sexually aggressive and very public behavior later at home.

Sandra scurried through the doors to the auditorium in time to see two men down near the stage, standing so close to each other their noses were almost touching, screaming at each other. She raced down the aisle, but before she could even inquire as to what it all was about, one of them, a bald, brawny bear of a man with a goatee lunged at the other man, who was also big and flabby but clean-shaven, so his multiple chins were pronounced, and wearing a Red Sox ball cap to cover up some of his greasy long hair. The two men, suddenly locked in a hug, looked as if they were dancing at first, but then they crashed into a crowd of worried onlookers, mostly women, and fell to the floor, where they rolled around, punching each other as hard as they could while wheezing mightily from the effort.

Sandra tried pulling the bald one off the flabby one, who was flat on his back now, covering his face with his hands as Baldy pummeled him with his fists.

The guy was at least three times the size of Sandra, so she had no luck stopping the fight. When a few of the other fathers, transfixed by this unexpected wrestling match, finally realized a pint-size woman, a U.S. senator's wife no less, was physically trying to stop this all on her own, their sense of duty finally kicked in, and they all converged to help her. One of the men managed to get Baldy into a headlock while a couple of the other dads helped haul Flabby to his feet and restrained him by pinning back his arms. Both men were red-faced and still fighting mad.

"What the hell is this all about?" Sandra shouted.

"His druggy daughter gave opioids to my youngest, a freshman!" Flabby screamed.

"That's a lie, you fat bastard! It was *your* punk kid who was the one selling pills to her fourteen-year-old classmates in the lunchroom!"

Sandra turned to one of the mothers, Mrs. Brandt, who was watching the whole scene with a horrified look on her face. "Where is all this coming from?"

"Where else?" Mrs. Brandt said. "Dirty Laundry."

Suddenly Flabby tore away from the two men holding him by the arms and slammed into Baldy, reigniting the brawl all over again. They tumbled into the first row of seats as a gaggle of women scattered to avoid getting body-checked.

Sandra had seen enough. After shouting one more warning, which unsurprisingly went unheeded, she snatched her phone from her purse and called 911.

She knew once the police arrived to break up the fight, her scheduled PTA meeting would have to be canceled. There was no way they would be able to get any school business done now. She would just have to postpone until everybody had a chance to cool down.

She could already hear Principal Hicks spinning the outburst as Sandra's inability to control her own meeting, how it might be best to have a stronger presence in charge in order to avoid another unfortunate incident such as this one. There was no doubt in her mind that this was going to be a gift to him. But despite her diminutive stature and ladylike demeanor, Sandra was a scrappy fighter and fully capable of defending her turf.

So bring it on.

CHAPTER FIFTEEN

After talking with the police officers who immediately managed to calm down the situation and send the two men home with a stern warning about how they would be arrested and charged if they ever resorted to physical violence again, especially on school grounds, Sandra excused herself and walked outside to her car. As she rummaged through her purse for her handy bottle of Advil, she ran smack into someone, who was staring at her phone and didn't see the collision coming either.

"Oh, I'm sorry . . . ," Sandra said to the surprised woman.

"No, totally my fault. I wasn't looking where I was going," the woman said with an apologetic smile.

Sandra was struck by how pretty the woman was, not pretty exactly, more beautiful, like a tall runway model, except much more casual. She fit perfectly into a tight pair of jeans and the white blouse and suede jacket she wore matched her long, curly raven hair and gorgeous brown complexion.

The woman quickly pocketed her phone and kept going. Sandra watched her head off and then called after her. "Do we know each other?"

The woman stopped and turned around. She seemed to recognize Sandra. "We went to high school together."

"We *did*?" Sandra asked, studying the woman's face. "I'm sorry, I don't remember. Sandra Wallage."

The woman smiled, not surprised. "I'm Maya Kendrick, but my maiden name is Ramirez."

"Maya Ramirez, of course! I remember you now! Do you have a kid who goes here?"

"Yes, a daughter."

"How have we not run into each other before this?"

Maya shrugged. "I don't make it to a lot of the PTA meetings unfortunately because of work."

"What are you doing now?"

"Private investigator."

Sandra perked up. "How exciting."

"It's really not."

Sandra couldn't help but stare at Maya. "Wow. You're just as beautiful now as you were in high school."

"Thanks. I honestly didn't think you would remember me."

"Why is that?"

"Well, we definitely ran in different circles. You were the fun-loving ponytailed-cheerleader type at the pep rally, and I spent most of high school hanging around the smoking area bumming cigarettes off the bad boys I met in detention."

Sandra chuckled. "I don't remember you that way. I

recall you being very sweet when we sat next to each other in chemistry class."

"That's because I was buttering you up so I could cheat off your paper."

"That wasn't very smart on your part. I think I failed chemistry."

"No, we both got C minuses. For obvious reasons. Luckily my daughter doesn't take after me academically."

Sandra laughed. "Neither do my sons, thank God! What's your daughter's name?"

"Vanessa. Vanessa Kendrick."

"I don't know her. Are you here to pick her up?"

"No, she already has a ride home."

"Well, if you're here for the PTA meeting, I'm sorry to say you came for nothing. I had to cancel it."

"No, actually I'm here on a work-related matter."

Sandra leaned in to her and in an excited, hushed tone, asked, "Are you working on a case?"

She noticed Maya was being very tight-lipped, but she couldn't resist asking more questions. "Is someone at the school in some kind of trouble?"

"I really can't talk about it."

"Teacher or student?"

"I really can't talk about it."

Sandra knew she was being annoying, but her curiosity was piqued, and once that happened, it was very hard to let something go.

"I understand. Maybe you could just nod yes or no. Student?"

Maya smiled, but it wasn't a full smile. She was just humoring Sandra. She gave a quick shake of her head just to appease her.

"So it's a teacher," Sandra exclaimed.

Maya gave her another shake.

"Someone in the administration."

"That's all you get. It was nice seeing you, Sandra."

Maya marched past her toward the entrance to the school. Sandra did an about-face and scurried along to catch up with her.

"I'll walk with you."

"I thought you were leaving."

"I think I left something in the auditorium."

"What?" Maya challenged her.

"My car keys."

"I saw your car. You don't need a key. It automatically unlocks when you touch the door handle."

"You really are an observant detective."

Once they were inside, Maya stopped and turned to Sandra. "This is where we part ways. The auditorium is that way, and I'm going this way."

Sandra was out of ideas on how to stall anymore, so she slapped on a smile and shook Maya's hand. "I hope we meet again."

Maya mumbled something, obviously not as keen as Sandra to rekindle any kind of friendship. And then she turned on her heel and walked in the direction of the administrative offices.

Sandra knew she shouldn't, but she waited a few seconds, and then quickly slipped out of her high heels and quietly padded after Maya in her nylon stocking feet, carrying her shoes by the white leather straps. Sandra stopped just short of the offices right around the corner, pressed her back to the wall, and poked her head around to see Maya knocking on the office door of Assistant Principal Maisie Portman.

Maya waited patiently for almost a minute and then knocked again.

Still no answer.

"Ms. Portman, it's Maya Kendrick. I need you to open up. We have to talk," Maya said.

She tried one more time.

Knock, knock, knock.

Nothing.

Sandra watched Maya try the door handle. It was unlocked. She slowly opened it and stepped inside the dark office. A light switched on, and Sandra heard someone gasp.

Unable to take the suspense anymore, Sandra tiptoed over and peeked inside the office.

Maya stood in the middle of the room, on her phone, talking to someone. Behind her, Maisie Portman dangled in midair, hanging from a rope that had been tied around a ceiling joist. There was an upended chair on the floor nearby and she noticed a note taped to the lapel of Maisie's purple long-sleeve cardigan. Her dead eyes stared right at Sandra.

Sandra heard screaming, which caused Maya to spin around in surprise.

That's when Sandra realized the screams were coming from her own mouth.

CHAPTER SIXTEEN

Maya moved quickly to usher the frantic, hysterical woman out of the office before she contaminated any evidence but not before Sandra had managed to push her way far enough inside to read the note pinned to the lapel of Maisie Portman's purple cardigan. It was hastily scribbled with a black felt marker on a yellow Post-it note.

I am the creator of Dirty Laundry. I am sorry I hurt so many people. The guilt was just too much to bear. Goodbye.

"You can't be in here," Maya barked as she gripped Sandra by the arm and led her back out into the hallway. "You might contaminate evidence."

"It was her . . . ," Sandra whispered, in a state of shock. "I can't believe it. . . . Why would she . . . ?"

"That's what I came here to find out," Maya said.

Sandra suddenly snapped out of her haze and zeroed in on Maya. "You *knew* she was behind the Dirty Laundry site?"

"Yes. I had a friend trace the IP address to a school computer and an email account linked to Maisie."

"But that's crazy. She was the *last* person—"

"It's always the last person you would expect," Maya said matter-of-factly.

They could hear sirens approaching in the distance.

"Wait here," Maya ordered before she headed back into the office to study the body.

"I thought you said we had to stay out here in the hallway so as not to contaminate evidence," Sandra said, folding her arms.

"*You*, not me. I'm a trained investigator," Maya called back.

"Well, whoop dee doo," Sandra huffed.

"Did you actually just say that?" Maya said from inside the office.

"Yes, I tend to trot out dorky phrases when I'm really nervous," Sandra explained. She couldn't resist peering back inside the office to see Maya standing close to Maisie Portman's dangling corpse, eyeing her neck with the rope tied tightly around the center.

Hearing the sound of approaching footsteps, Sandra turned to see a ruggedly handsome man in a green shirt and brown jacket that accentuated his soulful brown eyes, running down the hallway toward her. He stopped when he reached her.

"Detective Mateo Reyes," he said.

"Sandra Wallage."

Detective Reyes raised an eyebrow. "The senator's wife?"

"That would be me," Sandra said.

"Did you discover the body?"

"Yes; well, no, technically *she* did," Sandra said.

"She? She who?" Reyes asked.

"*Her*," Sandra answered, pointing inside the office.

He looked in the office and sighed. "Maya, would you come out here, please?"

Maya stepped out into the hallway. "Oh, hi."

Detective Reyes looked at Maya, surprised. "What are you doing here?"

"I was working on a case and came here to question Maisie Portman," Maya said.

"I assume that's who is hanging from the ceiling right now," Reyes said, jotting notes down on a small writing pad with a pen that he took from his breast pocket.

"You would be correct in assuming that, yes," Maya said.

"And why did you need to question her?" Reyes asked.

Sandra interrupted. "She's been secretly running a website called Dirty Laundry, and she's been posting all kinds of salacious rumors about people connected to this school online. Well, frankly, it's caused quite a ruckus in the community, and I am still stunned that Maisie was behind it because I was so certain it was a disgruntled student. . . ."

Detective Reyes nodded at Sandra, appreciative of the fact she was such a fountain of information. Then he turned back to Maya. "Who is your client?"

"I don't have to tell you that," Maya said.

Reyes gave her a withering look.

"But I will," Maya said. "My daughter. She wanted me to find out who was responsible for the site because she was afraid all the anger and finger-pointing was just going to get worse."

"And you called nine-one-one?" Reyes asked Maya.

"Yes, right after I found the body."

"She wrote a suicide note. It's pinned to her sweater. She explains everything, how the guilt became too much for her," Sandra piped in excitedly. "I can only imagine how she must have felt after seeing the consequences of her vicious website."

"I don't think she felt guilty about anything," Maya remarked.

Reyes looked at her curiously. "Why not?"

"Because I don't think this was a suicide."

"What? But the note . . . ," Sandra said.

Maya shrugged. "We don't know for sure she wrote it."

More sirens were blaring outside the building now, and within seconds they heard a bunch of pounding footsteps. Soon the hallway was swarming with police officers, including the two cops who had earlier responded to the fistfight at the PTA meeting, along with a forensics team. Reyes waved the CSI guys into the office before turning back to Maya.

"Are you suggesting this is a homicide?" Reyes asked, lowering his voice as he noticed a crowd of curious teachers and students down the hall being escorted out of the building by three uniformed police officers.

"I'm not completely sure, but I noticed Maisie has a straight-line bruise on her neck. Come with me. I'll show you."

Maya made a move to enter the office, but Detective

Reyes grabbed her by the arm, halting her. "I can't let you back in there."

Maya tried to shake free. "Oh, come on."

Reyes tightened his grip. "You're not a cop anymore. You're a civilian. Let the CSI guys do their job. You'll have plenty of time to explain your theory to me later. Now I need you both to follow Officer Kaplan outside the building."

Maya and Sandra turned to find a friendly, baby-faced officer in his midtwenties, standing directly behind them.

"This way, ladies."

Without saying another word, Maya and Sandra were led outside, where the local press was gathering, having heard the initial reports over their police scanners. The evacuated teachers and students were already huddled in small groups gossiping about the possible identity of the dead person inside the school, since Maisie Portman's name had yet to be publicly announced.

Sandra stepped closer to Maya, who was fuming. "Did that conversation with Detective Reyes strike you as slightly—?"

"Misogynistic? Egotistic? Completely condescending? Yes! Take your pick," Maya hissed.

"I thought so too. I'm glad we're on the same page."

"And to think Frances tried to fix me up with that creep."

"Who's Frances?"

"My partner. In my PI business. She's eight months pregnant, so she's kind of sidelined when it comes to a lot of the legwork in our cases."

"Oh, how wonderful. Boy or girl?"

"Boy. Man, you sure do ask a lot of nosy questions."

"It's in my nature. I can't help myself. So, anyway, what you said to the detective in there, about the straight line across Maisie's neck, what did you mean by that?"

"Usually when someone hangs himself, or herself, there is a V-shaped bruise on the neck, caused by the rope, but I noticed Maisie's neck bruise went straight across, which indicates strangulation."

Sandra gasped. "Which means . . . ?"

"Which means I think she was murdered."

CHAPTER SEVENTEEN

"My sister did *not* commit suicide, and that's that," Chelsea Portman declared as she sat in Maya's cramped, cluttered office.

Maya couldn't help but marvel at Chelsea's regal, graceful demeanor, almost swanlike, as she floated into the room, fresh off a flight from New York, wearing an expensive-looking cinch-sleeve white-and-tan-striped blazer, a tight-fitting white top and designer jeans, although Maya hadn't a clue who the designer was.

When Chelsea called and requested an appointment, Maya had no idea she was calling from her Upper West Side apartment in New York and would have to feign an illness to get out of her evening performance playing Glinda the Good Witch in the Broadway production of *Wicked* in order to catch a puddle jumper from LaGuardia to the Portland International Jetport. Maya was somewhat surprised that the rather reserved, unobtrusive, and plain Maisie Portman had such a beautiful, tall, glamorous sister who was a successful actress in New York.

Chelsea flipped her luxuriant, shimmering blond hair back and leaned forward, her ocean-blue eyes fixing on Maya. "I want to hire you to find out what really happened."

"The police closed the case a few days ago. They're ruling Maisie's death a suicide," Maya said softly, a sympathetic look on her face.

"I don't care what the police believe. They're wrong. I've known Maisie my entire life, and while we may have had our differences and gone in two totally different directions, we've remained very close. She would never, *ever* take her own life."

"When was the last time you spoke to Maisie?"

"The day she was found hanging in her office. I called her to invite her to New York to meet a new friend I had made, this up-and-coming playwright who is currently working on a new project for me to star in. I'm so ready to do something real and meaningful and not just the same old Broadway musical fluff I've been stuck in."

Maya wasn't sure why she needed to know all this, but she chose to play along. "Wow. Good for you."

"I offered to pay for her flight down to the city, but she said she had a lot going on with the new school year just getting under way."

"How did she sound when you talked to her?"

"Fine. Normal. I didn't pick up on anything unusual. She mentioned that one of her posts on her site was getting a lot of attention—"

Maya cut her off. "So you knew about her Dirty Laundry website?"

"Oh, yes. Maisie told me all about it. It was a nice little side project of hers. It allowed her to blow off some
steam, get a few things off her chest, which was a good
thing because, well, unfortunately, Maisie sometimes felt
stuck in my shadow."

"That's understandable," Maya said. "It must not have
been easy for Maisie to have a sister who is a gorgeous,
successful Broadway actress."

No harm in buttering up a potential client.

"Exactly!" Chelsea exclaimed, agreeing wholeheartedly with Maya's flattering assessment.

"Did Maisie run the Dirty Laundry site alone or did
she have help?"

"It was all hers, I think. Maisie had a lot of free time
when she wasn't working at the school, and she was always a bit of a computer nerd, so I'm sure she was capable of building the site on her own. I just didn't know it
was such a big secret or that what she wrote was so . . ."

"Scandalous?"

"Yes, it took a lot of guts to write the truth the way she
did."

"Some would argue that a lot of what she posted were
rumors and innuendo, maybe even outright lies . . ."

"I've always believed that where there's smoke there's
fire. Trust me, I've had a few horrible things written
about me on Page Six of the *Post*, and when I contacted
my lawyer to sue for libel, he had to remind me that you
can't sue if it's true. My bad," Chelsea admitted with a
wry smile.

Maya was starting to get a clearer picture of Maisie's
possible motive for starting Dirty Laundry. Maybe she
was depressed that her sister was living such a fast-paced,
flashy, fascinating life in the Big Apple while she was

stuck adhering to the whims of the pompous Principal Hicks at a small high school in southern Maine. Dirty Laundry could have been her way of making herself feel more important. But she wasn't about to share her theory with Maisie's younger sister because if Chelsea wanted to know any further information from Maya, she was going to have to pay for it.

"How did you find me?" Maya asked.

"I googled private detectives in the area and your name came up. The fact you are a woman was just an added bonus."

Okay, Maya was liking her a little better.

Maya's phone buzzed on top of her desk. She glanced down to see a text from Frances. *Still at the doctor appt. All good. Will call later.*

She had almost forgotten she had a partner, since Frances was hardly around anymore, but she kept telling herself Frances would have the baby and be back from maternity leave before the business went under. At least she hoped that would be the eventual outcome.

But with the bills still piling up every day and no active clients . . .

"Do you need to answer that?" Chelsea asked in a slightly irritated tone. She didn't appreciate Maya's focus drifting off her for even a few seconds.

"No, not at all," Maya said, smiling. "Is there anything else I need to know about Maisie? Was she dating anyone?"

Chelsea burst out laughing. "God, no! That's actually why I wanted her to come down to the city and meet this playwright. They are both boring bookish types, so I thought maybe they would hit it off and she would finally have a man in her life!"

"Did the police question you?"

"Briefly. Some detective with a sexy-sounding voice . . . Miguel or Manuel . . . ?"

"Mateo?"

"Yes! Mateo! He called me the day after it happened. I told him just what I told you. That Maisie would never kill herself. But he didn't seem to care all that much about what I had to say. He was more interested in locating her phone, hoping it might provide some clues about what was going on with Maisie. It wasn't on her, nor was it in the office where she was found, or in her car, or at home. Maisie always had her phone with her."

"That's odd."

"So will you take my case?" Chelsea asked, her big crystal-blue eyes wide-open as her perfect lashes flapped up and down expectantly.

Maya thought for a moment.

It would be an uphill battle convincing the police of anything now that they had so quickly and efficiently closed the case, so getting her hands on the autopsy report would be nearly impossible.

Plus there was the strong plausible argument that Maisie did feel guilty about the damage she had caused at the school with her irresponsible and gossipy website, enough for her to take such drastic action as to hang herself in her office.

But then there was the nagging evidence Maya had spotted at the crime scene. The bruise on Maisie's neck suggesting strangulation by an assailant. How could the cops have missed that? Or had they found more compelling evidence proving Maisie's death was indeed a suicide that she didn't know about? She could be totally wrong.

Finding Maisie's phone might lead to a treasure trove of useful information that could shed some light on Maisie's situation, but if the police had failed to locate it, her own chances were probably slim to none.

But as Maya's eyes settled on Chelsea's Fendi Runaway tote bag, which looked like one Vanessa had coveted once in a catalog and retailed at something like three grand, Maya had her answer.

If Chelsea could shell out that kind of money for a purse, then she could more than likely pay Maya's retainer and then some, and right now, she desperately needed a client with deep pockets.

"Yes, Chelsea, I'll take your case."

CHAPTER EIGHTEEN

"What the hell are you doing in my sister's place?" Chelsea screamed, as she charged into the one-bedroom apartment before Maya had a chance to stop her.

The man jumped back, startled. He was big, well over six feet, his towering frame a mix of fat and muscle. He was in a red tank top, and he had shoulder-length hair, a bushy beard, and quite a bit of curly shoulder hair. The apartment looked cluttered enough to have been ransacked. Maya and Chelsea had come to Maisie's apartment in search of clues and had already stumbled upon their first suspect.

Chelsea took one look at the unsavory dude and the open drawers and Maisie's clothing strewn about and quickly snatched her phone from her pocket. "I'm calling the cops!"

"No, wait," the man begged, taking a step forward.

Maya grabbed her Glock 19 handgun out of her bag and aimed it squarely at the man's chest. "Stay where you are!"

"Holy sh—!" he cried, shooting his hands up in the air. "Wait, I'm not a robber! Look, I have a key!"

He held up a hand, where a shiny key jangled off a scuffed rusted ring he held between two of his thick fingers.

Maya glanced over at Chelsea, who was ready to punch the last 1 in 911. "Hold on a minute."

She looked back at the man, gun still drawn. "Who are you?"

"Spencer. Spencer Jennings," he stammered, his voice shaky. "I am . . . I mean, I *was* Maisie's boyfriend."

"*Boyfriend?*" Chelsea gasped. "That's a lie! Maisie would have told me if she had a boyfriend!"

"You must be Chelsea . . . ," he muttered.

"That's right," Chelsea said warily.

"Yeah, she told me all about you," he sneered, shaking his head, before realizing Maya's gun was still trained on him and the fear of getting a bullet through his chest returned.

"So what did she say?" Chelsea demanded to know.

"How she didn't want to tell you about me because I'm currently between jobs, and she was afraid you'd judge me and her for dating me, and that you would try to poison our relationship. Her words, not mine."

"What? I would *never*!" Chelsea wailed.

Maya was leaning toward believing Spencer at this point but kept mum as she slowly lowered her gun.

"If you're not here to rob the place, then you're here looking for something. What is it?" Maya asked.

"A necklace. Cost me two hundred bucks at Kay Jewelers. I spent every last cent I had to my name, but it was Maisie's birthday a few weeks ago, and I wanted to get her something special."

"I'm sure she loved it," Maya said, suppressing the urge to inject a tinge of sarcasm.

"You bet she did. She was very impressed. She cried when I gave it to her. But then . . ." his voice trailed off.

Maya guessed the rest. "She hung herself a few days later, or so the story goes, and you thought maybe you could come back here with the key she gave you and retrieve the necklace so you could return it to Kay and wouldn't be out two hundred bucks."

"It's not like she wanted to be buried with it," he said defensively.

"You're right," Chelsea said, mouth agape. "I am so totally judging you right now."

Maya looked around. "Did you find it?"

Spencer shook his head. "No, I searched everywhere."

"How long were you and Maisie together?" Maya asked, keeping her gun close to her side in case she was wrong about Spencer and he wasn't as harmless as he was coming across.

"Six, maybe seven months. I didn't exactly keep track. But we had a good time together, and she told me she was getting ready to tell her family about us," he said, eyes narrowing as he glared at Chelsea.

"I don't believe you," Chelsea spit out. "In fact, I think Maisie finally realized what a loser you were and broke it off, and when she refused to give back the necklace you bought her, you killed her and staged her death to look like a suicide to throw the cops off your scent!"

"You're crazy, lady!" Spencer yelled, eyes wide. He shot a look toward Maya, hoping she might come to his defense.

But she didn't.

"I would never touch a hair on Maisie's head, I swear! I'm a good guy!"

Chelsea turned to Maya. "I still think we should call the cops."

Maya shook her head, her eyes fixed on a quivering Spencer.

"I'm going to do my homework on you, Spencer Jennings," Maya said calmly. "I'm going to turn over every rock and scour every corner, and if I find one hint of a history of violence, a police record, or even a jaywalking ticket, I will come after you, because even though I'm willing to give you the benefit of the doubt now, that could change in a heartbeat, do you hear me? I will hunt you down."

"I have a DUI!"

"What?" Maya asked.

"I got pulled over on my way home from a party a few years ago and got busted for drunk driving! It cost me fifteen grand and a year of substance-abuse classes, but I got my driver's license back and all is good now! It only happened once! Other than that, I have a clean record."

"Give me your license."

"What?"

"Your driver's license—let me see it."

Spencer hesitated, then reached into his back pocket.

"Slowly . . . ," Maya warned.

He pulled out his wallet and gently brought it around

in front of him. He opened it up and pulled the laminated card out and handed it to Maya.

She studied it.

"Forty-One Bridgeport Road, Brunswick, Maine," Maya said as she memorized it. "Now I know where you live."

She handed the license back to Spencer. "Get out of here."

Spencer nodded and started to leave when he stopped in front of Maya and stuck out his hand.

"Thank you," he said softly.

"For what?"

"For not calling the police. I really appreciate it."

"No problem, as long as Maisie gave you that spare key to her apartment and you didn't steal hers and have an extra made."

"No. She definitely gave it to me."

"Then we're good."

"Okay," he said, his face full of relief.

Maya waited for him to go, but he just stood there a few moments longer, staring at her.

"Was there something else?" Maya finally asked.

"Uh, I know this is a really inappropriate time to ask this given the circumstances, but . . ." he stopped himself, debating whether he should continue, but then he stupidly went for it. "Are you single?"

Chelsea gasped, appalled.

Maya gripped her gun and raised it slightly, enough for him to notice. "Do you actually hear yourself right now?"

Spencer's face went pale. "You're right. That was a really bad call. I never should have asked that. I can be really dumb sometimes."

"Well, we finally agree on something, but I got that impression from the moment you told me you drive drunk."

"You ladies have a nice evening," Spencer said as he gingerly slipped past Maya and scampered out the door.

"I can't believe you let him go," Chelsea barked.

"He won't go far, if we need to talk to him again," Maya assured her.

"Why would Maisie hide something like that from me? It doesn't make any sense."

It was clear that self-absorbed Chelsea didn't hear, or chose to ignore, the very probable reason, as Spencer spelled out in exquisite detail, as to why Maisie had shut her sister out on her romantic life.

But Maya wasn't about to upset a paying client.

"What really gets me is how he hit on you like that!" Chelsea said, infuriated.

"I've got to admit it was a pretty ballsy move considering I was packing heat," Maya laughed.

"No, I mean why would he pick *you* over *me*? I mean, seriously, I'm a successful Broadway actress who does Pilates six times a week."

Maya nodded, trying her best to be sympathetic.

"Do you know how many guys—from Wall Street hedge fund managers to hipster artists painting murals in the East Village—do you *know* how many of them take a whack at me every single day on the street on my way to the theater, at restaurants, the gym, gallery openings? It happens everywhere I go! I mean literally, it's insane!"

"I can only imagine," Maya said.

She had just deposited Chelsea's retainer-fee check using her phone and bank app, but it had yet to clear, so she really wanted to keep her happy until she knew for sure that the money was safely in her account.

"The guy obviously has a few screws loose," Maya added for good measure.

"*Right?* I totally agree!" Chelsea said.

Maya was wise enough to know it was not just the restaurant and retail businesses where the client is always right.

CHAPTER NINETEEN

His face looked drawn and tired. She worried that he wasn't getting much sleep behind bars. And she was probably right. He had entered the dayroom in handcuffs and wearing a tan jumpsuit that hung off his once-muscular frame. But she could see there was still a little twinkle in his eye, especially when he saw his beaming daughter excitedly waving at him.

As he approached and the officer who accompanied him released his wrists from the handcuffs, Vanessa impatiently shifted back and forth on the balls of her feet, anticipating the moment when she could finally make physical contact with her father.

When the officer snapped the cuffs on his belt and stepped back with a cursory nod, that was her cue. Vanessa rushed forward and threw her arms around her father, Max.

"I love you, Daddy!" she practically sang, holding him tight.

"I love you too, baby girl," he choked out, voice cracking, on the verge of tears.

Maya could tell how much he missed his only child. She surreptitiously checked her watch. Twenty-nine minutes and forty-six seconds left for this little family reunion.

Max noticed her checking the time and frowned. He knew she didn't like being here, exposing her daughter to a state prison and all that entailed, but they both knew there would be no living with Vanessa if Maya didn't at least agree to a few visits to see her incarcerated father. Early on, Max gently asked about conjugal visits, which to her surprise, were allowed at this facility, but Maya had quickly declined. That was right before she asked for a divorce.

When Vanessa finally let go first, they both sat down, smiling at each other. Maya folded her arms, choosing to take a back seat in the conversation.

"How's school?" Max asked.

"It's all right. I'm in the school musical."

"What are they doing this year?"

"*Hello, Dolly!* . . . again," she sighed. "We pushed for *Rent* but Ms. Callis is afraid it's too edgy and doesn't want any more controversy after she tried doing *The Full Monty* . . ."

Max chuckled. "Are you Dolly?"

"No, Minnie. She's whiny and hysterical and kind of fun to play."

"I'm proud of you," Max said sincerely, but then his smile faded. "What about boyfriends? You're not dating, are you?"

Vanessa blanched, covering her face with her hands.

"You better not be. I may be stuck in here, but I know people . . ."

"Max!" Maya admonished.

"What? I'm kidding. Just because I'm locked up and all my personal belongings are being stored in a metal box doesn't mean I have to put my sense of humor in there too, you know."

Vanessa deftly avoided the topic. "Any news on a parole hearing?"

"I think we're still a little too far out from that right now, baby girl," Max said.

Vanessa stared glumly at the floor. "Oh . . ."

Her disappointment was killing him, so he tried a more optimistic tack. "But we'll get there at some point."

Maya's heart broke for her daughter. Her father's arrest, which was all over the news at the time, had been especially traumatic for her, and then there was the pain of the highly publicized trial and conviction. Their house had been vandalized, their garage door spray-painted with the word *Guilty* even before Max's arraignment. What was remarkable was Vanessa's strength and determination to protect her father and not succumb to the public trolling of her social media accounts. But despite her steely resolve, Maya could tell the situation had been hard on her, and it pained Maya, as a mother, not to know how to make it any easier. The fact was, they were both still hurting and there was a big empty void left in their lives now.

Max and Vanessa engaged in some more small talk, and the time zipped right by. Maya was surprised when she glanced down at her watch and they had only three minutes left.

Max shot a look at the officer, who was getting ready to return him to his cell, and then returned his gaze to Maya. "Have you filed the papers yet?"

Vanessa pretended not to know what he was talking about, but she wasn't that good of an actress. She knew exactly what papers to which he was referring.

"Uh . . . no . . ." Maya said, fumbling.

He had a sad puppy-dog expression on his face, which Maya instantly resented him for, because it just made it that much harder on his daughter.

"They're still with the lawyer," she said quickly, hoping to end the conversation.

"It would mean a lot to me if you took a little more time before—"

She cut him off. "Let's not do this now, okay?"

He was taking advantage of Vanessa's presence. He knew better than anyone that Vanessa didn't want her parents to divorce, that she still held out hope that maybe once he was released they would be a family again.

But that was a fantasy.

Maya could never see that ever happening.

And there was absolutely no reason that either of them should give their daughter false hope.

Max bowed his head and nodded, very dramatically, in fact, so it would have maximum impact on his daughter's already scarred psyche.

But then, he was back to his usual chatty self for the remaining time he had left to visit with his family. "So I heard about your assistant principal's suicide at the school . . ."

"It's all anyone is talking about," Vanessa said breathlessly.

"Did she suffer from depression?" Max asked.

Vanessa shrugged. "Maybe, but it wasn't something anybody really knew about. Her sister doesn't think it was suicide at all, and she has hired Mom to prove somebody murdered her."

Maya sighed. Her daughter could be frustratingly loose-lipped, another trait she apparently inherited from her father.

"Wow, that's pretty dark," Max whispered before turning to Maya. "Any leads so far?"

"I can't really discuss the case," Maya said, trying to shut him down.

"You're a PI, not a lawyer. There is no attorney-client privilege."

"You're right, Max. There is nothing legally keeping me from talking about my work. I just don't want to."

Max cracked a smile. "Okay, I'll stop. But . . ."

Maya rolled her eyes. "Here we go."

"I was just going to say, if you need any help, I still have a lot of police contacts on the outside who would be happy to do me a favor."

"I'm sure they would. Thanks for the offer. If I need anything, I'll get in touch with you."

She had no intention of involving him in any of her investigative work, but there was no harm in just keeping the peace and telling him what he wanted to hear.

Mercifully the officer was back, handcuffs in hand, ready to escort Max away. Vanessa teared up as Max enveloped her in one last hug, squeezing her tightly, bending down to whisper in her ear that everything was going to be all right and they would one day be together again.

Maya felt her own emotions rising and tears welling up in her eyes, but she fought like hell not to cry. There was no way she was going to break down in front of her estranged husband, not after all the tears she had shed over him during his arrest and trial. She had thought that she had no more tears left at one point, but there was a small part of her who still cared for him. Probably because of what they would always share—a beautiful, kind, and thoughtful daughter.

The officer finally broke up the emotional goodbye, snapped the cuffs back on Max, and dragged him away. Max winked at Maya as he went past her, and she gave him a nimble nod.

And then she took her daughter by the hand and led her out of the prison and to the car, where they drove home in silence.

CHAPTER TWENTY

"You really didn't have to come with me tonight," Maya said as she sipped from a paper cup of coffee while sitting behind the wheel of her car.

"I'm done being uncomfortable sitting on my couch at home waiting for this kid to finally pop out," Frances said, tugging on the seat belt that was firmly strapped over her protruding belly. "I might as well be uncomfortable sitting here with you where we are actually doing something."

"Well, I appreciate the company," Maya said, smiling.

Frances grabbed a small bag of potato chips off the dashboard, ripped it open, and began devouring it. "I've had so many cravings lately. Right now I'm all about salt 'n' vinegar chips. I just can't get enough of them."

"There's a 7-Eleven around the corner if you run out,"

Maya said, her eyes trained on a seedy, run-down three-story apartment building across the street.

"I'm sorry I haven't been around more," Frances said with her mouth full. "I had no idea how being pregnant makes you so tired."

"I've been through it. I understand."

"Well, I know it's been tough on you, running the business on your own. I promise I'm not going to take much of a maternity leave, maybe a few weeks, just to get acclimated to the lifestyle change."

"You take as much time as you need."

Maya knew motherhood wasn't an easy adjustment, and that Frances, although a tough talker, was not fully prepared for what was going to happen once she gave birth to her son. So, for now, Maya was going to allow her to make all the big promises she wanted, and they would adjust expectations later.

Frances finished the chips, crumpled up the bag in her hand, and then stuffed it down in the cup holder next to her. "Hey, is that him?"

Maya whipped around to see a man coming out of the building. His head was down and his hands were stuffed in the pockets of his gray sweatshirt, but she instantly recognized him. "Yes, that's Spencer Jennings."

He unchained a motor scooter from a bike rack, hopped on it, and zipped off down the street. Maya turned on her Chevy Volt and peeled out of her parking space in pursuit.

"If you don't think this guy murdered his girlfriend, then why are we following him?" Frances asked.

"Because I'm not one hundred percent certain he's innocent, and he's the only suspect we've got at the moment. Maybe he might lead us to somebody else."

"Ow . . . ," Frances cried.

"You okay?" Maya said, turning to Frances, who rested a hand on top of her stomach.

"Yeah, he's a ruthless kicker. I'll be surprised if this kid isn't drafted by the Patriots in a few years."

Spencer made a few turns down some residential streets, leaving his shabby area and entering a more up-scale neighborhood with bigger colonial houses and immaculately landscaped lawns. Maya kept her distance, staying far enough behind him so as not to arouse suspicion. He pulled up in front of a yellow nineteenth-century three-story house, parked his scooter, and trotted up to the front door.

Maya pulled to the curb across the street and switched off her lights. She watched as Spencer rang the bell and waited. The door opened, and an attractive woman, probably in her early thirties, with long wavy brown hair and a tight-fitting halter top pressed against her chest, threw her arms around him and drew him in for a long, wanton kiss. Then she took his arm and pulled him inside the house and shut the door.

Frances opened the passenger's side door.

"Where are you going?" Maya asked.

"I'm going to go in for a closer look," Frances said, struggling to free herself from the seat belt.

"Absolutely not. You stay right here. I'll do it," Maya insisted.

"Listen, Maya, I'm pregnant, not disabled, okay? I want to feel like I'm doing something, and I've missed our girls' night stakeouts. I'll be careful. I promise. We can stay in constant contact by phone. I'll talk you through everything I see. And if I suddenly go into labor, which would be such a blessing at this point, then you can take over for me."

Maya was still resistant, but she knew how stubborn Frances could be, so there really was no use in arguing with her.

"Fine," Maya sighed.

Frances blew her an air-kiss and then struggled to haul herself out of the car. Maya watched as Frances swiftly crossed the street, her hands on her belly, and darted up the front lawn of the yellow house, pretty fast for a woman eight months pregnant. She bent down to stay below the sill of the front windows but had trouble because of her giant stomach. Finally, she disappeared for a few moments behind some freshly trimmed hedges and then raised her head slowly to peek in the window. Maya could see that Frances's phone was clamped to her ear, and hers was now ringing.

Maya answered. "What are they up to?"

"They're drinking champagne. I think it might be her birthday. He just gave her a gift, which she's unwrapping now."

"What is it?"

"Hold on . . ." Frances raised her head a little higher to get a better look. "A necklace. Looks expensive too."

"That lying creep. He *did* find it," Maya muttered to herself.

"What are you talking about?"

"He bought that necklace for Maisie Portman weeks before she died. We found him in her apartment looking for it, but he claimed he didn't find it."

"Well, he just regifted it. They're kissing now in front of a roaring fire. Man, this scene could not get any more clichéd. I feel like I actually want to throw up, and this is *after* all those months of morning sickness."

Maya laughed.

"Uh-oh . . . ," Frances said, her voice trailing off.

"Frances, what is it?" Maya said urgently, sitting up in her seat. From the car, she spotted a dog, maybe a pit bull, barreling around from the back of the house that was barking wildly and racing toward Frances.

Frances stood up, her arms outstretched, holding the dog at bay, talking to him softly. "Good dog . . . that's a good dog. . . ."

The dog was unamused. He kept barking, and from across the street Maya could see the whites of his sharp teeth.

The porch light snapped on.

"I'm coming to help," Maya said, about to leap out of the car.

"No, I can handle this. Stay where you are," Frances whispered urgently, still clutching her cell phone with one hand as the dog slowly, almost methodically advanced upon her.

Maya knew dogs. She had a lot of experience with them and had owned a few. This pit bull was fully ready to attack a pregnant woman. Maya certainly was not going to stay where she was. She had flung open the driver's side door and was halfway out when Spencer and his wealthy girlfriend rushed outside to see what had upset the dog so much.

"Remus, down!" the woman shouted.

The dog instantly stopped barking and sat down on his haunches in a completely docile state.

Maya could see the woman staring at Frances, and

through Frances's phone, she could faintly hear their conversation.

"I don't know you. Do you live in this neighborhood?" the woman demanded to know.

"Me? No . . . ," Frances said in the sweetest voice she could possibly muster since her normal personality was the furthest from nice and sweet as you could get.

"Then what are you doing here? This is private property, and you're trespassing!" Spencer bellowed.

Maya rolled her eyes. He was strutting around like a rooster, his chest puffed out, a far cry from the pleading sad sack she had encountered at Maisie Portman's apartment. This was definitely his way of showing off his manliness in front of his new girlfriend.

"I'm a representative of Planned Parenthood," Frances said.

Maya suppressed a giggle.

The woman sized up Frances's protruding belly. "Guess you didn't plan so well."

Spencer cracked up. "You kill me, Katie."

She had a name now.

Katie.

"What are you doing skulking around my house?" Katie asked, snapping her fingers at her dog, who jumped up and ran to her. She kneeled down to pet him but kept her mistrustful eyes trained on Frances.

Frances was always the ultimate pro, cool under pressure, able to come up with a believable story on the spot. And tonight she did not disappoint.

"I'm just here to meet a client. I was here a couple of weeks ago, and we scheduled a follow-up appointment."

Katie looked confused. "I live here alone, and for the record, I have no plans to be a parent."

"Not yet anyway," Spencer remarked, grinning.

Katie ignored him. "You must be at the wrong house."

Frances looked at the house. "I swear it was this house. I was definitely here before."

"When was your first appointment with this supposed client?" Katie asked, her voice full of suspicion.

Frances looked at her phone. "Let's see, I need to scroll back a couple of weeks on my calendar. . . . Here it is, the sixth of October. That was a Wednesday night."

Way to go, Frances.

She purposely chose the night Maisie Portman was found hanging in her office at the high school.

Katie thought about the date and then turned to Spencer. "Weren't you here that night?"

"Yeah, I think so. You cooked me that awesome casserole and then we . . . ," he said, chuckling, giving her a conspiratorial wink. "You know . . ."

Katie nodded and then turned back to Frances. "We were both here that night. All night. There is no way you could have been at this house."

Frances glanced at the house number. "Forty-three . . . Yes, I have it right here, Forty-three Blueberry Lane."

Katie sighed. "This is Forty-three Strawberry Lane. Blueberry is two streets over."

"Oh gosh, I . . . I am so embarrassed," Frances stammered. "I guess I really do have the wrong house."

"I don't recall a yellow house on Blueberry Lane. What is the name of your client?" Katie said, eyes narrowing.

"Oh, I couldn't possibly tell you that. We have a very strict privacy policy at Planned Parenthood."

Spencer took a menacing step toward Frances. "What kind of scam are you trying to pull here, lady?"

Frances suddenly opened her mouth and screamed.

She screamed so loud the startled pit bull began barking again.

Spencer and Katie stood frozen in their tracks, not knowing what was going on.

Maya dropped her phone and reached for her gun in the glove compartment.

"What the hell is wrong with you?" Katie yelled, clutching Spencer's arm as Frances continued screaming.

"Labor pains. I think my water just broke. I better have my friend take me to the hospital right away!"

Frances almost broke into a run as she scampered back down the lawn to the street. Katie had to grab her pit bull, Remus, by the collar to stop him from chasing after her. The dog kept barking ferociously as she wrestled him inside the house with Spencer's help.

As Frances hurried across the street, her belly bouncing up and down, she gave Maya an excited little wave, impressed by her own acting abilities.

Her run-in with the happy couple had proven fruitful.

If Katie was telling Frances the truth, then both she and Spencer had an alibi on the night Maisie Portman was killed either by her own hand or someone else's. There really wasn't a reason why either of them would have a reason to lie to a representative from Planned Parenthood.

So if Chelsea was right and Maisie did not commit suicide, then Maya had to keep digging to find out who would go to such lengths to murder her and make it look like a suicide.

And as of now, her suspect list was back down to zero.

CHAPTER TWENTY-ONE

"You're the senator's wife, if I remember correctly," the detective said, shutting off his desktop computer and leaning back in his rickety old metal chair.

"Yes," Sandra said with a bright smile only a politician's spouse could muster.

"I didn't vote for him," Detective Mateo Reyes seemed to relish adding.

Sandra refused to give him the satisfaction of reacting. She kept that polite smile plastered on her face. "That's quite all right. Fortunately enough people did."

He studied her for a moment, almost like a wolf sizing up a lost elk.

"So how can I help you, Mrs. Wallage?"

"I may have some pertinent information in the Maisie

Portman case," Sandra said, moving slightly closer to him and lowering her voice.

Detective Reyes took this in and then folded his hands and rested them on his desk. "That case has been closed."

"Yes, I know. But I have a feeling Maisie did not commit suicide."

"Oh, you do, do you?"

He couldn't have sounded more condescending if he tried.

She hadn't liked him from the moment she had first seen him at the crime scene and witnessed how he had summarily dismissed that female detective Maya Kendrick.

"You have a *feeling*? Like an intuition?"

Intuition.

Of course that was a dog whistle for sexism.

But she wasn't going to play into his hand.

She was determined to have him hear her out.

"Yes, I believe Maisie was murdered."

Detective Reyes couldn't help but crack a smile. She could tell he was humoring her and not taking her seriously. But she plowed ahead anyway. "And I'm afraid I have an idea who might have done it."

"Wow," he exclaimed. "Well, go on. I'm all ears. Don't keep me in suspense."

God, she wanted to slap him across that smug face of his, but she refrained. She was here on a mission, and she was not going to be kicked out before she got everything she had to say off her chest.

Even if at the moment he was actually staring at her chest.

"Maisie Portman hurt a lot of people with her salacious website, as I'm sure you are fully aware."

From the blank look on his face, it was obvious he wasn't aware at all. Once the case was sufficiently closed, he had clearly lost interest in anything related to Maisie Portman.

Sandra cleared her throat and continued. "One person in particular told me to my face that if he found out who was behind the Dirty Laundry site, he wouldn't hesitate to kill him or her . . ."

"And who is it we're talking about?"

"Joel Metcalf. He has a troubled son with a substance-abuse problem, and Maisie exposed it to everyone at the school, even making it out to be worse than it really was. I've known Joel for years, and believe me, I have never seen him so angry, so determined to get revenge . . . I've gone back and forth on whether I should have spoken to him about this first, but I decided you should know."

"I see . . . ," Detective Reyes said quietly, thinking, going through the motions of at least trying to pretend to be engaged.

"Maybe he somehow found out Maisie was the one writing those awful things about his son, blatantly and almost gleefully invading his family's privacy, and he snapped."

"Maybe he was just venting to you," Detective Reyes offered.

Sandra shook her head. "No, I don't think it was an empty threat."

"It's an interesting theory, but then again, Maisie Portman hung herself. There was zero evidence of foul play."

Sandra decided to keep pressing the point. "I've questioned all the teachers at the school, people who have worked with Maisie for years . . ."

He interrupted her. "You *questioned* them? Are you a

fully licensed PI or just an amateur sleuth on the side when you're not being a senator's wife?"

"I'm president of the PTA," Sandra said, seething. "I have a responsibility to know what's going on at the school."

"Oh, I see," he said, almost chuckling.

"Not one teacher, or student for that matter, not one of them, believes Maisie took her own life."

"People who are severely depressed can become quite good at hiding their darker emotions."

"I suppose that's true, but I also saw Maisie arguing with a woman I didn't recognize outside the school a few days before she died."

Detective Reyes stared at her, waiting for more.

"Well, it got very heated, to the point where I had to intervene. There appeared to be a serious conflict between them. Maisie was quite upset."

He didn't say anything. He just kept looking at her, eyes glazed over, as if he was waiting for her to finally be done.

"I'm simply suggesting that it might be something you could follow up on as well, in addition to talking to Joel Metcalf."

"Okay, Mrs. Wallage, I appreciate you bringing me all this information, and I will definitely look into it. But there is no further need to concern yourself with this any longer. So you can go back to your ladies' luncheons and visiting orphanages or whatever your duties are as a senator's wife—"

Orphanages?

What is this, a Charles Dickens novel?

Sandra stood up. "You have absolutely no intention of following up on any of this, do you?"

He considered his response very carefully, given the fact he was talking to the wife of a very powerful man in the state, but in the end, he couldn't help himself. "No, I don't."

"May I ask why?"

He waved at an in-box stacked with folders stuffed with papers. "Because I have a dozen or so cases I still have to deal with today, and probably five more that will be added to my workload before the end of the day, so I don't have a lot of free time to open up an investigation that has already been closed just because you have a *feeling*."

His self-satisfied expression said it all. His opinion of her had been cemented from the minute she had walked through the door. She was a bored busybody, a privileged U.S. senator's wife, who got her kicks out of sticking her nose into police business.

His tone and demeanor were insulting.

"Thank you for your time," she said calmly, standing up and marching out of the police station.

She almost turned around so she could catch him leering at her butt as she left, but again, she was not going to give him the satisfaction of knowing she actually cared.

CHAPTER TWENTY-TWO

"I'm sorry, who are you?" Frances asked, a puzzled look on her face.

"I'm Sandra Wallage."

Frances scrunched up her face, now completely confused and glanced at Maya. "The senator's wife?"

"Yes, *that* Sandra Wallage," Maya confirmed, nodding.

Frances shrugged, not all that impressed, and turned back to Sandra. "And what are you doing here again?"

"I wanted to speak to you about one of your cases."

Frances pointed to the hours posted next to the office door of their firm as they all huddled outside in the hallway. "As you can plainly see, our office hours are from nine to six daily, and it's almost seven, so I suggest you come back tomorrow."

Sandra frowned but respectfully turned to go away

when Maya suddenly stopped her, much to Frances's surprise.

"Which case?"

"I heard you're investigating Maisie Portman's death," Sandra said.

Maya and Frances exchanged baffled looks.

"Who told you that?" Maya asked.

"My son Ryan."

"And who told him?"

"I'm not sure. A friend, maybe. Someone at his school."

"How long have you been waiting out here in the hallway?" Maya asked, pulling her office key out of her bag.

"Not long. A half hour or so. I was just about to leave a note with my phone number when you showed up."

"We were on a stakeout," Maya said.

Frances raised an eyebrow. "Do you really think she needed to know that?"

"Something connected to the Maisie Portman case?" Sandra asked, suddenly intrigued.

"Look, why don't you come inside?" Maya said, brushing past Sandra to unlock the door to the office.

"Seriously?" Frances blurted out, somewhat aghast.

Maya opened the door and ushered Sandra and Frances inside.

"When's your due date?" Sandra asked, attempting a little small talk.

"Not a moment too soon," Frances barked, snapping on the light and waddling behind her desk to sit down and take a load off her feet.

"I can make some coffee," Maya offered.

"No, thank you. I won't stay long. I want to offer my help," Sandra said confidently.

"Help for what?" Maya asked, curious.

"The Maisie Portman case."

There was a pregnant pause as the pregnant woman behind the desk stared at Sandra before snickering and shaking her head.

"I have some information that might be important that the police, to be frank, had no interest in hearing about."

"Who did you talk to?" Maya asked.

"Detective Mateo Reyes."

"That figures," Maya grumbled, giving a little side eye to Frances.

Frances sat up, defensively. "He's a busy guy, Maya. He doesn't have time to listen to every gossipy housewife who has a dramatic story to tell. No offense, Mrs. Wallage."

"I'd say none taken, but I'd be lying. And as the president of the PTA, I ethically cannot tell a lie."

Maya smirked.

The lady had a sense of humor.

"Okay," Frances groaned, wishing to wrap this conversation up sooner rather than later. "What kind of information do you have?"

Sandra recounted exactly what she had told Detective Reyes at the station. About the mysterious woman arguing with Maisie Portman in the high school parking lot. About Joel Metcalf's direct threat to kill whomever turned out to be behind the Dirty Laundry site. Maya jotted down notes as she talked, but Frances just leaned back in her chair behind her desk, hands folded on her large protruding stomach, sighing skeptically.

"Is that all?" Maya asked quietly.

"For now, yes, but I was hoping . . ." Sandra let her words trail off as she debated with herself whether she should go on.

Maya was now even more interested in what she was going to say.

Sandra glanced at Frances, who stared at her intimidatingly, but then, gathering her courage, she decided to go for it. "I was hoping you would let me help you solve the case. I feel like I could be a valuable asset."

"You mean like team up?" Frances asked, incredulous.

"Yes, you wouldn't have to pay me. I would work for free. I just want to contribute to finding out what really happened to Maisie."

Frances burst out laughing.

Maya wanted to as well, but she politely refrained because she didn't want to hurt Mrs. Wallage's feelings. It was too late. Frances had already done the job.

Maya could see Sandra getting hot, her face a deep red as she stood up, both angry and embarrassed.

"I'm sorry, I don't mean to laugh," Frances wailed, wiping the tears from her eyes.

"Oh, I think you do," Sandra snipped. "You're just as bad as Detective Reyes."

Frances managed to calm herself for a moment. "What, did you expect a more sympathetic ear because we're women?"

"I suppose so, I guess, but now I see how foolish that notion was," Sandra said as she turned and headed for the door.

Maya stepped forward to intercept her. "Please, don't be upset. We're just not in the habit of taking on additional partners to work with us on a case. I'm sure you are a very effective investigator in your own right—"

Frances snorted and then raised her hands in surrender, unable to contain herself as she began to howl again.

Sandra took a deep breath and exhaled. "I'm very

good at reading people, knowing when they're telling the truth or not. It's a skill I developed from a very young age, and it has served me well in my husband's political career. But I know what I must look like to you, a bored housewife looking for some excitement. Well, that could not be further from the truth. But I respect your decision, and I appreciate you giving me your time. Good night."

And with that, Sandra did an about-face and marched out of the office.

Maya spun around and glared at Frances, who was still chuckling and shaking her head. "You could have tried to be a little more sensitive."

"Look, I'm sorry," she said, clutching her big belly. "But when she offered to become a private eye with us, I almost went into labor for real from laughing so hard."

Maya wished to herself that the meeting had gone better. But the outcome would have ultimately been the same. Frances may have been dismissive and tactless, but she was right. They had no time to break in a wide-eyed newbie with aspirations to be the next kick-ass female private eye.

CHAPTER TWENTY-THREE

J oel Metcalf breathed in the intoxicating aroma of the piping-hot portobello penne pasta casserole Sandra had wrapped in tin foil as she stood in the doorway.

"Sandra, you are too kind," Joel said, placing a hand over his heart.

"It's one of my favorites. I thought you and Kevin might like it," she said, holding up the glass baking dish.

"Please, come in," Joel said, stepping aside and ushering her in with a warm smile.

"Hey, Kevin, Mrs. Wallage brought us a casserole for dinner," Joel called out.

Sandra could see Kevin in the living room, his long, lean body draped over the plush couch cushions, his eyes glued to a large-screen TV mounted to the wall. He ignored his father, too distracted by what he was watching or just not caring to engage with them.

"How's he doing?" Sandra whispered to Joel.

He shrugged. "Okay, I guess. Lots of erratic mood swings, but nothing like the first few days after he got home from the hospital. I've been keeping a close eye on him to make sure he doesn't get his hands on any more drugs, but I can't be with him twenty-four-seven so it's been a challenge to say the least."

"He looks well," Sandra offered encouragingly.

Joel nodded. "He's definitely feeling better but not quite ready to go back to school just yet. Honestly I think it's more about the humiliation from those nasty stories that Maisie Portman wrote about him on her website than anything else."

It certainly didn't take him long to bring up Maisie.

Sandra had been wrestling with the guilt of her true motivation for showing up on the Metcalf doorstep with a homemade casserole. Yes, she wanted to make sure Kevin got a few home-cooked meals, since his Dad was admittedly a disaster in the kitchen, but what she really wanted was to casually question Joel about his intense negative feelings about Maisie and if they were strong enough to cause him to take matters into his own hands and do something about her abhorrent actions.

"I'm just going to heat this up for you," she said, slipping past him and parading into the kitchen.

He walked close behind her, and when she bent over to turn up the heat in the oven to 350 degrees, her butt bumped into him.

"Oh, sorry," she said, standing upright and spinning around.

He had a strange, expectant look on his face, which startled her a moment before she decided to brush it off.

"Once the oven's done preheating, just pop the casserole in for about thirty minutes, or until you see the cheese bubbling."

"You're not staying?" he asked.

"I have to go home and feed my own boys," she said.

She hadn't been sure how to approach the topic of Maisie Portman when she first arrived, but since he had already brought her name up, she felt she had an opening.

"Joel, you mentioned Maisie Portman, and I've been thinking about what you said—"

Before she managed to get another word out, Joel Metcalf's lips were pressed over hers, and he was forcing his tongue inside her mouth. He planted his hands firmly on her butt and drew her close to him. Sandra gagged and squirmed in his grip and then used her hands to forcibly push herself off his chest and away from him.

The sudden move surprised Joel, and he quickly released her.

"I didn't come here for that," Sandra said.

"I'm so sorry . . . ," he said softly, eyes downcast. "I thought when you showed up with dinner . . . I guess I misunderstood your intentions."

"Joel, I'm a married woman."

"Yes, I know. But I had the impression that you and Stephen were having troubles and . . ."

"What on earth would give you that impression?"

He knew he had stepped in it and was supremely embarrassed. "I read it on Dirty Laundry."

"And you assumed that it must be true? Oh, Joel, you of all people . . ."

"You're right. I'm a damn idiot. Here I was raging on about Maisie writing those awful things about Kevin, and then I buy right into her story about you."

"Just to be clear, my marriage is fine."

The words came out loud and confidently.

Even if they weren't exactly true.

She was actually surprised by how quick she had been to dispel the notion that there might be trouble in paradise. It was probably the knee-jerk reaction of any politician's wife. Always make sure to give the voters the picture of perfection.

Joel shrank back, suddenly flustered. "Please, Sandra, forgive me. I haven't been thinking straight lately. It's been really hard with Kevin these past few months, raising him on my own and everything . . ."

"I get it, Joel, I do, but—"

"And you're such an attractive and sweet lady, so when you showed up on my doorstep tonight with a casserole, I guess I thought . . . ," he muttered, shaking his head, disgusted with himself. "Well, I guess I didn't think."

She felt terrible about giving him the wrong impression. Perhaps it was her fault. Perhaps she had given off some kind of unintended vibe. Despite her protestations that when it came to her marriage, the ship was sailing along smoothly, there might have been something in her look or actions that suggested otherwise. Like the ship had already hit an iceberg.

Still, it was in her inherent nature to cover up any unpleasantness by pretending it didn't exist.

"We've both been victims of lies and rumors, Joel, so I think we can both be given a little leeway for getting our signals crossed."

"I appreciate you understanding, Sandra. Now where were we?"

"Maisie Portman."

He grimaced as the oven beeped, indicating it had reached the desired temperature.

Sandra opened the oven door and slid the casserole dish onto the rack and closed it again. "It's just that I'm not one hundred percent certain Maisie's death was an accident."

"Why do you say that?"

She set the timer on the oven for thirty minutes. "Well, there was some evidence at the scene that might suggest foul play, according to someone who would know, plus there were a lot of people who had a strong motive to see Maisie dead."

"Including me," Joel said matter-of-factly.

"Well, yes, I suppose," Sandra stammered, pretending the thought had just crossed her mind in that moment. "And me. Along with plenty of others too, given all the nasty things she wrote about the teachers and students at the high school."

"Do you want to ask me if I did it?"

"No, Joel. I don't think you killed Maisie," Sandra said, although not as convincingly as she had hoped.

Joel cocked his head and smiled at her. "I didn't know Maisie was behind the Dirty Laundry website until after she was dead," Joel said, folding his arms. "Anything else?"

"Right. Of course. It's just that I noticed you were not at the PTA meeting at the school on the night Maisie was found hanging in her office. . . ."

"I know. I'm really not the PTA-meeting type. Just tell me how much to write the check for when it's time to raise money for new football uniforms."

"Where were you?" Sandra asked, trying to make the

question sound offhanded and casual, but coming off more like Miss Marple in the drawing room at the end of an Agatha Christie novel.

"He was at a poker game."

Sandra whirled around to see Kevin standing in the doorway to the kitchen, looking withdrawn and spiritless.

"He's right. Guilty as charged," Joel said with a grin. "I play with the same group of buddies one night a week. I never miss it."

"I remember that night because you were going to skip it because of me," Kevin said.

"That's right," Joel said as he turned to Sandra. "Kevin was home from the hospital and I didn't want to leave him alone, but he insisted I go."

"I felt bad about all the stress I had caused Dad, and I wanted him to have a break and blow off a little steam, but he was worried I was going to relapse and overdose again, so he called Coach Cooper and some teammates to come by and check up on me. They never left my side all night, not until you got home, right?"

Joel patted his son on the back. "Right."

"Do I know any of these poker buddies of yours?" Sandra asked, with an air of nonchalance.

"No, I don't think so."

She waited for him to continue, but he didn't.

"So they don't have any kids who go to the high school who I might know?"

"No. Why?"

She knew she had just overplayed her hand.

"Just curious," she said breezily, trying to brush it off.

He didn't believe her. His face darkened, and his body stiffened, like he suddenly didn't trust her. And he certainly had no intention of sharing any more information with her.

"Kevin, why don't you set the table?" Joel said sharply.

Kevin eyed Sandra. "How many places?"

"Just two. Sandra's not staying."

Sandra knew she had worn out her welcome. She couldn't very well insist on getting all the names and numbers of Joel's poker buddies in order to corroborate his alibi. At least not right now after she had pressed him so hard and made him feel like he was a murder suspect.

But she just couldn't understand why he was being so demonstrably vague. Most people would just volunteer the names without a second thought.

But Joel Metcalf, who not moments ago had kissed her aggressively on the mouth, was now acting guarded and distant.

She was convinced he was lying to her.

And she needed to know why.

CHAPTER TWENTY-FOUR

Sandra stared at her reflection in the mirror and didn't recognize herself. The curly red wig and matching lipstick, the black leather skirt and tight-fitting green halter top, the copious amount of makeup slapped on her face. She had purposely dabbed her cheeks with too much rouge and lined her eyes with a thick trail of mascara, and slipped on clanging cheap gold bracelets on her wrists, all to make herself look, well, cheap.

And it had worked.

She looked like a cheap hooker.

It was objectively an insane plan, and she still was debating with herself on whether she should actually go through with it. But after getting summarily dismissed by both the police and her new acquaintance Maya Kendrick, not to mention her patronizing partner, Frances, Sandra had decided to take matters into her own hands.

And here she was about to go out on her first undercover assignment.

She had known in her gut that Joel Metcalf was lying to her when he told her about that weekly poker game. It was the way he had so quickly averted his eyes when she asked about the other attendees. He shifted them to the left as if he was trying to construct an answer in his head. He pulled his arms into the sides of his body, oftentimes a sign of being tense and nervous. But then there was the biggest telltale sign of all. He shook his head when he claimed to have been playing poker the night Maisie was killed, which was a big indicator that he was not telling her the truth and was subconsciously admitting it.

So where did he really go once a week?

Sandra had parked on the same street where Joel and Kevin lived, just a few houses down, and waited for him to leave the following evening, a Wednesday, the night of Joel's alleged weekly poker game, and sure enough, just after dinner, around seven o'clock, Joel emerged from the house, got in his car, and drove away.

Sandra had pulled out behind him and followed him to a warehouse on the waterfront with lots of activity, people—mostly men, many in business suits—coming in and out. She had spotted a few women entering and leaving, and from their slinky and risqué attire, she guessed they were professional sex workers, although in this day and age it was definitely harder to tell. Sandra suspected this warehouse was some kind of bordello on the down low.

Joel remained inside for about an hour or so before coming out, nodding to the giant doorman guarding the entrance, and driving off. Sandra had found herself jumping out of her car and marching toward the warehouse. She figured if she could find whomever Joel met with every Wednesday night, then perhaps the woman could give Joel a solid alibi.

However, the doorman, a hulk of a man called Tiny by one of the johns who had been leaving as Sandra approached him, had put up a huge beefy hand to stop her from going inside. He knew just by taking one look at her that she did not belong there, and there was no way he was going to let her inside. Sandra had tried to explain that she just needed to speak to someone, and it would take only a few minutes, but he was having none of it. He had turned her away. It was unlikely that she would be able to force her way inside, since the doorman with the ironic name Tiny was roughly five times her size, so she had politely wished him a nice evening and walked back to her car.

Never one to easily give up, Sandra had come up with her bold undercover-as-a-prostitute idea on the drive home. She knew she had the perfect wig and outfit from a costume party she and Stephen had gone to several years ago, dressing up as a hooker and her pimp. At the time, she had convinced herself it was a cute idea, but then, of course, the press got hold of a picture from the party and had gone to town on Stephen for exploiting and making a joke of the illegal sex-worker industry in a series of political-attack ads during his reelection campaign.

And so here she was dressed in her lady-of-the-night outfit and ready for action. She took a deep breath, told herself she wasn't being stupid, that this was a perfectly legitimate plan, and then got back into her car and returned to the warehouse, parking far enough away so as not to draw any attention. She slipped out and waited until she saw a gaggle of girls, their faces painted and their breasts spilling out of their tight tops, heading toward the warehouse, presumably ready to work the midnight-to-six shift. They were too busy gossiping and joking with each other to notice Sandra quietly falling in behind them, walking close enough to give the impression they were all together.

Tiny didn't even look twice when he opened the door and greeted the ladies, and before she knew it, she was inside. The warehouse was large and cavernous, but toward the back there were a row of offices that Sandra assumed were rooms where the women held their private sessions with their clients. The girls clustered around an area with water and snacks, and Sandra awkwardly stood by, not sure how she should proceed.

Before she had time to come up with a plan, a pretty African American girl in a provocative pink bikini top and a sizable weave, turned to her and said, "I haven't seen you around before."

"I'm kind of new," Sandra answered, trying her best to sound confident and tough. She had no idea if she was at all convincing.

"I'm Shania," the woman said, giving her the once over.

"Sandy."

"Like in *Grease*. I loved that movie. That's smart. Playing the innocent type. The guys here will love that."

Sandra forced a smile and nodded while trying to tamp down her nerves.

"You look a little jumpy, Sandy."

Sandra tried to pull herself together, but she was incredibly nervous. "I don't have a lot of experience with this kind of thing, but I really need the money."

"You're adorable and you seem sweet. That will definitely work in your favor. Just do as Aggie says and you'll be fine."

Sandra assumed Aggie must be the madam or the queen bee. It was good to know who she needed to avoid.

Well, now was as good a time as any to get started. Sandra looked around to make sure they were alone and then said to Shania, "I met a guy recently at a party who comes here a lot. He said he'd like to get together the next time he's here."

"Who's that?"

Sandra grabbed her phone out of her bag and pulled up a picture of Joel she had taken last year at one of the football games at the high school after a rousing victory.

"Oh, yeah, Joel—I know him. You're right. He comes here once a week like clockwork. Nice guy, and believe me, watch out, because there a few who are not."

"I'll be careful. Is there a specific girl he likes to see when he's here? Because I certainly wouldn't want to encroach on her territory."

"He spends a lot of time with Nell. But don't worry. She's cool. She won't give you any trouble if you get down with Joel. Nell's very popular around here."

"Where is she now? I'd like to introduce myself."

Shania arched an eyebrow. "Um, probably working. But this ain't some Sunday social after church services. We're here to make a few bucks and then get the hell out of here and go home."

"I understand. But can you point her out to me?"

Shania began eyeing her suspiciously. Sandra knew she was coming on too strong. She just wanted to talk to Nell and then be done with all this because her heart was pounding and she was so scared at the moment, she thought she might pass out.

Shania finally stopped staring, then looked around and shrugged. "I don't see her. But you can't miss her. Just look for the big blonde with the largest rack. Guys who have a thing for Dolly Parton always want Nell."

"Got it. Thank you, Shania. It was nice to meet you," Sandra said, scurrying away.

It took forty-five minutes to locate Nell because she was busy in one of the rooms with a client, but when she finally materialized she was a vision to behold. Everything about her was larger than life, her hair, her face, and yes, her breasts, everything except her itty-bitty waist.

She planted a kiss on a man's cheek and waved him away. "See you next week, Hank."

The man gratefully nodded, unable to speak he was so satisfied and happy, and then he scampered off like an obedient schoolboy.

Sandra wasted no time and quickly approached Nell. "Excuse me, Nell, I'm Sandy. I just started here. Can I have a word with you?"

Nell barely glanced at her. "I'm about to take my break."

Sandra had expected this. She pulled out a hundred-dollar bill. "I'll pay you for your time."

Nell eyed the money and grinned. "My rate is two hundred."

Sandra fished through her bag for another hundred and held both bills out to Nell. She snatched them from Sandra's fingers, stuffed them down her cleavage, and then waved Sandra into her "office."

The room was bare except for a double bed.

"I'd offer you a seat, but the sheets haven't been cleaned."

Sandra peered down at the unmade bed and couldn't help but scrunch up her face, which Nell found hilarious.

"You're a newbie," Nell said, laughing. "So let me give you some valuable advice. It's usually the men who pay for my services, not the other working girls."

"I know, but this is really important," Sandra said before raising her phone and showing Nell the picture of Joel.

Nell stared at the picture but kept a poker face, not indicating one way or the other if she recognized him.

"You a cop?" Nell asked evenly.

"Me? Oh, no! Hardly! Do I look like a cop?"

"No, but you can never be too careful."

"He's a friend of mine, and I'm concerned about him."

"Is he in some kind of trouble?"

"He could be. I'm trying to help him."

Nell considered all this and then folded her arms. "Yeah, I know him."

"When was the last time you saw him?"

"Tonight. He comes here every Wednesday, always the same time. In at eight, out by nine. Literally."

Nell howled at her own dirty joke.

"*Every* Wednesday?" Sandra asked.

"Hasn't missed one in almost a year . . . maybe once, right before Christmas."

Sandra believed Nell. There was no reason not to because she had absolutely no motive to lie.

"Is there anything else? Because I've only got ten more minutes to rest this weary body before my next appointment."

"No, I'm good, thank you, Nell," Sandra said before scooting out of the room and down the hall toward the exit.

Joel was in the clear. He could not have killed Maisie that night because he was with Nell. It was a huge relief.

Suddenly a hand clamped down on her shoulder. "I know all my girls who work here, and you aren't one of them."

The hand gripped Sandra tighter, and then she was spun around. She didn't know what to expect but was surprised to see a petite young brunette with a hardened face, in jeans and a white T-shirt. This had to be Aggie, but she certainly was not what Sandra was expecting. Some dolled-up, older woman, like the madams from the movies she had seen as a kid. No, this woman looked as if she were just out of Stanford and working in the tech industry in Palo Alto.

"This is private property, and you're trespassing," Aggie said in a cool, detached tone.

"I'm sorry, I was just leaving," Sandra said, quickly turning away and running smack into the big, broad, muscled chest of Tiny the doorman.

"My girls tell me you've been snooping around asking a lot of questions. Why? What's your deal?"

Sandra's lip quivered, and she thought she might burst into tears, but she forced herself to remain calm. "Look, I don't want any trouble . . ."

"Too late," Aggie said, feigning a sad face. "You got some. Tiny, why don't you take her outside and teach her a lesson?"

Tiny grabbed Sandra by the wrists so tight she yelped in pain.

"Maybe next time you'll think twice before coming into my backyard uninvited," Aggie said.

Tiny lifted Sandra up like a rag doll and carried her away under one arm. Before Sandra had the chance to cry for help, a giant paw of a hand clamped tightly over her mouth.

CHAPTER TWENTY-FIVE

Sandra struggled mightily in the giant's grip, using her fingers to try to pry his beefy hand loose from her lips. But anticipating the move, Tiny tightened his hand against her mouth even tighter, effectively muffling her screams and nearly suffocating her. He carried her behind the warehouse, into a dark alley near a couple of industrial-size dumpsters, and then dropped her. She hit the pavement hard, banging her knee and cracking her head. She felt dizzy and disoriented and had very little fight left in her. She could feel the blood dripping down her leg from her scraped knee, and her vision was a little blurry. When she finally was able to see straight, she gulped at the towering figure standing over her, staring menacingly down at her.

"You sure picked the wrong night to come out here,

sweet thing," Tiny said in a low, guttural Maine-accented drawl.

Sandra slowly began crawling away from him, keeping an eye on his sneering face.

Tiny shook his head. "Ain't nowhere to go, darlin'."

Sandra put a hand up and whispered, "Please . . ."

"Sorry, I don't get paid to be understanding. I make my living roughing people up, and the woman who pays my bills told me you need to be taught a lesson."

"Listen to me. I'm the wife of a United States senator. . . ."

Tiny stared at her, getting a good look at her trashy getup, and then his sneer widened into a big grin. "Yeah, and I'm Prince Harry."

"I'm serious," Sandra begged.

"So am I, babe."

He flipped open the top of the dumpster and then reached down and hauled Sandra to her feet.

"What are you going to do?" she asked weakly.

"My job. Put a few bruises on that pretty face of yours and then throw you away."

He hauled back, balling up his fist, and was about to punch Sandra in the face. She threw her hands up to block the inevitable blow, when suddenly from behind them, she heard a familiar voice.

"I wouldn't do that if you want to live."

Tiny spun around.

Maya had a gun trained on him. Next to her, a very pregnant Frances with one hand on her belly and breathing hard, clenched a gun in her free hand at her side.

"Who the hell are you two?" Tiny yelled.

"The two women who the police will not charge for putting a bullet through your forehead because they will say our actions were justifiable since you were about to physically harm our friend."

It was a lot for Tiny's small brain to process, but to his credit, he finally did, and he relaxed his fist and stepped away from Sandra.

Sandra, a wave of relief rushing through her entire body, fell against the dumpster and started to cry softly.

"So you're not cops?" Tiny asked.

"Nope. Just two concerned citizens making sure bullies like you don't assault a poor helpless woman. But we can call the cops, if you like."

Tiny's eyes popped open, panic rising. "Now I don't see why you have to do that. The lady and I here were just having a small disagreement, and it might have gotten a little out of hand. . . ."

"Is that what happened?" Maya asked Sandra.

Sandra debated whether she should insist on calling the police and having Tiny arrested, but then she considered the fallout and all the questions that would arise about why Senator Wallage's wife was dressed up like a hooker loitering around the waterfront and a known brothel. She decided it would be best not to push it.

"Yes, that about sums it up," Sandra said. "Let him go. I won't press charges."

Tiny exhaled, his fears allayed.

"We ever hear you raised a fist to a woman again, we'll be back," Frances promised.

Tiny nodded and then hustled out of the alley and back to the warehouse.

Sandra rushed to Maya and nearly collapsed in her arms. "Thank you so much, Maya!"

Maya pushed her away. "What the hell were you doing out here?"

"Well, when you and Frances refused to investigate Joel Metcalf, I decided to take matters into my own hands and—"

Maya stepped forward. "Are you seriously that loony? You put on some Halloween hooker costume and drove your fancy car out to this dangerous area crawling with lowlifes so you could play out some fantasy of being a private eye?"

Sandra's face flushed. She was taken aback by the sheer intensity of Maya's anger. "I know it was impulsive, but—"

Maya cut her off. "Not impulsive. Irresponsible. Where's your investigator's license? Do you own a registered weapon? How were you going to defend yourself?"

"I don't have a gun. . . ."

"Why not?" Maya snapped.

"Because I don't like them," Sandra said softly.

"Unbelievable," Frances scoffed, shaking her head.

"Just because we didn't team up with you doesn't mean we were going to ignore the information you gave us. We've been tailing Metcalf too. That's why we are here. We saw him show up at the warehouse earlier this evening, and then double backed to find out more," Maya said.

"It's a good thing too. Otherwise, you probably would have wound up in that dumpster, brain-dead or in a coma," a disdainful Frances spat out.

Sandra knew she had gotten in way over her head. And Frances was right. If they hadn't shown up when they did, she probably would have been a national news story by morning, if someone even found her. "I'm sorry."

Frances angrily approached Sandra. "That's *all* you have to say?"

"Frances, dial it down a bit. She's been through enough for one night," Maya said, resting a hand on Frances's arm, pulling her back.

"I'm sorry, but she needs to get it through her thick skull that we are not a team. This isn't some retro episode of *Charlie's Angels*. We don't need a third."

Maya adopted a more measured approach. "I know you were just trying to help, Sandra, and I applaud your determination to get to the bottom of Maisie's death, but with no formal training, you're just putting yourself in danger."

Sandra sighed, embarrassed. "I get it. I won't do anything like this again."

Frances opened her mouth to continue her tirade, but Maya stopped her abruptly with a tight squeeze to her arm. Frances obliged and kept her mouth shut.

Sandra nodded and then turned to leave. "Good night."

But before she took two steps, she turned back around. "For what it's worth, Joel Metcalf has an alibi for the night we found Maisie's body. He was with a sex worker named Nell. She struck me as credible, so I believe her. I think Joel is in the clear."

Maya gave her a half smile. "Thank you, Sandra."

And then Sandra fled to her car, where once she was behind the wheel, the floodgates opened and she sobbed, not because she was humiliated or embarrassed, but because she had just barely escaped being beaten within an inch of her life.

She had learned her lesson.

CHAPTER TWENTY-SIX

Sandra ignored her phone buzzing incessantly inside her bag for the whole drive back to her house. Only after she was parked in the driveway did she rummage through the bag for her phone to see who had been calling.

It was Stephen.

She listened to his voice mail message. No earth-shattering news or last-minute request to fly down to DC so she could be on his arm for some political fund-raiser or White House state dinner. He just wanted to check in and see how she was doing. He had been on pins and needles ever since his last visit home and was anxious to hear that everything was fine and that he didn't have to worry about the state of their marriage.

Sandra decided not to call back just yet, because the

last question she wanted to hear from him when he answered was, "What are you doing?"

What would she tell him? "Hi, honey, not much. I just went down to the waterfront to a brothel, where I posed as a hooker to get some information and nearly got my face smashed in by a three-hundred-pound thug. How was your day?"

No, that was not an option at the moment.

She had to clear her head first before she talked to her husband.

Sandra unbuckled her seat belt and got out of the car, crossing the lawn to the front door. The door was unlocked. She headed directly to the kitchen, where she opened the refrigerator, pulled out a half-empty bottle of pinot grigio and poured herself a generous glass. She gripped the stem and tossed the wine back into her mouth, finally relaxing, happy to be safe at home.

That's when she heard a cough.

It came from behind her.

Sandra slowly turned around to see her two sons, Jack and Ryan, along with Kevin Metcalf, and another player from Jack's football team whose name she could never remember, all sitting around the kitchen table. They stared at her, wide-eyed, their mouths hanging open.

"What, do I have something stuck in my teeth?"

None of the boys even attempted to answer her.

She suddenly realized what was so interesting to look at. She was still sporting her "hooker" look.

Oh God.

"Hi, Mrs. Wallage," the boy whose name she couldn't remember squeaked.

"Hi . . . ," she drew it out, hoping he would help her.

"Gary," he croaked, staring at her immodest green halter top that accentuated her ample bosom.

She folded her arms in a lame attempt to cover herself. "Hi, Gary. Have you boys eaten? I've got a casserole in the fridge I could heat up for you."

Kevin Metcalf's eyes were glued to her tight black leather skirt. "No, we had pizza earlier. . . ."

"Mom, what are you . . . ?" Ryan whispered, unable to finish his question.

Gary finally tore his eyes away from Sandra's breasts and turned to Jack, whispering, "Dude, when did your mom get so hot?"

Jack just shook his head, speechless.

Sandra pondered attempting a reasonable explanation but then sighed, deciding against it. The last thing she needed was for Gary to rush home and tell his parents about her extracurricular activities as an amateur gumshoe. And she certainly didn't want to alert Kevin to the fact that she had been investigating his father and had discovered that his weekly poker nights were actually trips to a prostitute to satisfy his carnal needs.

No, these boys, along with her own, were better off being left in the dark.

"I'm going to go upstairs and take a shower. If you boys change your mind, just give me a holler."

"Yes, Mrs. Wallage," Kevin said, nodding, eyes still fixed on the tight leather skirt.

Sandra instinctively pulled the skirt down a bit to cover more of her thigh before spinning around to leave.

There was a flash.

She whipped back around to see who had taken a picture.

It was Gary, capturing the moment for posterity, his phone held up in front of him. He quivered at the stern look on her face. "I just wanted to . . ."

Sandra marched over to the table and held out her hand. "Give it to me."

Gary wavered but knew he was not going to win this one, so, reluctantly, he handed her his phone.

Sandra deleted the photo of her bum he had just taken before handing his phone back to him.

Ryan leaned forward. "Mom, are you in a play or something you didn't tell us about?"

That sounded at least plausible.

"Yes, why? You don't have to be the only actor in the family, you know."

And then she got out of the kitchen as fast as she could before she had to suffer through any follow-up questions.

She raced up to her bedroom, where she pulled off the green halter top, shimmied out of the skintight leather skirt, and then stepped into the shower, where the cascading rush of water began to wash away the heavily caked makeup on her face.

Sandra was determined to rinse off every last remnant of her adventure as a lady of the night, hoping the traumatic memory of the experience would also swirl down the drain and be gone forever. Even though she had a strong feeling her days as a tenderfoot detective were far from over.

CHAPTER TWENTY-SEVEN

"I still can't believe she's gone," Principal John Hicks lamented as he sat slumped behind his desk, his face drawn and tired. He stared at his hands while he fiddled with his fingers, lost in thought. "It's been a shock for everyone here . . . especially the students. Those poor kids . . . I've brought in some extra counselors in case they need to talk to someone."

Maya sat opposite him, upright and legs crossed, all business. She had a lot of questions but didn't want to appear insensitive to his grief. So she remained silent until she felt he was ready.

Finally, she cleared her throat, pulling him out of his random thoughts. "Were you aware that Maisie was the one who was behind the Dirty Laundry website?"

This aroused him out of his mournful fog. "Good Lord, no! I had no clue! I was as surprised as everyone else when I found out. That website was horrible and cruel, and I still can't believe Maisie had anything to do with it."

"I heard rumors Maisie had a few conflicts here at the school last year," Maya casually mentioned.

"Who told you that?"

"I don't remember."

Of course she did.

Her source was Vanessa.

"Yes, well, it was nothing, really. Maisie had come to me, concerned about the moral decline at the school."

"Such as?"

"The usual stuff. Girls wearing tops that were too revealing. An abundance of public displays of affection in the hallways between boys and girls, boys and boys, girls and girls, you name it. She was very upset that the culture at the school, and society in general, had become so sexualized and permissive. It really bothered her. So she took it upon herself to try and restore a little modesty."

"In what way?"

"She tried revising the dress code to ban plunging necklines and skirts that were too short and too tight for the girls and require all boys to wear khakis and dress shirts, no jeans or T-shirts, She also wanted to divide the cafeteria into sections, one for the boys and one for the girls."

"Did her suggestions get implemented?"

Hicks chuckled. "No. We're living in the twenty-first century. It's hard to go back to the ways of the past. I've been here over ten years and I've seen each generation get more and more unrestrained, shall we say, about sex and all that."

"Do you think Maisie started the Dirty Laundry site as a way of calling people out for their immoral behavior?"

Hicks thought about it for a few seconds and then nodded. "It does make sense, I suppose," he sighed. "There was something virtuous about her intentions, if that's true, but she went way over the line. I mean, she dragged a U.S. senator's name through the mud, and he was only tenuously connected to the school by being married to the PTA president!"

"Sounds like she went a little off the rails," Maya commented.

"A *little*? There is a difference between attempting to rein in student behavior and attacking a man in public service with lies and innuendos!"

"So you don't believe there was any truth to her story?"

"Of course not! And even if there was, it's none of our business. That's between Senator Wallage and his wife. But Maisie was acting like the religious police in Saudi Arabia, you know, those men who go around arresting people for anything they personally deem objectionable. It was just too much!"

Maya paused, waiting for Hicks to calm down a bit, before plowing ahead. "Mr. Hicks, do you believe Maisie hung herself?"

Hicks flinched, bothered by the unpleasantness of her question, but then thoughtfully considered it and finally nodded. "Yes, yes, I do. The Maisie Portman I knew was a deeply unhappy woman. I was stunned when I heard she had died, but not surprised by the news that she took her own life. She was bothered by so many things. I mean, you never expect anyone to do something so drastic, but somehow it made sense to me, especially after what she did. I can't imagine anyone feeling good about willfully ruining people's lives."

"Putting your personal opinion aside for a moment, is there anyone you can think of who may have had a reason to want to see Maisie dead?"

Hicks's eyes nearly popped out of his head. "Here? At the school? No! Not at all. Even the people she wrote about on her site, I could never imagine any of them being capable of murder. Not one!"

"How did the students react to her proposed restrictions on their dress code and interactions with each other?"

"They didn't take her seriously at all," Hicks said, shaking his head. "They knew I would never go for it. They see me as a modern, cool guy who has his finger on the pulse of their generation."

Maya didn't believe a word of what he was saying. Anyone claiming to have a finger on the pulse of a generation usually did not.

"I can't think of any student who actually gave Maisie a second thought, other than a few disgruntled kids in the drama club."

"Drama club?"

"Yes, based on what happened last year."

He stopped, assuming Maya knew what he was talking about. She waited for him to continue, but he just sat there. Finally, she decided she needed to prod him along.

"What happened?"

"The drama club was going to stage *The Full Monty* for the school musical. I had never seen it, nor knew much about it, so I didn't really object at first. But Maisie went absolutely ballistic. She wrote me a long email calling the show filthy and disgusting. She said our school had no business mounting such a production. Well, I rented the movie and agreed. Come on, it ends with a bunch of men doing a striptease and then flashing their junk in front of the audience right before the final curtain comes down. I called the theater director, Georgina Callis, into my office and told her there was no way I would allow her to do anything remotely that lewd and indecent."

"Was that the end of it?"

"Oh, no. Georgina explained to me that she had no intention of allowing the boys to strip naked in front of their parents and that she had the costumer design flesh-colored underwear for them to wear. Not only that, she assured me there was a trick in the end with the lighting and a big flash would momentarily blind the audience from seeing anything too risqué. So I signed off on it."

"But Maisie wasn't satisfied, I take it," Maya said.

"Not in the least. She got just enough parents to sign a petition demanding we not do the show because it was too sexually explicit, and when the school board threatened to get involved, my back was to the wall, so I canceled the whole thing. I told Georgina to do *Oklahoma!* instead because that never fails to pack them in."

"That's right. I saw it. It was fun."

"That show is a national treasure, and Georgina is a talented director. She can make anything work. But she did that production under protest. She blamed Maisie for stifling the creative spirit of her students. It got rather messy."

"So Maisie and Georgina clashed over the petition?"

"I'll say they did! It got so heated at one point, I practically had to pull them apart in my office one night," Hicks said, before the light bulb finally went off in his head. "Dear God, I completely forgot about Georgina Callis! She despised Maisie!"

"Enough to do something about it?"

"Well, no, I don't think . . . Then again, I'd never seen so much rage in Georgina than I did when Maisie interfered with her project. Georgina got so fired up and . . . Well, I honestly don't know. Maybe she could have . . ."

That was all Maya needed to hear.

She needed to speak with Georgina Callis.

CHAPTER TWENTY-EIGHT

Georgina Callis—a short, brassy spitfire, with gorgeous dark skin and a mop top of frizzy black hair—was not pleased. She did not appreciate Maya's interrupting the final dress rehearsal for her production of *Hello, Dolly!*, which was to premiere in the high school auditorium Friday evening at eight o'clock sharp.

When Maya quietly approached the free-spirited, artsy Georgina, in her flowing caftan with an African-inspired print, she was sitting in the third row of the theater shouting directions at the six boys dressed as waiters dancing around the diminutive girl playing the title role of Dolly. Maya bent down and asked if she could have a moment with her and was met with a cold stare. Georgina was under enough pressure as it was getting the show ready for opening night, and the last thing she needed was a distraction from a stranger.

Georgina waved her off dismissively. "I'm sorry, we're in the middle of a dress rehearsal. I can't talk right now. You'll have to call my office tomorrow and make an appointment."

Maya wasn't ready to give up just yet. "It will only take five minutes. I promise."

Georgina's big brown eyes flared. How dare this woman linger when there was so much more work to do. "Who are you again?"

"I'm Vanessa's mother . . . Vanessa Kendrick?"

At the mention of Vanessa's name, Georgina's mood lightened considerably. "Oh . . . Vanessa's a wonderful talent."

Maya beamed proudly. "Yes, I know."

Georgina leaned in conspiratorially and whispered, "I would have cast her as Dolly, but she's my utility player; I can plug her into any role, and she was the only one who really nailed Minnie in the auditions."

"She speaks very highly of you. She considers you a role model," Maya said, not above using flattery to get what she needed.

And Georgina was not above eagerly accepting compliments. "That's so sweet. I just try to guide her and offer her my support, and maybe a few pearls of wisdom when it comes to performing onstage, but she's got a good head on her shoulders, that one."

Vanessa, who had heard from one of her friends that her mother was in the auditorium, came out from backstage with an annoyed look on her face. "Mom, what are you doing here?"

"I just need to speak with Ms. Callis for a few minutes," Maya said.

Vanessa, embarrassed that her mother had crashed their rehearsal, huffed and stomped offstage.

Georgina suddenly looked worried. "Is this about Vanessa?"

"No, it's about Maisie Portman."

Georgina's face fell. "What about her?"

Maya leaned in and spoke softly. "I'd prefer it if we could talk somewhere more private."

Georgina stood up from her third-row seat to address the boys onstage. "Look, I know none of you are professional dancers, and a lot of you have absolutely no rhythm, at least none that I can see, so while I'm outside talking with Mrs. Kendrick, can you please go over the dance steps one more time together as a group so you're all at least moving in the same direction when I get back? Can you do that for me, *please*?"

The boys mumbled yes and nodded their heads.

"Thank you!" Georgina sighed, before stalking up the aisle and out of the theater as Maya followed close behind her.

Once they were outside in the deserted hallway, Georgina began to fidget, a bundle of nerves. "Those boys are a disaster. They dance like elephants, and not like the ones from *Fantasia*! I recruited them from the soccer team because I felt athletes might have some inkling about graceful movement, but I couldn't have been more wrong. I had to use all my regular boys from the theater department, the talented ones, to fill out the speaking roles, so I didn't have much of a choice."

Maya nodded understandingly, and then tried to get on point. "I was hoping you might shed some light on—"

"I really hope that old cliché about lousy dress rehearsal/great opening night holds true, because this rehearsal ranks as one of the worst in all my years directing shows, otherwise we are totally screwed," Georgina wailed to herself before noticing Maya. "But Vanessa is doing a stellar job. She's like the glue holding the whole damn thing together. Katharine, the girl playing Dolly, is acting like a total diva, which is insane, because she can't even hit the high notes!"

Maya tried again. "I know you've got a lot on your plate right now, so I'll make this quick—"

Georgina, who clearly wanted to get back to rehearsal, beat her to the punch. "What do you want to know about Maisie?"

"I heard you two had problems."

"Where did you hear that? Principal Hicks? Well, you heard right. I hated that uptight, horrible woman. She gleefully undermined me and sabotaged my production of *The Full Monty* last spring. There was no reasoning with her. I almost quit on the spot. It was only the unwavering support from my students that stopped me."

"So you probably were not upset when you found out she died?"

"I'm not a monster. I have empathy for anyone who finds herself in such a dark place that she would take her own life, but that doesn't change what she did or how I felt about her. Maisie Portman still haunts me. Thanks to her, I'm stuck doing *Hello, Dolly!* for the fourth time because it has been deemed acceptable content by the school board. She may be dead, but her censorship agenda lives on! I really wanted to do *Rent* for the fall musical, but no chance of that! Thank you, Maisie!"

"The reason I'm asking around about Maisie's death is because I believe—"

Georgina was on a roll and didn't let her finish. "The

one I truly feel sorry for is Maisie's sister, Chelsea. She couldn't be more different. Talk about a talented actress! Have you seen her work?"

"No, but actually Chelsea is the one who has hired me to—"

"That one's going to win an Oscar someday. Mark my words. We got to know each other in high school doing plays together. Not mindless crowd-pleasers, but real, authentic avant-garde pieces, works that mattered, shows that had the potential to change people's thinking!"

Maya's only hope of getting the conversation back on track was for her to try a bit of flattery again. "The school is so lucky to have an artist like you."

That did it. Georgina stopped her passionate monologue and managed to focus again. "Aw, you are too sweet. You mentioned something about Chelsea hiring you?"

"Yes. Chelsea doesn't believe Maisie committed suicide. She is convinced someone murdered her."

Georgina's face fell again. "She what?"

"I'm not sure if you are aware of this, but I am a licensed private investigator."

"No, Vanessa never told me what her mother did for a living. How interesting," she said, those big brown eyes bulging. "But why do you need to talk to me? Is it because of what Hicks told you? About my fractured relationship with Maisie? I've directed enough Agatha Christie murder mysteries to know you probably consider me a suspect!"

"I'm certainly not singling you out," Maya lied. "I'm talking to everybody who worked with Maisie."

"I will admit if what you're saying is true, if someone staged that scene to make it look like Maisie hung herself, then I would be a likely suspect given my directing experience. But for the record, I am a genuine pacifist, Mrs. Kendrick. Just the idea of taking another human life is incomprehensible to me."

"Did you have rehearsal the night Maisie was found?"

"Yes, but I finished early because of the PTA meeting."

"So you were at the school?"

"Yes, in my office, working on the choreography for the big Harmonia Gardens 'Hello, Dolly!' number, the one we're rehearsing now. Clearly my plan failed."

"Alone?"

"Yes, alone. I don't group-think my choreography. I do everything myself."

"Okay, thank you, Ms. Callis."

Georgina looked stricken and worried. "I didn't do anything to harm Maisie, I swear. Although I'd be lying if I told you I never thought about it."

"I appreciate your honesty," Maya said, turning to leave.

"Don't go yet. I'm going to dismiss the rest of the cast and keep those lead-footed jocks here until we get it right. You can take your daughter home."

Georgina disappeared back inside the theater.

Maya waited, replaying their conversation in her mind, convincing herself that Georgina was probably telling the truth. It was a gut feeling. But Maya believed her.

"Maya?"

Maya spun around to see Sandra approaching.

"Sandra, what are you doing here?"

"I got a text from my son to come by and pick him up after rehearsal."

"Well, he should be out any second. Ms. Callis is letting most of the cast go for the night," Maya said.

Students began filing out of the auditorium and out the door to the parking lot. Maya and Sandra waited patiently for their kids, but after what seemed like an interminable and awkward wait, with the two mothers ignoring what had happened at the docks the night before, they decided to head back inside to find them.

Georgina was now onstage, yelling at the boys, who were still sadly messing up her intricate choreography. In the otherwise empty auditorium, both Maya and Sandra saw at the exact same time, two students near the back row, in a shadowed corner, locked in an embrace, passionately making out.

Maya had to squint to get a better look, but it wasn't hard to identify her daughter, Vanessa, as one half of the head-over-heels-in-lust young couple. She turned to Sandra. "Is that—?"

"Yes," Sandra sighed. "That's my son."

CHAPTER TWENTY-NINE

The South Portland High School's production of *Hello, Dolly!* roared onto the stage in the 250-seat auditorium the following evening, full of unbridled energy and an infectious spirit. At least, that was how Sandra would have described it if she were writing a review. The cast appeared to be having such a good time the few noticeable mistakes that occurred throughout were forgivable, such as Dolly singing "Put on your Monday clothes" instead of "Sunday clothes," or when one of the tap-dancing waiters tripped and fell into the boy playing the maître d', or when her own son Ryan went blank on his lines at one point in the second act and had to be prompted by his costar and current girlfriend apparently, Maya's daughter, Vanessa.

Sandra sat in the front row, cheering the kids on as loudly as she could as the official Wallage representative since Stephen was in DC and Jack had an away game. She even led the standing ovation during the final bows before the curtain fell and the lights went up. She resisted the urge to run backstage with a bouquet of flowers and dole out universal praise to everyone in the cast. Ryan had given her strict instructions not to cause a scene, which, as a proud mother, she was prone to do. Instead, she waited in the hallway outside the auditorium for Ryan to wash off his makeup and get back into his street clothes. All he wanted to do to celebrate opening night was go out for a pizza. Sandra had encouraged Ryan to invite the entire cast, her treat, but he had declined the offer, wanting something a little more low-key, which in her mind meant a more intimate evening with his brand-new girlfriend. So she was hardly surprised when Ryan finally showed up with Vanessa hanging off him, clutching his hand.

The night before, when both Sandra and Maya had caught their kids making out together in the back of the theater, they had tried playing it cool, pretending not to be surprised or bothered by the fact that their kids were officially an item.

"You were great!" Sandra cooed. "Both of you!"

"Thank you, Mrs. Wallage," Vanessa said, beaming.

"I was a disaster! I can't believe I forgot my lines outside of the Harmonia Gardens at the top of Act Two!" Ryan wailed.

"Oh, honey, I didn't even notice," Sandra lied.

Ryan threw his hands up in the air. "Everybody noticed! Didn't you hear people in the audience laughing?"

Vanessa kissed his cheek. "Nobody cared, because you were so handsome and charming."

Sandra was struck by how poised and sweet Vanessa

appeared to be. "We're going out for pizza, Vanessa, would you like to join us?"

"I can't. My mom's here," Vanessa said, pointing behind Sandra.

Sandra turned around. Maya stood down the hall, waiting by the exit door. She waved at them with a tentative smile.

Sandra waved back. "Well, she's welcome to join us."

She half expected Maya to say no to dinner, given the simmering tension between them after Sandra's ill-advised undercover assignment and how she had to be rescued by Maya and her partner, Frances, but Maya was in a celebratory mood. Her daughter had killed it in the role of Minnie. Within twenty minutes, the four of them were at a long table with a checkered tablecloth, waiting on a large pepperoni pizza. Sandra and Ryan on one side, Maya and Vanessa on the other. Ryan's and Vanessa's hands were clasped together, resting on the table next to two shakers, one with Parmesan and the other with red pepper flakes. The two teenagers gazed into each other's eyes and whispered private jokes to each other, giggling and cracking each other up as their mothers sat across from them, feeling completely excluded from the conversation.

Sandra and Maya awkwardly smiled at each other, not knowing if they should attempt to try some small talk.

Sandra finally turned to Vanessa and said, "Did you know your mother and I went to high school together?"

Ryan seemed annoyed that Sandra was interrupting his quality time with Vanessa, but Vanessa politely nodded. "Yes, she told me."

"She knows we weren't really friends," Maya quickly added, before catching herself. "What I meant to say is, I mentioned that we ran in different circles."

There was an awkward silence.

Sandra could only imagine how Maya must have described her when she was in high school. She was painfully aware of the kind of reputation the popular-cheerleader type probably had with the cooler students.

Ryan's cell phone buzzed on the table, and he glanced at the screen. "It's Dad." He scooped it up and answered. "Hey, Dad . . . Yeah, it was okay, but I messed up my lines. . . . No, seriously . . ."

"His father is working in DC and couldn't make it up for opening night," Sandra said in an almost apologetic tone.

Maya folded her arms on the table. "I understand. He is a very busy man."

A college-age waitress—with a gloomy face that couldn't hide that she wished she were anywhere else—arrived with the pizza and set the tray down on top of a metal rack.

"Careful, it's hot," she warned before grabbing the empty plastic pitcher on the table. "I'll get you a refill of soda."

As she lumbered away, Sandra homed in on Ryan's conversation with Stephen. "Her name's Vanessa. . . . Uh-huh . . ."

He was beaming now.

"An eleven, definitely an eleven."

Sandra knew Stephen was asking about Vanessa's looks on a scale of one to ten and didn't appreciate it. Especially given recent events involving the now-shuttered Dirty Laundry site. She also didn't like him encouraging his sons to objectify women, but that was a whole other matter.

Vanessa, on the other hand, was loving every minute of it. She picked up the spatula that came with the pizza and adoringly served Ryan a slice on a paper plate first before dishing out one for herself. She then set the spatula down on the table, ignoring her mother and Sandra, who were left to serve themselves.

Ryan finally looked up at Sandra. "Do you want to talk to Dad?"

"No, I'll call him when I get home," Sandra said with a thin smile.

"She'll call you later," Ryan said into the phone, before finishing up the conversation. "Love you too, Dad." He ended the call, set his phone down on the table, and grinned at Vanessa. "My dad says hello."

"I can't wait to meet him," Vanessa purred, leaning in close enough to his face that he was able to steal a quick kiss on the bridge of her nose.

Oh, to be a high school student and in love again.

From that point on, Ryan and Vanessa were too into each other and their pizza to care about what their mothers had to say. They basically tuned them out, leaving Sandra and Maya to entertain each other.

Maya was the one to break the ice first. "It must be difficult raising two boys when your husband is gone so much of the time."

Sandra had always been sensitive about how much time she and Stephen spent apart. But there was no judgment in Maya's voice. She had a much tougher situation than Maya. Her husband was serving time in prison. At least Stephen made it home every other weekend.

"It can be. Especially now when their hormones are raging like a category-five hurricane," Sandra cracked.

Maya chuckled, casually eyeing Vanessa, who was practically wrapped around Ryan at this point. "It's not just the boys, believe me."

By the time the pizza disappeared, so did Ryan and Vanessa, who spotted some castmates at another table and bolted away from their mothers to go socialize with people their own age.

Sandra's discomfort around Maya seemed to melt away as the two women began communicating as mothers. Maya explained how hard it had been for both her and Vanessa after Max's arrest and trial. As a politician's wife, Sandra could relate to weathering a scandal, but she was amazed at Maya's grace and fortitude as well as her single-minded determination to protect her daughter throughout the entire ordeal. For Maya's part, she proved to be a sympathetic ear when Sandra finally opened up about the pain of the Dirty Laundry article, although she decided to remain mum about Stephen's past infidelities. She was trained to keep uncomfortable truths that could hurt the family's reputation in Washington tightly under wraps.

Sandra sensed a bond slowly developing with Maya and felt obliged to say, "Listen, I want to apologize for the other night. You were right. I had no business running headlong into danger like that."

"No worries," Maya said, waving it off.

"No, really. I was extremely lucky you and Frances were there, otherwise . . ."

"I understand. You want answers. So do I. That's why I showed up at the rehearsal last night. I wasn't just there to pick up Vanessa. I wanted to talk to Georgina Callis."

Sandra sat up, puzzled. "Georgina?"

"Apparently she and Maisie Portman had a very contentious relationship."

"I heard there was a small kerfuffle last year over the spring musical . . ."

"It was more than just a kerfuffle. They despised each other, and Georgina's alibi on the night Maisie was killed is a bit wobbly. She was in her office alone."

"I had no idea. . . ."

"She got *very* uptight the more I questioned her. She finally shut me down, but I have a feeling she has more to say. She's just not going to say it to a private investigator."

"I can get her to talk," Sandra said confidently.

Maya raised an eyebrow. "How?"

"Stephen and I have donated thousands of dollars to the theater department. We are big believers in the arts. In fact, our donation helped build that state-of-the-art theater where we just saw *Hello, Dolly!* tonight. In other words, Georgina owes me. Big-time."

Maya leaned forward on her elbows. "I'm listening. . . ."

"Well, as a valued patron, I'm sure Georgina would feel obligated to answer a few questions, especially from a concerned mother and president of the PTA, at least for now anyway."

Maya grinned, "You sure are determined to be a detective, aren't you?"

"I just want to be helpful," Sandra said, although she could tell Maya wasn't buying any of it, because it was true. Sandra was hooked. "Georgina and I both take a cooking class on Saturday afternoons, which happens to be tomorrow. That will be the perfect time to grill her . . . pardon the pun."

Maya laughed heartily.

Sandra felt a surge of excitement. After the debacle at

the warehouse brothel, she now had a chance to prove herself again to Maya, and she was not going to screw it up.

The question was, however, why was it so important to her? Maya was almost a complete stranger, a woman she hadn't really spoken to since high school and barely back then. Why was she so stubbornly firm in her resolve to show how capable she was? She knew she envied Maya's investigative skills and coolness under pressure and wanted to be like her, but now there was a fondness growing for Maya too. Sandra was also anxious to prove her worth as a friend. Because at the end of the day, besides her husband and sons, she didn't have a lot of friends.

Close friends anyway.

CHAPTER THIRTY

Sandra made sure she secured the spot directly next to Georgina Callis at their Italian cooking class that was held every week at Luigi's Ristorante in the Old Port. Today's lesson was on how to make the perfect chicken Parmesan. Luigi, a larger-than-life bear of a man with a messy black beard with specks of gray, always showed up for class wearing all white, including his signature chef's hat. He played the role of the Italian lover to the hilt by flirting with all the ladies in class, especially the older ones. But it was all in good fun, and no one ever called him out for being inappropriate.

Luigi partnered up his students and assigned them to different workstations in the kitchen to handle the various stages of preparing the dish. Since Sandra was standing right next to Georgina, they were paired up and placed at the stove, where they would fry the chicken according to Luigi's instructions after it was breaded by another team. Luigi took his time walking them all through the process, pontificating about the importance of seasoning the meat just right before adding the homemade tomato sauce and mozzarella cheese. And without fail, he would usually wind up telling a long colorful story from his childhood about growing up in Palermo and how he learned to cook from his beloved grandmother Carlotta.

As Sandra and Georgina patiently waited for the breaded chicken to make its way to them and Luigi was preoccupied playfully complimenting a grinning, giggly seventy-five-year-old woman on her "sexy" new hairstyle, Sandra whispered to Georgina, "I just have to tell you, you did a wonderful job directing *Hello, Dolly!*"

"Thank you so much," Georgina said with a radiant smile.

"Ryan has learned so much from you, and I appreciate the way you have cultivated his talent as an actor. He's looking into applying to Juilliard next year."

"Well, he can count on me for a glowing recommendation. He is one of my best students. You should be very proud of him."

"We are. Stephen's worried about how he will fare in the real world after high school. He thinks the competition is too fierce and Ryan should have some kind of backup plan just in case the acting doesn't work out, but I have always believed in following your heart. And if acting is what the kid wants to do, then he should give it one hundred percent."

Georgina nodded, but it was obvious she was suddenly distracted.

"Did I say something wrong?"

"No. Not at all."

Sandra could tell Georgina wasn't being truthful. In fact, she hadn't even mentioned Maisie Portman yet, but she already had the feeling she had somehow upset Georgina.

Georgina's face was flushed red, and she was fidgety as Luigi arrived at the stove, and with great fanfare delivered the freshly breaded piece of chicken to the frying pan.

"Now it looks like you have just the right amount of olive oil heating. You can also use butter if you wish, so let's now cook the coated breast, about two minutes on each side, until golden. Not too much, because it will finish cooking in the oven. Why don't you do the honors, my lovely Georgina?"

Georgina took the freshly coated breast and carefully set it down in the sizzling oil. Then Luigi was off on another tangent, recounting the time as a boy he was on a bike ride and got caught in a thunderstorm and showed up at a house in a nearby village to get out of the rain and ended up cooking a seven course meal for a family he had never met.

"I think the last time I tried to make chicken Parmesan was for that potluck dinner that doubled as a fund-raiser for Mrs. Rossi's Italian class to go to Rome," Sandra said before casually adding, "Maisie Portman said it was the worst chicken Parmesan she had ever tasted."

Actually Sandra had made veal piccata and Maisie loved it, but it was not as good a segue, so she changed a few details.

Then Sandra frowned and slowly shook her head. "Poor Maisie . . ."

Georgina ignored her and kept her eyes fixed on the chicken and checked her watch, counting down the two minutes until she could turn the chicken breast over in the pan.

"You know, there are rumors going around that Maisie didn't commit suicide, that she was actually—"

"Do we have to talk about this now? I'm trying to concentrate on the chicken Parmesan."

"I'm sorry, Georgina, I didn't mean to upset you."

"I'm not upset! Why would I be upset?"

"Well, it's no secret that you and Maisie had a somewhat checkered history."

"What are you implying?"

"Nothing, I didn't mean to imply anything. . . ."

Georgina was now totally discombobulated and gestured wildly with her hands. "Why does everybody keep bringing up Maisie Portman to me? It's not like I had anything to do with what happened to her! She was a lonely, miserable woman who hated her life and was tired of living it! End of story!"

"But are you sure Maisie was *that* unhappy?"

"I don't care! I never want to hear that woman's name again! Would you please stop bringing her up?"

Sandra attempted to lower the temperature in the room.

"Georgina, please forgive me. I always seem to put my foot in my mouth. My husband, Stephen, tells me it's one of my greatest talents."

Sandra laughed, trying to lighten the mood.

But it only seemed to distress Georgina even further.

She was now a downright emotional mess.

"I try to be a good person and live an honorable life, but no one is perfect, okay? We all have our secrets! I just can't deal with this interrogation right now!"

What was she talking about?

Sandra had hardly even gotten the chance to ask any questions about Maisie yet, and Georgina was already losing it right in front of her.

That's when she noticed the smoke billowing up from the stovetop.

Georgina had plumb forgot about the chicken.

It was well past golden and heading straight for blackened.

"Georgina!" Sandra cried, grabbing the spatula to scoop up the burning chicken from the hot oil.

Georgina practically body-checked her and wrenched the spatula away from Sandra. She picked up the chicken and hurled it across the room to the sink. It missed and landed on the floor. Some hot oil splattered out of the pan and onto a dish towel Georgina had left right next to the burner, and it suddenly went up in flames. Georgina screamed and grabbed some pot holders to beat down the flames, but then the potholders ignited.

Luigi was so busy wrapping up his long story he didn't even notice the kitchen fire at first, but when the smoke alarms overhead began blaring, that finally caught his attention. Luigi ordered his students to evacuate as he first tried to snuff the fire out with one of his pot lids and, failing that, began pouring baking soda on it. Sandra tried to hand him a nearby fire extinguisher, but he refused, fear-ing it would contaminate his kitchen. Sandra decided to call 911 as she filed out of the restaurant with the rest of Luigi's cooking students.

Outside, Georgina purposely avoided Sandra as the five women and two men milled about waiting for the fire department to arrive.

It was obvious in Sandra's mind that Georgina Callis was definitely hiding something.

The question was, what?

CHAPTER THIRTY-ONE

S andra's heart sank when she arrived at Maya's office and spotted through the window on the door Maya's partner, Frances, sitting across from her on a small couch, her feet up on a weathered off-white ottoman, her hands resting on her big, round belly.

Sandra considered doing an about-face and hightailing it out of there before knocking, but Maya, who was behind her desk, spotted her and was already standing up and crossing to the door.

At least Maya smiled when she opened it to greet her. "Hello, Sandra."

It wasn't exactly a warm welcome, more confused and tentative, but Sandra could tell Maya's opinion of her had greatly improved after they bonded over pizza.

Sandra kept an eye on Frances, who grimaced at the sight of her. "I don't mean to bother you . . ."

"No bother, come on in," Maya said, stepping aside and ushering her inside.

Sandra nodded at Frances and tried a breezy tone. "Hi, Frances!"

Frances audibly groaned as Sandra swept into the office, but after a sharp look from Maya, she begrudgingly shrugged and grunted, "Hello."

It was clear Frances was annoyed by her presence, and so Sandra didn't want to drag this out any longer than she had to, so she got right to the point. "I spoke to Georgina Callis at my cooking class today."

Maya closed the door and walked back behind her desk. "And?"

"She got so upset over me questioning her that she nearly burned the whole restaurant down," Sandra reported breathlessly.

"Who is Georgina Callis?" Frances asked, slightly curious but not wanting to engage Sandra too much.

"Drama teacher at the high school who had a very combative relationship with Maisie Portman," Maya said before turning back to Sandra. "Coffee?"

"No, thank you," Sandra answered.

Frances tried sitting up on the couch, but her massive pregnant belly made it difficult, so she had to swing her feet off the ottoman, plant them on the floor, and use her hands to lift herself into a manageable position. "Wait a minute . . . why were *you* questioning her?"

"I didn't get anywhere trying to talk to her, so Sandra volunteered to give it a try, since she has a little political clout as the PTA president," Maya said.

Frances was now struggling to stand up but couldn't. "So when did you two collude together and decide to send Sandra out in the field . . . again."

"Calm down, Frances," Maya said, laughing. "She wasn't exactly out in the field. They just take a cooking class together."

"You haven't answered my question," Frances said, still laboring to rise up off the couch.

Maya finally crossed to her and took her hands and hauled her up on her feet. "Our kids are in the musical together at the high school, and we took them out for pizza after the show, and we were chatting. There is nothing sinister about it. I'm not looking for a new partner."

Frances shot a glance at Sandra and then turned back to Maya. "Of course I know that. You'll never find anyone better at this job than me. And once I pop out this baby, I'll be back one hundred percent, that I can promise you."

"It's all good, Frances, really," Maya said soothingly. "You can take all the time you need. Don't pressure yourself."

Sandra smiled. "I remember when I was carrying my first child, Jack, and he was such a kicker, I mean constantly, and one night—"

Frances cut her off. "Was there anything else?"

Sandra shook her head, deflated. "No, that was it. But if you want my opinion . . ."

Frances opened her mouth to speak, but this time Maya interrupted her before she had the chance. "Yes, Sandra, please, tell us what you think."

Maya stared at Frances, silently warning her to behave.

"Well," Sandra said, clutching her purse. "Georgina is clearly hiding something, so I would suggest we, I mean you, do some kind of stakeout and follow her around."

Frances sighed. "To what end?"

"Well, if she *was* responsible or had a hand in Maisie's murder, then she might somehow make a mistake or show her true colors."

"That's a pretty broad canvas for a stakeout," Frances argued. "Tailing a drama teacher on the off chance she might be connected to a death that the cops ruled a suicide."

"We have a paying client, Frances, who wants us to prove her sister was murdered, so I think Sandra is right. We need to follow every lead, even if it's just a feeling that Georgina is hiding something."

"Fine. Whatever," Frances huffed.

Maya took a deep breath and treaded carefully. "And maybe it wouldn't be such a bad idea if Sandra joined us on this one—"

"*What?*" Frances cried.

"Hear me out. She knows everybody at the school, and she can get to people we don't necessarily have access to, and with you about to go into labor at any moment . . ."

"I'm not going anywhere until my water breaks, do you hear me? I can do the job, Maya," Frances said, seething.

"I know you can, but what's wrong with enlisting a little free help?"

"Help? She's not a professional. The woman has absolutely no experience, and she has no idea what she's doing! She nearly got herself killed! She will just get in the way!"

Sandra could see Maya trying to play the diplomat but just getting caught in the middle, so she decided to intervene. "Frances is right, Maya. I'll be honest. I scared myself silly playing detective the other night and have no desire to ever put myself in such a dangerous situation again. So I'm just going to go home and let the professionals handle this."

"I promise to keep you in the loop," Maya said.

"I would appreciate that. Thank you," Sandra said, before turning to Frances and trying one more time. "Good luck with the baby, Frances. You're going to love being a mother."

It didn't work.

Frances just stood there, eyes blazing.

Sandra knew it was time to leave. "Have a lovely evening, ladies."

"'Bye, Sandra," Maya said with a rueful smile.

Sandra slowly backed out of the door, leaving it open a crack, and then clattered off down the hall before realizing she was walking in the wrong direction and returned, passing the office door, heading the other way.

She overheard Maya scolding Frances. "You didn't have to be so rude."

But Sandra knew Frances didn't care about her and was just happy to hear that she was not going to be sticking her nose into their business again anytime soon. Frances was finally rid of her.

CHAPTER THIRTY-TWO

"For an artsy type, she sure is the most boring person we've ever staked out." Frances sighed, biting into the burger they had picked up at a McDonald's drive-through before parking in front of Georgina Callis's modest house on a quiet residential street in East Deering, situated between Munjoy Hill, North Deering, and the neighboring town of Falmouth.

Behind the wheel of her car, Maya sipped a Diet Coke. "We've only been here a couple of hours. Let's give her a chance to prove you wrong."

"I'm not holding my breath," Frances said, shifting her body in the passenger's seat, trying to get her belly in a more comfortable position. "What's she got on the TV? Can you tell?"

"I think it's one of those Real Housewives shows, but I'm not really sure," Maya answered, squinting her eyes, trying to get a good look through the living-room window.

"She hasn't gotten off the couch since she went to refill her wineglass. God, what I would do right now for a glass of pinot noir," Frances said wistfully. "I'm betting she's in for the night. Want to call it quits?"

Suddenly there was a loud rap on the driver's side window, startling them both. Frances let out a surprised yelp. Maya whipped her head around to see an elderly man, thin, pockmarked face, a few wisps of white hair sprouting off the top of his otherwise bald head. He was holding a dog leash.

Maya pressed the button to put down her window.

"Evening, ladies," he said, staring at them through Coke-bottle glasses.

Maya nodded. "Evening."

"Do you live around here?" he asked, inspecting Frances's pregnant stomach.

Frances noticed and tried to sit up straight. "What's it to you? Are you the neighborhood-watch captain?"

Maya shot her a stern look to keep quiet as she tried a more diplomatic approach. "No, we were just in the neighborhood for a Tupperware party."

"I see," the nosy man said, glancing in the back seat to see if they had actually bought any Tupperware. "I saw you two just sitting out here as I was walking my dog, Priscilla, and, well, the neighbors around here tend to look after each other, keep an eye out for any sign of trouble, you know."

Maya leaned out the window slightly and looked down to see a scrawny, little fluffy dog with a pink bow tied to the matching pink leash, panting with her tongue hanging out.

"Cute dog," Maya remarked.

This seemed to win her a few points with the local crime stopper. He smiled and said, "Priscilla thanks you, don't you, precious?"

The little dog wasn't listening. She was distracted by another dog being walked by its owner farther down the street.

The man lowered his thick glasses to the bridge of his nose. "Did Georgina host the party?"

"Who?" Maya asked, feigning ignorance.

"Georgina Callis," the man said, pointing at her house. "She lives right over there."

Maya shook her head. "No, why do you ask?"

"I just saw you looking at her house a lot when Priscilla stopped by that tree to take care of her business."

He held up a plastic bag with dog poop inside it, causing Maya to cringe until he finally lowered it out of her view again.

"No, we don't know anyone named Regina . . . ," Maya said with a tight smile.

"Georgina. I haven't heard about anyone hosting Tupperware parties in the neighborhood. Who did you say it was?"

"We didn't," Frances interjected, on the verge of lunging at the nosy, annoying old man.

He noticed her burger. "No food at the Tupperware party?"

Frances looked down at her half-eaten burger and frowned. "I'm eating for two."

"Looks yummy. Did you know McDonald's burgers are made to order now so they are fresher? It makes a huge difference. Priscilla loves them!"

Maya checked her watch. "Fascinating. We better get

going. If I get home past ten o'clock, I'm going to be on the hook for an extra fifteen dollars for the babysitter."

"I won't keep you," the man said. "Let's go, Priscilla."

"Good night," Maya chirped, offering a friendly wave and then pressing the start button of her Chevy Volt. She glanced in the rearview mirror to see the old man making a note of her license plate.

"We can wait until he's gone and circle around the block and park again," Maya said.

"Come on, Maya, let's call it quits. Georgina's not going anywhere," Frances pleaded, finishing the last of her Quarter Pounder.

"Fine. We can come back tomorrow," Maya sighed, about to pull the car away from the curb when she suddenly stopped. "Wait!"

She slammed on the brake, and they both jolted forward, stopped only by the straps of their seat belts.

"Seriously, Maya, you want me to go into labor right here?" Frances wailed.

"Look," Maya said, eyes glued to a car pulling up in front of Georgina Callis's house. "She has company."

A man got out of a silver Mercedes sedan and walked up the driveway. His back was to them so they couldn't get a good look at his face. He rang the bell, and they could see Georgina shoot up from the couch, turn off the television, check her hair in a wall mirror, and then scurry to open the door. It flew open, and with her arms outstretched, Georgina greeted her visitor. He slid his arms around her waist and drew her closer to him. She wrapped her arms around his neck and he bent down and kissed her softly on the lips. She seemed to melt in his embrace.

The man glanced around to make sure they weren't being watched, missing the car parked across the street with the two women staring at them, and then gently pushed Georgina inside the house and shut the door.

"Who do you suppose it is?" Frances asked.

"I don't know," Maya said, raising her phone. "Maybe we'll get a better view once they're in the living room."

Through the windows, they saw Georgina cross to the bar to make the man a drink while he loosened his tie. She poured him a bourbon and handed it to him, but he was still turned to enough of an angle where he was facing away from them.

"Come on . . . come on . . . turn around . . . ," Maya said as if trying to send some mental telepathy his way.

Georgina returned with her own drink, a clear drink, like vodka with an olive in it, and smiled at him. He stroked her face, and she leaned into his palm, appearing to shiver at his touch. She turned, and he playfully patted her on the behind before she wandered back toward the couch.

She plopped down and disappeared from view as the man stood in front of her, gazing down, smiling.

Maya quickly grabbed her phone and snapped a photo.

"Maybe I can get Mateo to run a facial-recognition program or something," Frances offered.

"You don't have to do that," Maya said, still staring at the man, who was now bent over kissing Georgina.

"Why not?"

"You don't know who that is?"

"No, should I?"

"You should if you ever turn on the news."

"I work full-time and I'm eight months pregnant. I don't have a lot of free time to watch any talking heads on cable. So don't keep me in suspense. Who is it?"

"That's our United States senator from Maine. Stephen Wallage."

Frances's eyes widened. "Wait, you mean . . . ?"

Maya nodded. "Yup. Sandra Wallage's husband."

"Oh boy."

At this point, Stephen Wallage had just dropped to his knees and vanished from their viewing vantage point. They could only surmise that he and Georgina were now passing third base on the couch.

"What should we do?" Frances asked.

Maya shook her head. "I don't know."

"Should we tell her that her husband is cheating on her with her kid's drama teacher?"

Maya didn't answer.

She just stared straight ahead.

"Maya, are you still with me?"

"I'm thinking."

After a long pause, Maya shifted the gear into drive and sped off down the street.

They drove in silence for a bit before Frances couldn't take it anymore. "Well . . . ?"

"I think maybe we should tell her," Maya said, eyes glued to the road.

"Really? If we keep digging and it turns out Georgina had nothing to do with Maisie Portman's death, and her only big secret is that she's having an affair with a married man, then that's her business, not ours."

"But Sandra . . ."

"Sandra is a pain in the butt! She's not our bestie, this is not *Sex and the City*, we barely know her! We should just stay out of it!"

Maya gripped the wheel and kept driving. Frances leaned back and shifted her belly one more time, under the impression that the whole matter had been mercifully settled.

But then Maya had the final say. "I would want to know."

CHAPTER THIRTY-THREE

Maya's stomach did a flip-flop when she saw Sandra pull into the parking lot of the old-fashioned fifties diner from her booth next to the window. When she had called Sandra the following day and asked if she would be available to meet her in the late afternoon for coffee, Sandra had instantly agreed, suggesting a time and a place. Maya feared Sandra might be under the impression that she and Frances had changed their minds about her helping them out and quickly noted that what she needed to discuss had nothing to do with the Maisie Portman case. Sandra didn't seem at all fazed by that clarification.

Maya had shown up early to mentally prepare for their conversation, ordering a cup of coffee from the harried waitress, who was the only server on duty during an un- expectedly busy predinner rush. The waitress hustled toward the table, balancing a tray with three plates of the fried chicken special on one hand and a pot of coffee in the other. She stopped to refill Maya's white mug before continuing on her way to feed the three loud and raucous teenage boys at a table in the back.

Maya watched through the window as Sandra got out of her car. It was starting to drizzle rain, so Sandra quickly slammed the driver's side door shut and dashed inside the diner. She looked around for Maya, who smiled and waved at her, and then hurried over, sliding into the sky blue vinyl booth opposite her.

"Traffic was a nightmare. I hope I'm not too late," Sandra said.

"No, not at all. Are you hungry?"

Sandra scooped up the large plastic menu and perused it. "I haven't eaten all day. I'm craving something sweet. I love their desserts here."

Maya hated that she was so nervous. She had broken the bad news to many clients that their spouses were cheating on them. But Sandra was different. Her husband was well-known, a political rock star in the state, and besides that, Maya actually was growing fond of her. She watched Sandra scan the list of choices and then flag down the waitress.

Sandra smiled at the stone-faced, seen-it-all waitress. "I'll have the bread pudding."

The waitress scribbled on her pad. "Ice cream or whipped cream on top?"

"Definitely the vanilla ice cream," Sandra said.

"Got it," the waitress grunted before sliding her pen behind her ear, dropping the writing pad into the pocket of her apron, and moving off toward the kitchen.

"My grandmother used to make the most amazing chocolate bread pudding when I was a little girl. But after she died, we couldn't find her recipe. It had been passed down in the family for generations. I've tried re-creating it, but so far, no luck."

"That's nice," Maya whispered before getting right to the point. "Thank you for meeting me."

"I have a feeling I know what this is about," Sandra said with a sly smile.

Maya raised an eyebrow, surprised. "You do?"

"I was very curious after you called. You were so mysterious about what you wanted to talk to me about, but I'm guessing it has something to do with our kids' budding relationship."

"Oh, no, that's not it," Maya said, her stomach doing another flip-flop.

This was going to be much harder than she had expected.

"They're getting quite serious, if you haven't noticed," Sandra said.

"Believe me, I've noticed," Maya said. "Vanessa's face lights up every time Ryan's name is even mentioned."

Maya took a sip of her coffee, stalling the inevitable.

Finally, Sandra couldn't take the suspense anymore, and leaned in, elbows on the table. "So what's up?"

Maya took a deep breath and just started talking. She knew the words were spilling out of her mouth so fast they were almost incomprehensible, but she just wanted to get everything out—the stakeout with Frances outside Georgina Callis's house the night before, the man who showed up at her door, how it was obvious that Georgina and this man were sexually involved, how she managed to take a picture of him, how it was dark and grainy, but that didn't matter, because Maya had recognized the man from watching him on the news.

Sandra kept a smile fixed on her face throughout, up until the moment when Maya said she knew the man from his news appearances on TV. Then, imperceptibly, the smile cracked a bit before it slowly faded altogether. Maya paused, steeling herself to come out with it, but from the frozen look on Sandra's face, she knew Sandra was already aware of what Maya was about to say.

Maya spoke quietly. "It was your husband, Sandra. It was Senator Wallage."

There was a slight nod from Sandra as she took this in, but otherwise her face was a mask of calm. Maya looked down at Sandra's hands, which were now flattened on the table. She noticed a slight tremor from her left hand's index finger. As if she was fighting to keep all her emotions inside and under control but was physically unable to keep her body from reacting in some small way.

Finally, after what felt like an eternity, Sandra cleared her throat and said, "That's impossible."

"I'm afraid it's true. I saw him—"

Sandra abruptly cut her off. "It *wasn't* him."

Maya slowly reached down and picked up her phone. She punched in her code and then swiped until she found the photo that she had taken the night before. She set the phone down on the table with the screen facing up so Sandra could look at the picture. She stared at it and then pushed the phone back toward Maya.

"You can hardly see the man's face in that photo. That could be anyone."

"I know it's a bad photo. But I saw him with my own eyes, Sandra. It was the senator."

"It can't be."

Sandra looked away, refusing to make further eye contact with Maya.

"Sandra . . ."

"Stephen was in DC last night. He called me from his apartment on K Street and again this morning before heading into a committee meeting at the Capitol."

"Are you sure?"

"Yes, I'm sure. The man you saw last night with Georgina Callis is not my husband, but I appreciate you trying to warn me . . . or protect me. . . . Frankly I don't know what you were trying to do. . . ."

"I just thought you should know."

"Well, thank you," she said brusquely, checking her watch. "I forgot I promised to take Jack to get his haircut downtown. I really should be going."

"I understand," Maya said with an apologetic smile.

"It was nice seeing you," Sandra said before abruptly jumping up and rushing out the door.

Maya watched Sandra run to her car, her hand over her head in a vain attempt to protect her hair from the buckets of rain that were now pouring down from the sky.

The waitress arrived with the bread pudding with a heaping scoop of vanilla ice cream on top. "Where'd she go?"

"She left."

The waitress dropped the plate of bread pudding down in front of Maya. "You want it?"

"Sure, why not?" Maya said, picking up a spoon and

cutting into it. That could have gone so much better. Maya wanted to kick herself for not handling it more sensitively. But in the end, there was only so much she could do, especially if Sandra refused to face the truth.

Because one thing was certain. The man Maya had seen on Georgina Callis's doorstep was definitely Senator Stephen Wallage from the great state of Maine.

CHAPTER THIRTY-FOUR

Sandra pulled her car into the driveway. She was re-lieved that the days of reporters camping out on her lawn were mercifully over. At least for now. But she knew the reality of being married to a public figure, and there was no guarantee that they would not flock to her house again at a moment's notice at the slightest whiff of further scandal.

She was happy to be home, especially after nearly sideswiping a city bus when she blew through a stop sign because her mind was so preoccupied. Luckily the bus driver swerved fast enough to avoid a collision but couldn't resist flipping her the finger as he pulled over at his next stop to pick up some waiting passengers huddled together in the rain.

Sandra tried getting a grip on herself before heading into the house. She had been deeply disturbed by what

Maya had told her. Of course her first reaction would be to deny it, that's what her role as a senator's wife was supposed to be. The ultimate denier. "No, you obviously don't know my husband," or "My husband would never do that." She had all the lines down cold from her nearly two decades of experience.

However, in the past few years, it had become a little more difficult to believe them.

But this one she was fairly sure about. Stephen was in DC. She had spoken to him just this morning. He could not have been anywhere near Georgina Callis's house last night. And that picture Maya had served up as proof? Yes, the man resembled Stephen closely, but it was so dark, and honestly, how many men with the right height and hair color could be out there in the world? She wasn't going to automatically assume Stephen was up to his old tricks again. The least she could do was give him the benefit of the doubt.

Sandra got out of her car, shut the door, clicked the alarm on her remote, and walked up to the front door. When she entered the foyer, she could hear laughing coming from the living room. She hung her bag on the coatrack in the corner as Jack and Ryan argued over who was more of an expert at some video game. And then she heard a third voice playing referee, and her heart nearly stopped.

She slowly made her way around the corner to see Stephen nestled on the couch between his two sons, as they nudged each other, frantically pressing buttons on their Nintendo controller pads while playing a game, all their eyes glued to the mounted TV on the wall above the fireplace.

"No!" Jack cried.

"Dude, you're so going down! I own you!" Ryan said triumphantly.

Stephen finally tore his eyes away from the TV after noticing Sandra.

"Hi, babe . . . ," Stephen said, grinning. "I'm losing badly. I'm a terrible Dragon Slayer, or Dragon Hunter, or what is this one again?"

Jack sighed. "Dragon Ball FighterZ."

"Yeah, that. Apparently I suck at it," he said, chuckling.

Sandra tried keeping her cool and spoke softly. "What are you doing here?"

"Senate recessed early after Kramer did a little legal maneuvering and blocked a filibuster so we could take a floor vote on the farm bill," he said. "So I caught the first flight that had room for me."

"When did you get in?"

"Midday, around three, I think," he said, shrugging.

"I was here when he got home," Jack said. "He took me to get my haircut. You like?"

It was practically a buzz cut. Jack hated any hair getting into his eyes when he played football, so he kept it close-cropped for most of the season.

"I was supposed to drive you," Sandra said evenly.

"Yeah, I meant to text you that Dad was here so you didn't have to," Jack said, oblivious to his mother's rigid tone. "Luckily Sam was able to squeeze me in a little earlier."

"What's for dinner?" Ryan asked, dropping his controller down on the glass-top coffee table. "I'm starving."

"I haven't really thought about it. I have enough in the kitchen, so I can whip up something that you'll eat," Sandra said.

Stephen suddenly noticed that something was bothering her and stood up and crossed to her, enveloping her in a hug. "Forget it. I'll take us out. You deserve a night off from slaving in the kitchen."

Sandra stared at him. "I'm not sure if I'm up for going out."

"Come on, Mom," Ryan wailed. "By the time you change and figure out what to make, it's going to be after eight o'clock, and I don't think I can make it that long!"

She didn't want to go out. She was too tired to keep a fake smile on and pretend nothing was wrong. She just wanted to slap together a few sandwiches for them, feign a headache, and disappear upstairs to bed.

But it was three to one.

She had already lost the vote.

"Okay, how about that new Indian place?" Sandra offered. "I hear their coconut curry is to die for."

"Sounds like a plan," Stephen said, kissing her on the cheek. "Let me just go change my shirt."

He bounded up the stairs.

Sandra turned to her sons. "Be ready in five minutes. I don't want to be out late."

"Can I call Vanessa and have her come join us?" Ryan asked as he headed for the stairs.

"No," Sandra answered.

Ryan stopped in his tracks. "What?"

"Let's just keep it to the four of us tonight," she said.

"Why?"

She didn't want to tell him that Vanessa's presence would only remind her of Maya and what she had told her today, but she couldn't do that, so she had to come up with something else. "I'm just tired, that's all. You can have her over later this week. I'll make something nice."

"Fine," Ryan huffed as he stomped up the stairs, annoyed.

Jack disappeared into the downstairs bathroom off the foyer to check himself out in the mirror as he was prone to do.

Sandra marched up to the master bedroom, where she found Stephen, shirtless, rifling through his row of casual button-down shirts that hung on his side of the walk-in closet.

He didn't notice her at first.

She marveled at how handsome she still found him to be.

No wonder he got 58 percent of the female vote in his last election.

"Did Ryan tell you all about opening night?"

"Yes, he did. A smash hit, according to just about everyone!"

"You would have loved it. He's a star in the making. He stole the show."

"As I would expect him to do," Stephen said, selecting a striped polo and slipping it on his broad shoulders.

"Georgina did a fantastic job directing," she said quietly.

He was looking down, tucking the shirt into his pants. "Who?"

"Georgina Callis. The drama teacher at the high school. I'm sure you remember her."

"Oh, right," Stephen said, turning to her and smiling.

He didn't even blink.

My God, Sandra thought. *I never realized it before. He is so good at lying.*

It came so easy to him.

And that's what she found the most disturbing.

How effortlessly he could look her in the eye and lie to her. It had to be what made him such a successful politician.

Sandra had become adept at pretending. It was how she was going to get through this dinner and not burst into tears. She was very good at putting on a mask when she had to, and now it was again one of those times because she was not quite ready to confront her husband.

Not yet.

However, one thing was crystal clear in her mind. Stephen did not catch the first available flight home today. He was already home in Portland last night. At Georgina Callis's house.

CHAPTER THIRTY-FIVE

Maya was happy to hear that Frances's baby daddy, Coach Vinnie Cooper, had decided to move into her apartment right before Frances gave birth. She liked Vinnie, he seemed like a solid guy and a source of emotional support for the sometimes volatile and moody Frances. Maya had even agreed to help Vinnie move his stuff in early the following morning since she didn't want Frances lifting any heavy boxes in her present condition, or more to the point, to stop her from lifting any heavy boxes, since Frances stubbornly believed she was capable of doing anything, eight months pregnant be damned.

Vinnie had recruited a substitute to fill in for him in his classes but planned on being done and back at the high school in time for football practice after school. Maya showed up with doughnuts and coffee, and Vinnie excitedly munched on a delicious-looking one with cream filling and chocolate smeared on top.

Frances, meanwhile, busily sifted through some of his sports memorabilia in the back of his rented U-Haul truck, nixing a giant oil painting of Joe Namath from the 1970s he wanted to hang in their bedroom as well as a giant flower vase made in the shape of a Michigan Wolverines helmet. She used the excuse of having very little extra room in her small one-bedroom apartment, but Maya could tell the real reason Frances told Vinnie to take them directly to his recently rented storage unit was because she found them infinitely tacky.

Once the task of actually moving the Frances-approved items from the truck into the apartment began, Frances stood on the curb supervising while Maya and Vinnie carried the items to the lobby and up the stairs to the second-floor walk-up. After dropping off the first load, they turned to head back down to the U-Haul.

"What's happening with the Maisie Portman case?" Vinnie asked casually.

"You don't know? I'm surprised Frances hasn't been keeping you in the loop," Maya remarked.

"No, she doesn't really talk about it much."

"We've been following a few leads, but so far, we haven't got much. I feel bad for our client, Maisie's sister. She wants answers."

"You think maybe the police are right that Maisie hung herself?"

"They would like nothing more than a closed case, but based on what I saw at the scene, and my own gut feeling, I don't think it was anything close to a suicide."

"Yeah, Maisie loved messing with people too much to want to end her own life early," Vinnie cracked.

This stopped Maya. "What do you mean by that?"

Vinnie thought about what to say. "She was kind of miserable to be around."

"That's what I've been hearing. Did you personally have any run-ins with her?"

"Not just me. Everybody at the school did."

"What happened between you two?"

"Promise me you won't say anything to Frances."

That was an odd request. But Maya was too curious at this point to argue. "I promise."

They were back outside now, where Frances waited for them. She had dug out another item from the truck and was holding a Freddie Freeman Atlanta Braves auto-graphed baseball sealed inside a glass case.

"You can keep this in the apartment, just not in the living room," Frances said.

"Got it." Vinnie smiled, resigned to keeping her happy.

Maya lifted a plastic bin of baseball cards, and Vinnie grabbed a gym bag full of clothes and his signed baseball, and the two of them marched back toward the building. Once Frances was out of earshot, they continued their conversation.

"A few years ago, after Maisie started working at the school, she asked me out on a date. It was long before I had even met Frances, let alone started dating her."

"So why be secretive about it?"

"Come on, Maya. We both know Frances can be insanely jealous."

"That's an understatement," Maya said, laughing.

"Anyway, we went out a couple of times, nothing serious, mind you—a dinner in the Old Port, a Red Sox game in Boston, but after a few weeks, it was obvious we didn't have any chemistry, so I stopped calling her."

Maya was getting a little winded carrying the plastic bin full of cards up the stairs to the apartment. "Did she get stalkery after that?"

"No, not really. She sent me an email asking if she did or said anything wrong, but I told her I wasn't feeling it and that maybe it would be best if we just stayed friends."

They finally reached the apartment, and Maya dropped the bin down on top of the kitchen table and stopped to catch her breath.

Vinnie set the gym bag down and took his signed baseball in the glass case into the bedroom. When he returned, he was using a towel to wipe the sweat off his brow. "I thought that was the end of it, but that's when things started getting weird."

"Weird how?"

"Well, she started acting really cool toward me, refusing to make eye contact during staff meetings, making cracks about my weight in front of my students. I was a little heavier before I met Frances, and Maisie bought me a gym membership for my birthday," Vinnie said, chuckling.

"Was that it?"

"No. Then she took it up a notch. We'd be in budget meetings and she would advocate cutting money designated for the athletic department. She even went after my salary, saying it was disproportionate to my contribution to the school. I mean, it was like she had a real vendetta. Luckily Hicks put the kibosh on her proposals. But that just made her madder. There were a couple of kids I cut from the team for blowing off practice too many times, and one of them was African American, so Maisie started a whispering campaign that I was some kind of racist. It was crazy, man!"

"She really had it out for you."

"All because I broke up with her. After an internal review, the school board decided I was not some kind of white supremacist and dropped the whole matter. But then she started that Dirty Laundry site, and stories started popping up again that I was seen going to Klan meetings on the weekends. It was completely nuts!"

"So you knew Maisie was behind the Dirty Laundry site?"

"I didn't have any proof, but yeah, I had my suspicions."

"Why didn't you say anything to Principal Hicks?"

"Because, frankly, she was out of her mind, and I didn't want to find myself in her crosshairs again. I figured eventually she'd get bored writing lies about me and move on to someone else. By then, I was dating Frances and I was happy, and I just didn't want to stoke the fire, you know what I mean?"

Maya nodded.

Still, in the back of her mind, Vinnie had just confessed to a motive for getting rid of this thorn in his side for the past three years.

"Vinnie, I have to ask, where were you the night Maisie was found hanging in the office?"

Suddenly a voice from behind interrupted them. "What are you doing?"

Maya and Vinnie spun around to see Frances hovering in the doorway to the apartment.

"Nothing," Vinnie said guiltily.

Frances studied them for a few moments and then said, "Vinnie, why don't you go back down for another load. I want to talk to Maya."

Vinnie, not in the mood to quibble with his girlfriend's wishes, dashed out the door in a flash.

"What are you *doing*?" Frances asked.

"What do you mean?"

"Why are you interrogating my boyfriend?"

"I'm not interrogating him. We were just talking."

"That's not what it sounded like to me. If I hadn't had to come up here to use the bathroom, which I'm doing about forty times a day at this point, I wouldn't have caught you."

"Caught me? You make it sound like I'm doing something bad."

Frances glared at Maya, her eyes wild with fury. "You're treating my boyfriend like he's some kind of murder suspect."

She was right.

In Maya's mind, everyone was guilty until proven innocent. And sometimes Maya could be like a dog with a bone until she learned the whole unvarnished truth. Maybe she had crossed a line with Vinnie by asking him where he was the night Maisie was killed.

Frances stepped forward, a hand on her belly. "What did he say to you that made you so suspicious of him?"

"Maisie had posted some things about him in the early days of her Dirty Laundry site, and I'm just questioning everyone she had written about."

"What kind of things?"

"He asked me not to say."

Frances scoffed. "He didn't want you to tell *me*?"

Maya nodded slightly.

"Fine. I don't care. You don't have to tell me. What I do know is that he had nothing to do with Maisie's death."

"I know, I was just being my usual—"

Frances cut her off. "How could you for one minute think Vinnie was capable of harming anyone?"

"It's what I do. I can't help—"

"I think we've got the rest of this. There are only a few boxes left in the truck. You can go."

"Frances—"

"Thanks for the coffee and doughnuts."

Maya opened her mouth to speak but stopped herself. She knew it was pointless, because once Frances was on a tear, there was no calming her. It was best to let her cool down until she called and apologized for overreacting. They had been through it so many times before.

So Maya just gave her partner a shrug and a thin smile and walked out the door.

CHAPTER THIRTY-SIX

When Maya unlocked the door to her apartment and entered, she instinctively knew she was not alone. There was a Cardi B song playing on the Alexa speaker, and Maya heard soft moaning coming from the living room. Her guard instantly came up. Vanessa had told her that morning that she would be at her friend Kristy's house, studying for a chemistry test, but that story was quickly disproved when Maya entered the living room to find Vanessa sprawled out on the couch with Ryan lying on top of her, their lips locked and their bodies gyrating. The only saving grace of the situation was that both teens were fully clothed, at least at this point.

Maya loudly cleared her throat, startling them both, and Ryan quickly sprang up from the couch, wiped the sweat off his brow with his forearm before extending a hand and smiling at Maya. "Hello, Mrs. Kendrick. Nice to see you again."

Maya glanced down at Vanessa, who had a hand stuffed down the front of her shirt, frantically adjusting her bra.

As most teenagers do when caught doing something they shouldn't be doing, Vanessa adopted a confrontational tone as she glared at her mother. "What are you doing here? I thought you were helping Frances move!"

"I was. I got done early," Maya said flatly.

"Oh," Vanessa said. "Well, you could have called and told me."

"Are we really doing this? Shifting the blame to me because you lied about where you were going to be today, and now I've walked in on you sucking face with your boyfriend and about to do God only knows what else?"

Vanessa straightened her shirt and rolled her eyes at her mother. "Mom, please!"

Maya ignored her. She turned to Ryan. "And where did you tell *your* mother you would be right now?"

Ryan wavered a moment, not sure if he should admit to a lie, but then, giving up, sighed. "Cast photo shoot for the school newspaper."

Maya raised an eyebrow.

Ryan threw up his hands defensively. "Which is technically true. We did have a cast photo shoot after school today. But it only took ten minutes, so when we were done Dylan dropped us off here where we could . . . hang out."

"*Hang out?*" Maya asked, folding her arms.

"Yeah. . . ." Ryan nodded, wincing.

"Maybe you ought to go home now, Ryan," Maya suggested.

"Yes. Good idea. Thank you," Ryan said, nodding again and heading for the door.

"Mom, he doesn't have a car, and it's over a three-mile walk to his house," Vanessa complained.

"What about an Uber?" Maya offered.

"My mom canceled my credit card after I took a bunch of my friends to Ruth's Chris Steak House after play rehearsal last spring, so my app doesn't have an up-to-date payment method."

Maya certainly was not going to pay for this kid's ride herself. She reached for her cell phone.

Vanessa looked worried. "Who are you calling?"

"His mother. We exchanged numbers when we went out for pizza the other night," Maya answered.

"Mom, no! Don't bother Mrs. Wallage! She's a very busy woman!" Vanessa pleaded.

"So am I," Maya growled.

Ryan kept his eyes fixed on the floor. He knew not to argue with Maya. She was intimidating enough as it was.

The call went directly to voice mail. Maya waited for the beep and then calmly spoke. "Hi, Sandra, this is Maya Kendrick. Your son is here and has no way of getting home, so if you wouldn't mind swinging by and picking him up at some point, I sure would appreciate it. Thank you." She ended the call. "Now why don't we watch a little TV while we wait for her to call back."

Vanessa and Ryan sat down on the couch, frustrated. Vanessa reluctantly picked up the remote and turned on a movie channel that was playing one of those old Lord of the Rings movies.

Without missing a beat, Maya sat down, squeezing in

between them, to keep them physically apart, her eyes glued to the television set. "I don't think I've seen this one."

Sandra called back fifteen minutes later to tell Maya she had just arrived home and could be there in twenty minutes. Sandra arrived soon after, bearing a casserole dish, which she held out to Maya when she answered the door. "I know you are out working on your cases all day long, so I thought it might be nice if you didn't have to think about dinner tonight. This is one of my mother's recipes. Ham, potato, and broccoli casserole."

"You are too sweet," Maya said, smiling, accepting the gesture.

"You just need to heat it up at three hundred and fifty degrees for about thirty minutes. I figured you don't need my help with the actual investigating, but maybe I could be useful making things a little easier on you by helping this way."

Genuinely touched, Maya smiled. "Thank you, Sandra, it looks delicious."

Sandra, still standing in the doorway, leaned in closer to Maya. "What did you catch them doing? Please tell me they used protection. . . ."

"They didn't get that far thankfully," Maya sighed. "But if I hadn't come home early, there's no telling what kinds of questions we'd have to be asking now."

"I let his father explain to him about the birds and the bees, so who knows how helpful that information was. Do people still say the birds and the bees?"

"I know I do," Maya said, smiling. "Please, come in."

Sandra entered, marching toward the living room, where Ryan and Vanessa sat upright on the couch, at least twelve inches between them so as not to arouse any more ire in their respective mothers.

"Come on, let's go," Sandra said quietly as Ryan shot up to his feet to follow his mother out the door.

Maya looked down at the casserole she was holding and then back up at Sandra. "Vanessa and I couldn't possibly eat all this. Why don't you two stay for dinner. I mean, if you don't have to get home right away?"

Sandra thought about it for a second. "No, we don't have to get home. Jack is out with some teammates tonight. We'd love to stay, wouldn't we, Ryan?"

Ryan looked as if he wasn't sure how he was supposed to answer. Was his mother just being polite? Was this some kind of trap? Was there a correct answer? He ultimately decided the best course of action was to just shrug and follow his mother's lead. "Sure."

"Great," Maya said before turning to her daughter. "Vanessa, why don't you set two more places at the table?"

Vanessa, who was still shell-shocked by what was happening, not sure what to make of this growing friendship between her own mother and the mother of her boyfriend, simply nodded and walked like a zombie into the kitchen and began rifling through the silverware drawer.

Ryan and Vanessa stayed relatively silent throughout dinner, mostly just exchanging nervous glances, not sure what the fallout would ultimately be for getting caught lying in order to pave the way for them to fool around. Maya and Sandra, on the other hand, were chatty and gregarious, and Maya finally had to admit to herself that she was really starting to like this woman, this woman she had very little in common with. That day, especially, Maya needed someone to talk to, after Frances had unceremoniously kicked her out of her apartment, and Sandra not only seemed to be a sympathetic ear, but she brought dinner to boot.

When Maya stood up to clear the plates and pour them some coffee, she excused Ryan and Vanessa and told them they could adjourn to the living room. But she also warned them that she had excellent hearing and would be able to hear any smacking lips or soft moaning.

"You never know, I might even have a nanny cam installed somewhere, so think about that when you consider entwining any body parts."

Red-faced, Vanessa threw her head back dramatically. "Stop embarrassing me!"

Ryan actually chuckled over that one, but his smile quickly faded when he glanced over at his own mother, who stared at him, stone-faced. "I won't try anything, I promise."

"You better not," Sandra warned. She tended to believe him, but there was a tiny part of her that didn't trust him. After all, he had been swimming in his father's gene pool.

The kids walked out of the little dining area and disappeared into the living room, leaving the two mothers to talk some more.

Sandra listened as Maya quickly explained that she had an argument with Frances earlier that day, not getting into too many details. Sandra offered a few words of encouragement, how it would probably blow over soon, and how envious Sandra was of Maya's strong bond with Frances, both as partners and as friends.

Maya explained to Sandra that Frances could oftentimes be mercurial and self-absorbed, and when Maya

herself had first met Sandra, she thought—as a fancy
U.S. senator's wife—she would be the stereotype of one
of those ladies who lunch, a shallow fashionista, ob-
sessed with her image. But Sandra had surprised her. She
was nothing like that. In fact, in some ways, Maya envied
Sandra. She had financial security. Something Maya sorely
lacked at the moment. And she told her so.

Sandra laughed bitterly. "I guess that's something."

Maya hadn't seen this side of Sandra before. She had
always been so positive and perky, but now she appeared
angry.

Sandra finally snapped back into the moment and
touched Maya's hand. "Well, I have to say, I admire, no,
I'm downright jealous of, your independence."

"I didn't ask for it," Maya snickered. "When they
carted my husband off to prison, it was sort of forced
upon me."

"Well, I wish I had more of it. I'd trade half my financial security for just a smidgen of your independence."

"Right back at you," Maya said quietly.

Sandra leaned back, making sure the kids were out of
earshot, and then, satisfied they couldn't hear, leaned toward Maya. "I'm sorry I didn't believe you."

"About what?" Maya asked, though she strongly suspected what Sandra was talking about.

Sandra sighed. "The whole Stephen thing. Deep down
I knew you were right. I just wasn't ready to accept that
he had lied to me again."

"*Again?*" Maya asked, quickly regretting it the second
the word rolled off her tongue.

Sandra nodded. "It's not the first time. In fact, I'm not
sure if it's the second, or third, or twentieth time. I de-

cided to brush all those negative thoughts under the carpet for years, not really wanting to know. Sometimes it's easier to just stay in the dark."

"And now? What are you going to do?"

"I don't know," Sandra said solemnly. "I honestly don't know."

CHAPTER THIRTY-SEVEN

Maya hadn't finished her first cup of coffee that she had picked up at Starbucks on her way into the office before there was a knock at the door. Without waiting for an answer, Chelsea Portman blew in, bedazzled in expensive jewelry, a smart tight-fitting pink top that boasted a smidge too much cleavage and dark blue-tinted sunglasses that hid her eyes even though the window shades were drawn and there was very little light seeping into the cramped office.

"Chelsea, I thought you were in New York," Maya said, jumping to her feet and scurrying around her desk to greet her. "I was going to call you."

"Good, because I've been waiting for what seems like forever for some kind of update, and I'm *still* waiting," Chelsea sniffed, more than a little perturbed.

Maya geared down into her professional mode, calmly reassuring the client. "We've been following up on a few leads, talking to a few people, and should know more by the end of the week."

"That sounds like detectivespeak for 'we have nothing to report so far,'" Chelsea growled, lowering the sunglasses down to the bridge of her nose so Maya could see the displeasure in her eyes.

Maya tried to make direct eye contact, but Chelsea had already pushed the sunglasses back up to shield her eyes. "We've made some headway, I promise. We just need a little more time."

"*We?* You keep talking about we, but I've never met anyone else but you," Chelsea exclaimed.

"My partner, Frances, is pregnant—eight months, in fact—so she's been out of the office a lot, but I can assure you she's heavily involved in the investigation."

"That really doesn't appear to be the case," Chelsea barked. "I try to be nice; I work hard not to allow myself to be taken advantage of, but I always wind up disappointed. I'm paying you a handsome fee for results, Maya, and I'm starting to lose my patience."

Starting?

Maya held her breath, waiting for the inevitable ax to fall.

"If your partner is AWOL, then I suggest you find someone else to help you, otherwise I will have no choice but to enlist another detective agency to find the answers I'm looking for," Chelsea warned. "An agency that boasts more than just one harried, overworked investigator."

Maya silently breathed a sigh of relief. She was not

going to get fired. Yet. Which was definitely a good thing, because she desperately needed this case.

"Am I making myself clear?" Chelsea asked.

"Crystal," Maya said, wondering what happened to the charming young woman who had breezed into her office to hire her a week ago.

"Thank you. You have my number. Call me. *Soon*," Chelsea said before dramatically whipping around like a seasoned soap actress and marching back out the door, effectively slamming it shut behind her.

Maya rubbed her eyes. She was already tired, and the day had barely started. Chelsea was right. The client was always right. She needed to get some results and fast, or she was going to lose her biggest client. Okay, if she was being honest with herself, pretty much her only client. She just couldn't afford that. And with Frances not speaking to her after the Coach Vinnie debacle, she was working this important case solo. She needed help. And she knew who she could call to get it. But if she did, Maya felt in her gut that there would be no turning back. It would be like bringing a puppy home from the pound temporarily to see how it adjusted but knowing you could never take it back once he staked out his territory.

Still, she didn't have a choice.

Maya picked up her phone and made the call.

Sandra arrived within a half hour. It was almost as if she had been waiting by the phone, ready to suit up like Wonder Woman and fly over in her invisible plane to answer the distress call. She even had time to stop for bagels and more coffee, and before Maya even had the chance to slather some cream cheese on her poppy-seed bagel with a plastic knife, Sandra had already rolled up her sleeves and was sifting through a pile of Maisie Portman's personal papers that Maya had taken from Maisie's apartment without Chelsea's knowledge. Maya considered asking for permission, but she was worried Chelsea might not agree if they were too personal, so she just casually slipped them inside her briefcase and walked out with them. Frances had promised to go through them but never did. Frances had always been better at reviewing paperwork than Maya. But Sandra was a speed-reader, absorbing the tiniest details in seconds. It was truly amazing to watch.

"Have you always been able to read this fast?" Maya asked, impressed.

Sandra nodded. "When I was twelve, I must have read a hundred books during my summer vacation, and after I married Stephen, he'd send me the bills he had to vote on. Sometimes they were close to a thousand pages, and I'd tell him exactly what was in them by the time he finished watching his cable news shows at night."

Sandra could barely contain her excitement. She was so enthusiastic, in fact, that Maya felt the need to tamp it down just a bit. "This is not a permanent situation though, Sandra, I could just use another set of eyes until Frances gets back."

"I totally understand," Sandra said, before looking up with concern. "I hope there are no complications with her pregnancy."

"Oh, no, it's nothing like that. She is just feeling a bit overwhelmed as the due date gets closer," Maya lied.

"Well, been there, done that. In my last trimester with Ryan, I could barely get off the couch."

"Don't you want a bagel?" Maya asked, pushing the plate toward her.

Sandra waved her off as she studied some papers. "I already ate two on my way over here. So Chelsea didn't know you took these papers from Maisie's apartment?"

"No. Why?"

"It's just that I came across a life-insurance policy."

Sandra handed the stapled papers to Maya, who perused them.

"It's for one point two million dollars," Sandra said. "And take a look at the primary beneficiary."

Maya scanned down the page. "Chelsea Portman."

"The sister. Your client," Sandra said, tapping her finger on the desk a few times.

Maya wrinkled her nose. "But that doesn't make any sense. Why would Chelsea go to the trouble of hiring me to prove her sister was murdered if she was the one who did it? Why not just keep quiet and collect a big fat check once the police ruled Maisie's death a suicide?"

Sandra shrugged, stumped.

"Besides, Chelsea is a successful actress on Broadway. It's not like she needs the money anyway," Maya added.

Sandra perked up. "*Actress?*"

Maya nodded. "Yes, she's literally the exact opposite of Maisie. It's hard to believe they were sisters."

"I love flying down to New York and seeing Broadway shows. Stephen hates going and usually falls asleep five minutes after the curtain goes up, so I tend to go alone or with a girlfriend. I bet I've seen her in something."

Sandra grabbed Maya's laptop and spun it around so it was facing her. Then she typed Chelsea's name in the Google search box. A dozen rows of images loaded and Sandra's mouth dropped open in surprise.

Maya noticed her wide eyes staring at all the pictures of Chelsea. "What is it?"

"I know her," Sandra whispered.

"You do?"

"Well, not know her really, but I've definitely seen her before," Sandra said, pointing at the screen.

"What show was it? She says she's appearing in *Wicked* at the moment."

"It wasn't a show," Sandra said solemnly. "It was at the high school in the parking lot. I saw her in a heated argument with Maisie."

"When was that?"

"About a week before we found Maisie dead."

"But Chelsea went to such great lengths to tell me how close she was to her sister," Maya said.

"Maybe they were, but they certainly weren't that night," Sandra said, closing the laptop. "I'm afraid if I hadn't shown up, they might have killed each other."

"Did you hear what they were fighting about?"

Sandra shook her head. "No, but I think we have enough to take a closer look at Chelsea and her relationship with Maisie."

"But again, why go to the trouble of hiring a detective if the sister you despised is already dead and you have a fortune coming to you from a life-insurance policy?"

"Perhaps there was another reason why Chelsea Portman hired you other than to prove Maisie was murdered," Sandra said her mind racing. "We just need to find out what it is."

Maya couldn't help but smile at Sandra's focused determination. For the first time in a while, she felt like she
had a fully committed partner who was totally on board
with the case. And it made her feel like she wasn't a solo
act anymore.

CHAPTER THIRTY-EIGHT

The Top of the East bar, with its expansive floor-to-ceiling windows and boasting the most breathtaking view of Portland and Casco Bay, sat on top of the Westin Portland Harborview hotel. It was a must stop for a cocktail on any night out on the town. Sandra had been there with Stephen and friends numerous times and was a big fan of their Bayside Basil, a yummy concoction consisting of Cold River gin, St. Elder natural elderflower, Dolin Blanc vermouth, and grapefruit juice. She knew when she walked in that the bartender Lori, a pretty young redhead working her way through the University of Southern Maine, would recognize her once she found a place at the bar. Sandra knew she looked good in her cobalt-blue connected-sequin lace sheath dress that she had recently bought on sale at Macy's along with her silver pumps, especially since a gaggle of businessmen seated at a table in the corner had abruptly stopped their conversation and were now staring at her.

It was happy hour, so the bar was crowded. Sandra scanned the patrons, settling on one sitting at the bar, sipping a Rose Kennedy. She was blond and beautiful and shouldn't have had a care in the world, but tonight she looked miserable. She sat in a high-back chair, slumped over a bit, staring into her rose-colored drink.

Sandra turned her head to the side and spoke in a whisper. "I see her. She's at the bar."

She heard Maya's voice in her ear. "Is she alone?"

"Looks like it. There's a man sitting next to her. It looks like he's working up the courage to talk to her."

"Can you get anywhere near her to strike up a conversation?"

"The bar's pretty busy. I'm going to order a drink and wait for something to open up."

"Okay, don't be too obvious, play it cool. You're very approachable, so you don't have to try too hard."

"I've been charming my husband's constituents for years. I got this," Sandra said confidently as she sashayed across the bar, passing the table of men, who were still gaping at her, and stood at the bar until Lori noticed her.

"Mrs. Wallage, how nice to see you again!"

"Hello, Lori. When do I have to start calling you doctor?"

Lori laughed. "I'm getting my master's in nursing. Adult-gerontology acute-care nurse practitioner, if you want to get technical. I have another year and a half to go."

"Impressive. I'm so proud of your career goals. Most young people I come in contact with just want to make YouTube videos and get famous."

"I'm too shy for that kind of stuff," she said, chuckling. "You want the usual?"

"Please," Sandra said, spotting an older couple putting some money down on the bar and getting up to leave. "I'll be right over there."

She walked over and smiled at the couple who passed her and moved off toward the elevator, and then she climbed up on one of the free chairs. Lori quickly removed their empty glasses, wadded up napkins and the cash tip, and then wiped the bar clean with a towel before heading off to make Sandra her drink.

Sandra casually glanced over in the direction of the blond woman, but Chelsea Portman hadn't noticed her yet, or maybe she already had and had chosen to go back to drowning her sorrows in her Rose Kennedy.

One of the businessmen at the table with his buddies got up and crossed over to Sandra and the empty chair next to her. He leaned down close to her, resting an elbow on the bar, and mustered up the most dazzling smile he could. "Is this seat taken?"

Sandra turned and said with a wan smile, "I'm waiting for a friend."

"Well, why don't I keep it warm until he gets here?"

"I'm married," she said coldly, holding up her ring finger.

"What a coincidence. So am I," he said, raising his own ring finger, not willing to give up just yet. "Looks like we have something in common."

"He's really handsome. I mean really handsome. If I was going to cheat on him, you'd have to be the spitting image of Benedict Cumberbatch. And sadly you're not, so read my lips: Not . . . going to . . . happen."

She could hear Maya laughing in her ear.

Sandra felt comforted by the fact that Maya was parked outside, right across the street from the hotel, ready to rush in if she needed her.

But Maya wasn't going to have to, because the businessman deflated right before her eyes and shuffled dejectedly back to his buddies, who were guffawing over his big fail.

Lori slid a red cocktail napkin in front of Sandra and set a Bayside Basil down on top of it. "Here you go."

"Thank you, Lori."

"How's Mr. Wallage; I mean *Senator* Wallage?"

"Down in Washington fighting to make all our lives better," she said. It sounded like a joke, but it wasn't. Despite his shortcomings, Stephen was one of those rare cases of a politician who was in it for the right reasons. He was sincere, at least in his work. It was one of the reasons she had fallen in love with him all those years ago when they met in college at a campus protest. She couldn't even remember what they were protesting, but Stephen had a bullhorn and had organized everyone. He had invited her over to his dorm room to help make signs, and when they finished at three in the morning they made love for the very first time. They had been a team ever since.

"My father didn't vote for him," Lori said matter-of-factly. "But my mother did, just to make my dad mad because he knows she has a *huge* crush on him."

Sandra giggled. "I like your mom."

Lori ambled off to wait on another customer waving an empty glass, and that's when she finally noticed Chelsea Portman looking at her.

"That same guy tried hitting on me right before you came in," Chelsea said.

Sandra grinned. "I guess he's not having a good night at the plate. His batting average sucks."

Chelsea chortled.

Play it cool, Sandra.

Don't come on too strong.

Sandra casually took a sip of her drink and looked away.

Luckily Chelsea wasn't done talking to her.

"I'm sorry, I couldn't help but overhear your conversation with the bartender. Is your husband a senator?"

Sandra turned back and nodded. "Senator Wallage. Stephen Wallage."

"Of course! I knew you looked familiar!"

This was her moment. Her time to reel in the fish. She had practiced it outside in the car several times with Maya.

"Well, truth be told, I recognized you the minute I came into the bar," Sandra said, almost shyly.

Chelsea lit up. "You did?"

"I took my sons to see *Wicked* in New York a few weeks ago. You were a brilliant Glinda the Good Witch."

"Thank you!" Chelsea cooed.

It was a slam dunk.

She had her right where she wanted her.

Sandra had gambled that Chelsea would not remember her from the night that she had intervened while she and Maisie were fighting in the high school parking lot. It was dark, and Chelsea had been too upset and distracted to pay much attention to her.

"You have no idea how much I needed to hear that tonight. I'm going to buy you a drink!" Chelsea said, flagging down Lori.

"Seriously, you don't have to do that."

"I want to. When do I have the opportunity to buy a drink for an honest-to-goodness U.S. senator?"

"Wife, I'm just the wife," Sandra said.

"Well, maybe you should be a senator. We need more women senators," Chelsea exclaimed before slamming down the rest of her Rose Kennedy.

"I'll drink to that," Sandra said, raising her Bayside Basil.

Lori appeared, and Chelsea, who was still technically sober, but not for long, leaned in to her. "We'll have another round. Just put it on my tab."

"Coming right up," Lori said before walking away.

Sandra lifted her glass to Chelsea. "Thank you."

There was a pause, and then Chelsea, eyeing the empty seat next to Sandra, gently asked, "Mind if I join you?"

Mission accomplished.

It had been so easy.

She knew Maya was listening and hoped she would be proud at how effectively and efficiently Sandra had handled the situation.

"Of course. We can fend off the wolves together as a team," Sandra joked, pointing to the table of businessmen in the corner.

Chelsea left her empty glass and walked around the bar to Sandra. "I'll be right back. I'm just going to go to the little girls' room. Save my seat."

Sandra nodded, and Chelsea bounced off. The minute she was gone, Sandra waved down Lori and handed her the nearly full cocktail glass with her Bayside Basil. "Do me a favor and dump this."

Lori took the glass, confused.

"And no matter how many more of the Bayside Basils I order, make them without alcohol, would you, please?"

"Really?" Lori asked, a puzzled look on her face.

Sandra reached into her clutch bag and pulled out a twenty. "I'll match this at the end of the night if you serve me nothing but virgin cocktails for the rest of the time I'm here."

Lori snatched the twenty out of Sandra's hand. "Whatever you want, Mrs. Wallage."

Lori wasn't about to ask any more questions if it meant pocketing a forty-dollar tip at the end of the evening.

Chelsea, looking refreshed but slightly tipsy, returned from the restroom and jumped up on the chair next to Sandra just as Lori returned with their drinks. Chelsea eyed Sandra's cocktail. "So what is that?"

"A Bayside Basil," Sandra answered.

"Mind if I try it?"

Before Sandra had a chance to stop her, Chelsea scooped up the drink and knocked back a healthy swig. She slammed the drink down as she tasted it and scrunched up her nose. "It's a little weak."

Sandra grabbed the drink and took a sip. "I don't know. I think it's got a nice kick to it."

But Chelsea was already waving at Lori, who made her way over to them. "I don't taste any alcohol. Could you make her another one, please?"

Lori stood there, not sure what to do. Sandra nodded to her, and Lori picked up the glass and went to make another Bayside Basil.

"I want to see how you make it," Chelsea said, slurring slightly, as she pounded down another Rose Kennedy.

Lori prepared the drink and returned with it. She was

about to set it down in front of Sandra, but Chelsea plucked it out of her hand before she had the chance and taste tested it. "Now this one is much better!"

She handed it off to Sandra, who took a slight sip. Lori had added a double shot of gin, and Sandra's eyes practically watered. She turned and eyed the restroom before turning back to Chelsea. "My turn. Looks like I should have gone when you did—now there's a line." She held up her Bayside Basil. "I'm going to need this to keep me company while I wait."

Sandra slid off the stool and marched to the restroom. There was a potted plant between the men's and ladies' rooms. She surreptitiously poured the drink out into it, and after waiting the appropriate amount of time since she didn't have to really go to the bathroom, returned to the bar with the empty glass and set it down.

"Looks like I'm going to need another, Lori," she said to the bartender with a wink.

Lori knew exactly what she was up to and raised the glass with a smile.

Chelsea spent the next twenty minutes asking about what parts of *Wicked* Sandra's sons enjoyed the most, and Sandra dutifully told her that both Jack and Ryan were enamored with her performance as Glinda, gushing about her beautiful singing voice and perfect comedic timing.

Finally, she heard Maya's voice in her ear. "You're overdoing it."

"Sorry," Sandra said without thinking.

Chelsea raised an eyebrow. "Sorry about what?"

Sandra could have kicked herself. Rule number one about wearing a wire: never speak to the person who is not in the room and talking to you through an earpiece. But Sandra was caught off guard for only a few seconds.

"Sorry to go on and on like this, but it's rare I get to hang out with a famous actress."

"That's so sweet of you to say, but I'm not really that famous," Chelsea said, feigning a modicum of modesty.

"Nice recovery," Maya said in her ear.

"Thank you," Sandra said, then bit her lip.

Did she really just do it again?

"For what?" Chelsea asked, now thoroughly confused.

"Thank you for . . . sitting here with me and having a drink. You must have so many people who want to spend time with you."

"You'd be surprised," Chelsea said bitterly, staring into the bottom of her glass, lost in thought.

There was a long pause of silence with only the tin of the other patrons in the background chattering away and the sounds of glasses clinking filling the air before Sandra felt compelled to speak. "What brings you to Portland?"

Chelsea took a deep breath and sighed. "Technically I'm here on family business . . ."

"I knew your sister. I worked with her in the PTA," Sandra said solemnly.

Chelsea seemed surprised for a moment that Sandra knew Maisie, but then after a moment, she relaxed. Sandra could see Chelsea's mind putting it all together. Maisie worked at the high school. Sandra had two teenage boys. Of course it made sense that they knew each other. And it was obvious she had no clue that Sandra was the woman from the parking lot.

"Yes, it's tragic what happened to Maisie," Chelsea said. It was obvious she had no desire to take the subject any further. "But the real reason I'm here . . ." Chelsea stopped herself, not sure if she should divulge anymore.

She took another gulp of her Rose Kennedy, debating with herself.

Sandra could hear Maya breathing through the earpiece expectantly, waiting impatiently to find out.

"To see my boyfriend," Chelsea said quietly.

"Oh," Sandra said, astonished a beautiful actress like Chelsea wasn't dating a hedge fund manager or a theater director back in New York. "Is he meeting you here?"

Chelsea's face soured. "I got a text from him earlier. He's not coming."

"I'm sorry," Sandra said softly.

"It's the age-old story," Chelsea said, raising a finger and pointing it down at her glass to alert Lori that she needed a refill and pronto.

Lori was happy to oblige.

"Married?" Sandra guessed.

"Yup, and for two years he's been promising to leave his wife. I played the role of the other woman for two years on a soap, and I still couldn't see the signs in front of me."

"We never do," Sandra said, touching her arm. "My husband promised me we would never live apart, and now he spends most of the year living in a duplex apartment on K Street down in DC."

Chelsea seemed to appreciate the physical contact and leaned into Sandra, bumping shoulders with her. "I guess we gals have to stick together."

"I'll drink to that," Sandra said, guzzling her nonalcoholic beverage. "Hey, I don't want to go all fangirl on you, but can I get a selfie? My sons will love it."

"Absolutely," Chelsea said, batting her eyes, flattered.

Sandra pulled her phone out of her purse and snapped

a few photos, both women checking to make sure they looked good.

"Hey, can you send those to me? I'll post them on Instagram," Chelsea said.

"I'm too drunk to type in your info. Why don't you take a few with your phone?" Sandra wailed, pretending to be intoxicated and nailing it.

"Okay," Chelsea said without a second thought. She rummaged through her bag and found her cell phone. She punched in the six-digit security code. 030690. Sandra made a mental note of it.

Chelsea put an arm around Sandra and snapped away. They had become fast friends, and after a few more rounds, Chelsea was literally swaying from side to side as she talked about the horrors of the casting couch that she had had to endure while coming up as an actress before the onslaught of the Me Too moment. Her words were almost unintelligible now, and Sandra knew it was time to call it a night.

"Where are you staying?" Sandra asked.

"Right here in the hotel," Chelsea said, climbing down off the chair and stumbling, nearly falling to the floor.

Sandra caught her, and held her up. "Here. Let me take you. What's your room number?"

"Four-twelve," Chelsea slurred.

Sandra and Maya already knew Chelsea was staying at the Westin. She stayed there every time she came to town. And after Maya questioned a few contacts she had at the hotel, she knew Chelsea had been coming to the top-floor bar every night, so it had been surprisingly easy to track her down.

"Good night, Lori," Sandra said as she slapped down another twenty and dragged Chelsea off.

"Get home safe," Lori said, winking. She knew Sandra was stone-cold sober.

After taking the elevator down to the fourth floor and convincing a half-conscious Chelsea to hand over her key card, Sandra managed to get Chelsea into the room. It was a plush one-bedroom suite. Sandra half dragged, half carried Chelsea into the bedroom, where she flopped down on top of the comforter, arms and legs spread-eagle. Sandra pulled off Chelsea's high heels but left her dress on. It would take too much effort to roll her over, unzip it, and get her deadweight out of it.

Chelsea was now flat on her back, head tilted to one side, snoring softly.

"Chelsea? Are you awake?"

No answer.

Sandra retrieved Chelsea's phone from her bag and punched in the code number. 030690, which, according to her driver's license that was in a side pocket, was Chelsea's birthday. March 6, 1990. Sandra scanned down her emails, but nothing stood out to her. She then went into her texts.

"Find anything?" Maya said in her ear.

"No, a lot of texts from her manager and castmates from *Wicked*. There are some texts from someone who she just refers to as *Him*. It's a local number, but she never refers to him by name. Just a constant stream of phone sex I won't bore you with and making plans to meet whenever she's in town."

"What about Maisie?" Maya asked.

Sandra scrolled down and found Maisie's name. She opened the texts. "Oh boy . . ."

"What?"

Sandra was too busy reading to answer her.

"Sandra? What's happening? What are you doing?"

"Hold on," Sandra sighed, continuing to read down through all the texts. "Okay, it sounds like there was no love lost between these two sisters."

"Why? What do they say?"

"From what I can gather, Maisie found out about the married man Chelsea was secretly seeing and didn't approve. You should see some of the names Maisie calls her. There are a few here I've never even heard of."

"What else?"

Sandra skimmed down the texts some more. "Apparently whomever Chelsea's been sneaking around with works at the high school with Maisie, and Maisie is pretty furious about that. Although she doesn't come out and say it, it's pretty obvious that Maisie is extremely jealous about the relationship, just from her tone. She clearly has feelings for this man herself. . . ."

Sandra suddenly gasped.

"What? What?" Maya cried in the earpiece.

It was like Sandra was immersed in a juicy summer beach read. "Maisie just threatened to expose the whole affair on her Dirty Laundry site if Chelsea doesn't stop seeing him!"

"That's cold," Maya said. "No wonder nobody liked Maisie."

"That had to be what they were fighting about when I saw them in the parking lot that night," Sandra said. "Maybe Chelsea told this mystery man what Maisie was threatening to do, so he was the one who killed her in order to keep her from splashing all the sordid details of the affair all over her website for the whole world, not to mention his wife, to see!"

"So either Chelsea hired me sincerely, not knowing that her boyfriend was the killer, or she did know and wanted to cover it up, and hired me under the guise of finding out who murdered her sister . . . ," Maya said.

"But why would she do that?"

"The first time we met she mentioned that Maisie's cell phone was not recovered at the scene, and she seemed real eager to find it. All the texts you are reading on Chelsea's phone would be on Maisie's as well."

Sandra was getting excited. "She was doing all of this for him. Hiring you to find the killer but she really wanted you to find the phone. Chelsea didn't want Maisie's phone to fall into the wrong hands because if those texts got out there, it would be deeply embarrassing and professionally detrimental for her lover."

"Well, yes, Sandra, but more important, it would expose him as the killer."

"Right, of course. That would probably take precedent. Remember, I'm new at this."

Sandra heard Maya chuckling.

"You're doing just fine," Maya said. "Chelsea knew if I recovered the phone during my investigation, I wouldn't know the security code to gain access. I wouldn't be able to see the texts. But once the phone was back in Chelsea's possession she could destroy it and fire me, and that would be the end of it. The world would be left believing Maisie committed suicide, and Chelsea's secret boyfriend would be in the clear.

"Okay, get out of there and meet me outside," Maya ordered.

"Roger that," Sandra said. She had always wanted to say that.

Sandra noticed a piece of chocolate in a gold wrapper on the pillow next to Chelsea's head and grabbed it. She was starving. And then she headed out of the bedroom.

She was just reaching for the door handle to leave when suddenly there was a knock on the other side.

Sandra gasped and jumped.

She heard Maya in her ear. "Sandra, what is it?"

CHAPTER THIRTY-NINE

There was another knock on the hotel room door, this one louder and more insistent.

Sandra stood frozen in place for a moment before quietly reaching over and snapping off the lights.

"Someone's here," Sandra whispered, panic rising.

Suddenly Sandra heard a whirring sound.

Someone was using a key card to enter the room.

She quickly spun around and ran back into the bedroom of the suite.

"Sandra, what's happening? Talk to me!" Maya yelled in her ear.

Chelsea was completely passed out on the bed, oblivious to the knocking or commotion of Sandra running around trying to find a hiding place.

She heard a man's voice. "Chelsea, are you here?"

The voice seemed familiar, but she couldn't place it in this context.

She dropped down to her knees to hide under the bed but there just wasn't enough space between the bed and the floor to squeeze through. She popped back up on her feet and was about to slide open the closet and hide in there when the man suddenly appeared. It was dark, and the curtains had been drawn closed, but there was a crack open enough for some moonlight to stream through. He would at least be able to make out that there was someone else in the room if he looked in her direction. But at the moment, the man's back was to her as she flattened herself against the wall. There was enough moonlight for her to see him standing over Chelsea's limp body on the bed. He reached down and stroked her hair.

"Hey, babe, you awake?"

He shook her gently.

She stirred a bit, mumbled something, but didn't wake up.

"Babe?"

He sat down on the edge of the bed next to her. "I'm sorry about tonight. I was halfway out the door when she came home from her night out with the girls unexpectedly. Apparently she had a spat with one of her friends over something silly and it soured the whole evening. . . ."

Chelsea moaned and turned over on her side.

"I'm sorry," the man said. "I shouldn't bore you with why I stood you up. But I'm here now."

That voice.

Sandra knew that voice.

There was a crackling in her ear.

"Sandra . . . what . . . doing . . . talk . . ." Maya's voice cut in and out. The crackling got so distracting that she reached up and pulled the earpiece out and pocketed it. Maya wouldn't be helping her out of this situation.

Sandra watched the man pull back Chelsea's tangled hair and kiss her on the cheek. Then he stood up. His back was still to her, and she pressed her body against the wall as much as she could, knowing that if he turned around, despite the darkness, he would see her in plain view.

He removed some cuff links and dropped them on the side table and then began unbuttoning his shirt.

Sandra used the distraction to slip into the bathroom.

Her mind raced. How was she going to get out of here? She was trapped. What if he found her? What would he do? She scanned the basin, and the only weapon she could find was a plugged-in hair dryer. She couldn't very well blow hot air in his face in order to make her escape.

She heard him cough. He was now much closer to her than before. He was coming into the bathroom! Sandra climbed into the bathtub and quietly closed the shower curtain just as the light snapped on and he stepped to the basin and ran the water. He was only inches away from her. What if he decided to take a shower? She would be caught. She slowly, carefully reached over and with two fingers drew back the shower curtain just an inch so she could try to get a good look at him.

He was bent over, shirtless, still in his pants, splashing water on his face. She could tell he was older, maybe in his fifties, with a hairy body with tufts of gray everywhere. He was thick, but not fat, more of a dad's body. Finally, after washing his face for what seemed like an eternity, the man sprang back up and grabbed a white towel from the basin to wipe his face. When he dropped the towel, she could see his reflection in the mirror.

Sandra had to cover her mouth with her hand to suppress a surprised gasp.

It was Principal John Hicks.

She couldn't believe it.

Chelsea's married man was the high school principal.

Maisie Portman's boss, to whom she had been devoted.

No wonder she had not approved of the affair.

Hicks unscrewed the cap over a tiny bottle of mouthwash and poured it in his mouth, swishing it around before spitting it back out in the sink. Then he rubbed a hand through his chest hair as he examined himself in the mirror before heading out and turning off the light.

Sandra waited a few minutes before pulling the shower curtain back slowly and quietly stepping out of the tub. She inched her way to the door and peeked into the bedroom to see Hicks climbing into bed with Chelsea and wrapping an arm around her waist, pulling her into him. Chelsea mumbled some more but said nothing coherent. She would be out until morning and then probably nursing a massive hangover.

Sandra waited and waited. Hicks cleared his throat a couple of times. She knew he hadn't fallen asleep yet, and it would be too dangerous to make a move, but eventually he began snoring. As it grew louder in volume, she made the decision to drop to her knees and crawl from the bathroom across the carpet of the bedroom and out to the main room of the suite. Once she was past the bedroom, she crawled to her feet and scurried to the door. She reached for the handle and turned it slowly. There was a loud click. She stood very still. Hicks had stopped snoring in the bedroom. Had the sound awakened him? She waited a few more seconds and then pulled open the door. A flood of light from the hallway poured in right past the bedroom door that was open.

"Who is it? Who's there?" Hicks shouted.

She was out the door in a flash, running down the hall in her high heels, stumbling a couple of times, nearly spraining her left ankle at one point, until she rounded the corner and stopped to catch her breath.

She poked her head around the corner to see if she was being followed, and there he was, in his underwear, sprinting down the hall in hot pursuit.

Sandra bolted toward the elevator and pressed the button. The door immediately slid open. It was her lucky day. The elevator was already at her floor. She rushed inside and pressed the button for the lobby. That's when she realized she had made a huge mistake. The elevator waited a few seconds before the doors started to close. Enough time for her to hear Hicks huffing and puffing as he ran for the elevator to catch up with the person who had been in Chelsea's room. She kicked herself for not escaping down the stairwell. She scooted to the side to hide as the doors finally began to close, and she saw Hicks's hand try to wedge itself between the doors to get them to open again. But he wasn't fast enough, and the doors locked shut, and she breathed a heavy sigh of relief as the elevator began its descent.

She thought he might try to intercept her by beating her down to the lobby using the stairs, but he was a high school principal with a reputation to maintain, so it might not be the best idea to fly into the lobby in just his underwear.

The elevator doors opened and the lobby was pretty much empty because of the late hour. Just a clerk behind the check-in desk. She nodded at the young woman, who looked up from her computer and with a bright smile said, "Good evening."

Once outside, Sandra spotted Maya's car across the street. She ran over and jumped in the passenger's side.

Maya stared at Sandra. "What the hell happened?"

"The boyfriend showed up! You will never believe who it was!"

Sandra excitedly told Maya all that had happened, and when she was finished, she threw her head back and smiled.

Maya shook her head, amused. "You really are loving all this private eye stuff, aren't you?"

"I was *this* close to getting caught, but I got away and he didn't see me! What an adrenaline rush!"

Sandra couldn't hide her exhilaration. Maya was right. She had not felt this alive in a very long time.

CHAPTER FORTY

When Alice Hicks opened the door and greeted Sandra and Maya with a warm smile, Sandra's stomach dropped. Of course she had expected her to be at home this early in the morning, but when she saw her sweet, unsuspecting face, oblivious to her husband's infidelity, Sandra suddenly felt nervous and unprepared.

"Sandra, what a pleasant surprise," Alice said, grabbing her in a hug before turning to Maya and sticking out her hand. "Hello, I'm Alice Hicks."

"Maya Kendrick," Maya said, shaking it.

"Maya's daughter, Vanessa, is a student at the high school. She's in this year's production of *Hello, Dolly!*" Sandra said.

"Oh yes. She's playing Minnie. She's a wonderful little actress," Alice said sincerely.

"Thank you," Maya said.

Sandra could tell Maya was feeling sick to her stomach now too. They had decided they needed to confront Principal Hicks about his affair with Chelsea Portman, and better it be done at his home rather than at the school, where there would be an abundance of prying eyes and ears. But they had ignored the fact that Mrs. Hicks, who was a part-time realtor, would not be out showing a house at this early hour. Sandra suddenly felt guilty for showing up unannounced to confront Hicks. The last thing she wanted was to do it in front of his innocent wife. Sandra knew of all people what it was like to be blindsided by a husband's dirty secrets. There was no way she wanted any part of causing this woman pain in her own home.

"Are you here to see John?" Alice asked brightly, waving them inside.

"Yes," Sandra said, stepping into the foyer.

"He's in the kitchen eating his breakfast. He's a little grumpy because he worked very late last night. Let me go get him," Alice said, shuffling off.

Sandra and Maya exchanged a look.

"We should have thought this through more," Maya groaned.

Sandra nodded.

They both looked around at the charmingly appointed house full of antiques and mementos from the couple's world travels. Their kids were off to college, but a number of framed photos of them throughout the years lined the wall going up the staircase.

John Hicks bounded in from the kitchen. His dress shirtsleeves were rolled up and a lobster-print necktie was tossed over one shoulder. He was holding a half-eaten piece of sourdough toast slathered with butter in one hand and a wrinkled cloth napkin to wipe his mouth with in the other. He looked surprised to see Sandra and Maya together.

"Ladies . . . ," he said warily.

"Hi, John. We were hoping to speak to you about something," Sandra said.

He checked his watch. "This couldn't wait until school hours?"

"No, I'm afraid not," Maya replied brusquely.

There were a few worry lines on his forehead. He wasn't sure what this could possibly be about, so he seemed to go over a few subjects in his mind, finally settling on one that made sense. "Is this about you resigning as PTA president?"

Sandra opened her mouth to answer just as Alice returned with two piping-hot cups of coffee. "I took the liberty of making you gals some coffee. Hope you like cream and sugar."

"Thanks, that's very kind of you," Sandra said.

Alice hovered, curious as to why they were here.

Hicks patiently waited for Sandra to answer his question.

"Yes, it's about the PTA," Sandra lied. "Is there somewhere we can talk in private?"

Alice got the hint and grabbed her Hermès bag that was hanging on a coatrack by the door. "Sorry to run off like this, but I have an open house clear across town and I'm already running late. Nice seeing you, Sandra. Nice meeting you, Maya."

She flew out the door, shutting the door behind her.

Hicks stared at Sandra and Maya, suddenly suspicious. "I get the feeling this is not about you stepping down as PTA president."

Sandra took a deep breath and exhaled. "No, John, it's not."

"Then what?" Hicks demanded to know.

"It's about Chelsea Portman," Maya said flatly.

Hicks flinched, then quickly regained his composure and took a bite of his toast, chewing it thoroughly before swallowing and responding. "Is that Maisie Portman's sister, the actress?"

Sandra suppressed a laugh. This whole act of pretending to vaguely know of her was both laughable and insulting to their intelligence. "Yes, that's right."

Sandra noticed his hand holding the napkin was trembling slightly.

"What about her?" Hicks casually asked.

Maya was losing patience. "We know you're having an affair with her."

Hicks responded like most men confronted with the truth. His first instinct was to react surprised, genuinely stunned as to how anyone could possibly believe such an outlandish lie. And he did so like a true adulterer. "What? Who said that . . . ? That's the most preposterous . . ."

But he could tell from their dead stares that they were not believing him for a second, so after a little more effort to deny, he gave up and his shoulders slumped. "Where did you get this information?"

"Nobody told us anything. We just know," Maya said.

Hicks eyed Maya, a little intimidated by her all-businesslike tone. And then he turned to Sandra and gave her the once-over before it dawned on him. "You . . . That was *you* in our hotel room. I saw the back of your head as you ran off down the hall, and I remember thinking the woman looked like you."

Sandra didn't answer, but her guilty expression gave her away.

Hicks was getting more discombobulated by the minute and shouted, "What were you doing there?"

"I ran into Chelsea at the hotel bar and when she had a little too much to drink, I helped her to her room."

"I find it difficult to believe that you just happened to be cocktailing in the Top of the East bar."

"It's a gorgeous bar with excellent drinks," Sandra said flippantly.

"What's really going on here?" Hicks wanted to know.

"I'm a private investigator," Maya sighed. "And I'm looking into Maisie Portman's death."

Hicks glared at her. "Maisie Portman committed suicide."

"I'm not so sure," Maya said.

"Well, the police are. The case is closed," Hicks seethed before turning his attention to Sandra. "And what are you? Detective in training?"

Sandra shrugged. "Something like that."

"Who hired you?"

The question caught them both by surprise, since the answer was so ludicrous.

"Chelsea Portman," Sandra muttered.

"Wait just a minute. Chelsea hired you? Does she think *I* killed her sister?" Hicks cried, panic rising in his voice.

"No, we're just looking at different angles, and following every lead available to us . . . ," Maya said, attempting to calm him down.

"And we found a life-insurance policy . . . ," Sandra added.

Maya shot her a look, and Sandra shrank back, kicking herself.

"What life-insurance policy?"

"Maisie took out a life-insurance policy naming Chelsea as her primary beneficiary," Maya said, sighing.

"Chelsea hired you to find out if her sister was murdered, and now you think she was the one who did it? This is insane!" Hicks bellowed as he began putting the pieces together. "So you befriended her at the bar in order to see if she would slip up and say something incriminating, but then you saw me when I showed up to meet her at the hotel!"

"If it makes you feel any better, it was a complete surprise. We had no idea . . . ," Sandra said.

"Let me put your minds at ease. I did not kill Maisie. Check out my Facebook page. I was doing a live event for hundreds of followers in the cafeteria before the PTA meeting that night, talking about the special things we've been planning for the fall semester. There was no way I could have done it."

"We'll be sure to check it out," Maya said, not quite convinced of his innocence just yet.

"As for Chelsea, she was home in New York at a Sam Smith concert with a bunch of girlfriends. They must have posted a thousand Instagram photos. So I'm sorry to report that we both have well-documented alibis all over social media. Now, is there anything else?" Hicks huffed.

"No, that about wraps it up," Maya said.

"Well, I appreciate you waiting until my wife left before hurling all these ridiculous accusations at me," Hicks spat out.

Maya clearly wanted to bite her tongue and keep mum but couldn't. "Most of them, anyway."

"Most of them what?" Hicks asked.

"Most of them are ridiculous," Maya said, unable to resist a final jab.

Hicks fought to keep his cool, but it was getting harder. He glared at Sandra. "I trust you're not going to go blabbing to Alice at your next knitting circle or something?"

Knitting circle?

Sandra had no idea John Hicks was such a sexist pig.

"No, what you do in your private life is none of my business," Sandra said.

"Apparently that's not entirely true since you're here in my house right now," he said angrily.

"Thank you for your time," Maya said, as both she and Sandra turned to leave.

"Oh, Sandra . . . ," Hicks said.

Sandra spun back around. "Yes?"

"Have you made a decision yet? Will you be resigning as PTA president?"

She thought about it for a few seconds. "I haven't made up my mind yet."

"Not that what I think means anything, but God, I really hope you do."

Sandra gave him a thin smile. Her days of respecting him as the principal of the high school were officially over. "Well, I appreciate your opinion. You've given me a lot to think about. I'll keep you posted. Goodbye, Johnny." Hicks flinched and Sandra smiled. "Isn't that what Maisie used to call you? Johnny?"

He didn't answer her.

Sandra followed Maya out the door and to the car, and before either of them had the chance to strap on their seat belts, Maya's cell phone was chirping.

She checked the caller ID.

"It's Chelsea Portman."

"I knew John would have her on speed dial, but boy, that was fast," Sandra remarked with a chuckle.

Maya pressed the answer button on the screen and put the phone to her ear. "Hi, this is Maya."

Maya sat there listening. After a few seconds, she nodded and said, "I understand."

And just like that the call was over. Maya dropped her phone in the cup holder between them and said, "Well, I can't say that wasn't totally unexpected."

"What did she say?"

"She just fired me."

CHAPTER FORTY-ONE

Maya opened the drawer of her desk and pulled out the half-full bottle of Jim Beam and poured some into two shot glasses. She handed one to Sandra, who sat opposite her in a rickety old chair.

Sandra leaned back and held the shot glass close to her mouth. "You remind me of one of those grizzled old private eyes who keep liquor in a drawer to ease the pressure when a case hits a dead end."

"That pretty much sums it up," Maya said with a wry smile. "You like bourbon?"

"Not really, but I don't see the ingredients I need for a cosmopolitan in that drawer."

The two women laughed and then clinked their glasses and swallowed the bourbon. Sandra had to suppress a cough as the bourbon burned through her throat.

Maya slammed her shot glass down on the desk. "You okay?"

Sandra nodded as she put a fist to her mouth, waiting to see if she was going to erupt in a coughing fit. "My husband always said I would never be a professional drinker."

"I think that might be a good thing. My husband never said that to me, probably because we met in a bar."

Sandra giggled. "Was it was one of those god-awful singles' bars?"

"No, just your typical neighborhood watering hole a few blocks from the police academy. I was a cadet and went out with some other recruits after a day at the shooting range to blow off some steam, and he was there with some fellow officers hanging out and playing darts. Our eyes met, and before I knew it he had sent a drink over." Maya rolled her eyes. "I know, I know, oldest trick in the book, and I fell for it."

"I think it's sweet."

"Not really. It was more calculated than that. Max had spotted me on my first day at the academy, when he gave an orientation speech. He knew the cadets went to the same bar every night after training, and so he made sure he was there when I showed up."

"Do you have a picture of your husband?"

"Just google him. He was all over the internet when they arrested him for corruption. You might even be able to find his mug shot."

There was an uneasy silence before Sandra spoke. "I'm sorry."

"Don't be. It's just a fact of life. You know, the funny thing is, when I was in high school I always chased the bad boys, the dangerous-looking ones who smoked pot and drove fast cars and skipped school all the time. I thought they were exciting and unpredictable and so sexy . . . but then when I met Max, I thought maybe I was finally growing up, finally changing, and making more responsible choices. I mean, hell, he was a police officer! It was like a one-eighty-degree turn from my previous boyfriends. And then, in the end, he turned out to be just another bad guy, and I realized I hadn't changed at all."

More silence.

Sandra leaned forward. "I could use another shot."

Maya raised an eyebrow. "Seriously?"

Sandra nodded.

"Okay, but I'm sending you home in an Uber. I don't need my new partner getting arrested too."

"Deal."

Maya poured more bourbon into the two shot glasses.

"I wish I remembered more about you when we went to high school together," Sandra remarked, smiling.

"Girls like me weren't really friends with girls like you," Maya said. There was no bitterness in her tone.

"What do you mean?"

"You know what I mean. You were the typical high school success story. Captain of the cheerleading squad—"

"I wasn't captain!" Sandra shouted defensively.

"Maybe not, but you were the most popular! All the boys had a crush on you. You dated the class president, if I recall."

"Yeah, and he cheated on me too," Sandra muttered, shaking her head at the memory.

"What?"

"Yes. I should have learned my lesson right then and there. Never date a politician. But did I? No, I'm a sucker for any man who tells me he wants to make the world a better place with progressive, humane policies. In Danny Ludwig's case, that meant putting a soda machine in the cafeteria. With Stephen, that meant expanding health care in the state of Maine. Either way, I bought into it."

"What a pair we make. One of us is still hitched to a convicted felon and the other is tied to a serial philanderer," Maya said.

"Girl power," Sandra replied.

They clinked their glasses again and downed their second shot.

"Maybe we could have been friends in high school," Maya remarked. "We could have bonded over our terrible taste in men."

Sandra laughed.

Suddenly the door flew open and a very pregnant Frances shuffled inside the office, stopping short at the sight of Maya and Sandra doing shots together.

"I'm sorry, I didn't mean to interrupt—" Frances said with a surprised look on her face.

"Don't be silly," Maya said, jumping up. "We were just chatting."

"I swear if I don't drop this bowling ball soon, I'm going to go out of my mind!" Frances wailed as she crossed to the other side of the room and sat down at her own desk in the corner.

Sandra wasn't sure if she should stay or leave, so she just sat still for the time being.

"Can I get you something to drink, Frances? Coffee? Water?" Maya offered.

"No, I'm fine, but I was just sitting at home alone and I was going stir-crazy, so I thought I would take a chance and find you still here so I could"—her voice lowered into a whisper; this wasn't easy for her—"apologize."

Maya walked over to her desk. "Frances . . ."

Frances held up a hand. "No, I never should've yelled at you like that. You were just doing your job, following the leads wherever they took you; it's what we're supposed to do, but I couldn't handle it. . . ."

Frances opened a drawer in her desk. There wasn't a bottle of bourbon in it, just a mound of assorted candy bars. She plucked one from the drawer, unwrapped it, and began taking big bites of a Milky Way. "At first I blamed the pregnancy for my appalling behavior, but I knew pretty soon I wouldn't have that excuse anymore, so I just had to face reality. It's totally me. I've been acting like a real bitch, and I'm sorry. Can you forgive me?"

Maya smiled.

"You're my best friend, and I don't think I'll survive if you can't forgive me," Frances said, her eyes brimming with tears. She wiped them away with her index fingers. "The crying I can still chalk up to the pregnancy."

"Of course I forgive you, Frances," Maya said, walking around the desk and leaning down to hug her.

"I know I've been a terrible partner lately, but that's going to change. I'm going to be around a lot more so you don't have to—"

Sandra winced. Frances caught herself before finishing the sentence, but they all knew the gist of what she almost said. *So you don't have to find a new partner.*

Sandra knew that was her cue.

Sandra stood up. "I better get going. . . ."

Maya crossed back around Frances's desk. "You don't have to leave right away."

"Don't leave on my account," Frances said. "I can live vicariously watching you two do more shots."

Sandra was taken aback by Frances's almost jovial tone. She had never heard her sound friendly before. She feared it might just be an act, a way to show Maya she wasn't jealous of their budding friendship, and the last thing Sandra wanted to do was to cause more tension between the two best friends.

"Good luck with everything. I'm sure you two will have the case wrapped up in no time," Sandra said before turning to Maya. "Thanks for the bourbon."

Sandra scooted out the door. Maybe it was time to stop playing private eye and deal with the problems she was facing at home.

CHAPTER FORTY-TWO

"I'm so proud of you, baby," Max said, his eyes welling up with tears, reaching out to squeeze Vanessa's hand.

Maya wasn't sure if he was crying because he was happy for Vanessa's tour de force or sad that he was stuck in prison and couldn't physically be present to see his daughter shine on the stage in *Hello, Dolly!*

They were back in the small windowless visiting room, Maya and Vanessa sitting opposite Max in those hard uncomfortable folding chairs. Several armed guards stood by stoically, keeping watch over things.

"She has an incredible singing voice," Maya added.

"No surprise there," Max said, grinning and winking at Vanessa. "She obviously gets that from me. Your mom can tell you, I used to kill at karaoke."

Vanessa giggled. "She doesn't have to. I remember when I was little, you used to come into my room and perform 'Stairway to Heaven.' I was like your captive audience."

Max did his best Marlon Brando impression. "I coulda been somebody. I coulda been a contender."

The reference was totally lost on Vanessa.

Maya noticed Max looked more tired and drawn than the last time they had visited. She wanted to ask what was going on, if he was dealing with stress on the inside—more than the usual rigors of fear and violence one had to cope with in prison—but she was afraid to ask in front of Vanessa because she didn't want her daughter to hear about it if her father was being threatened. Word inevitably got around when a cop was forced to serve time, and revenge-seeking convicts were always eager to put a bull's-eye on his back.

Maya reached into her bag and rummaged around for some loose bills. She handed a five to Vanessa. "Why don't you go to the vending machine and get us a snack? I'm craving a bag of salt 'n' vinegar chips."

Vanessa eyed her suspiciously. "Are you trying to get rid of me so you can talk to Daddy in private?"

Max leaned back in his chair and folded his arms. "That skill she has of reading people, that she gets from you."

"Five minutes," Maya said to Vanessa.

Vanessa held out her hand after pocketing the five. "I'm thirsty. I could use a Diet Coke too."

Maya sighed, reached in for another five and slapped it in the palm of her daughter's hand. "Don't hurry back."

Vanessa got up and ambled away.

Maya turned back to Max. "You don't look too good, Max."

He shrugged. "Typical stuff. There are a lot of bullies who like messing with me in the yard, but I can handle it."

She noticed a Band-Aid on his arm. "Did someone attack you?"

"I wouldn't call it an attack. I went for the last dinner roll in the cafeteria, and this dude decided he wanted it so he bit me on the arm before I could even open my mouth to take a bite. But it was no big deal. I jabbed him in the forehead with my fork to teach him a lesson."

"You don't call that an attack?"

"Not a real one. I've dealt with plenty of those. You should see the big scar on my torso from a shiv in the shower last March."

Maya shuddered. "Oh, Max . . ."

They sat in silence for a few minutes. Max stared at the floor before finally looking up at Maya. "I want to get the hell out of here, babe . . ."

"I know. Just stay positive. Your parole is coming up in a few months."

"Ten. Ten months. That's almost a year."

She didn't know how to make him feel better, so she just resorted to more small talk about Frances's due date, how Frances was finally moving in with Coach Vinnie, how she had been getting help with her case from a new friend, although she neglected to mention it was a U.S. senator's wife. Max took it all in, happy for the distraction.

"Well, like I told you before, I still have a lot of connections on the outside, so if you need any help . . ."

"I appreciate it, Max, thank you," she said, although

she still had no intention of ever taking him up on the offer. However, she was curious. "So who do you still talk to?"

"My old partner, JC. He keeps me up to speed on everything that's going on, all the dirt. Apparently there is a big internal-affairs investigation unfolding right now, and according to JC, a lot of officers are about to get caught up in it. The IA is casting a pretty wide net."

"What kind of investigation?"

"Big corruption case. Racketeering and robbery. A bunch of guys have been targeted from my old division, both active duty and retired. Apparently they've been out of control, like thugs with badges, stealing cash, reselling seized narcotics, sticking illegal GPS trackers on the cars of their robbery targets, mostly drug dealers flush with cash, and lying under oath to cover their tracks."

"Oh my god . . ."

"Yeah, it's pretty bad. JC, one of the good ones by the way, is assisting IA in identifying the ringleader, but he's conflicted because he feels like he's snitching. I told him it was his duty to find the bad apples so they don't destroy the credibility and reputation of the whole department. Ironic, right?"

Max laughed as he looked around at his surroundings.

Maya forced a smile, but she didn't find any of this funny.

"Guess I'm trying to make up for my past sins," Max muttered.

"Does JC know who the ringleader is?"

Max nodded. "Yeah, but I don't know him personally. He started after I left, or I should say, after I was forced to leave," he said with a trace of bitterness. "I hear he's got a golden-boy reputation and a sledgehammer approach to his homicide cases."

"So he's a detective?"

"I've probably said too much already."

"Max, who is it?"

"I really can't tell you. I wouldn't want the guy some-how getting tipped off or find out that it was JC who fin-gered him. Not until IA makes a move on him and he's safely in custody."

"Do I know him?" Maya asked, curious.

Max hesitated. "I don't know. I think Frances might. She worked with him briefly when she was still on the force. But that's all you get."

"You just told me you want to help me out. Why are you holding back on me now?"

"Because this has nothing to do with any of your cases. This is some dirty, dangerous stuff that you don't need to get involved in."

A name popped into Maya's head and she suddenly sat up straight. "Reyes? Is it Detective Mateo Reyes?"

Max didn't have to answer her question.

She could tell from the tense, agitated expression on his face that she had just guessed correctly.

Mateo Reyes wasn't just an acquaintance of Frances.

He was a close friend.

Close enough that Frances had gone to the trouble of setting Maya up with him on a date.

Frances had to be warned.

CHAPTER FORTY-THREE

Frances sat stone-faced on her ratty old couch that was in desperate need of new upholstery. She gently placed a hand on her giant stomach as Maya stood a few feet away, arms folded, having just explained what Max had told her about Mateo Reyes.

Maya spoke softly. "I know this is a lot to take in right now, but I felt you should know. I didn't want to hide anything from you."

"It just doesn't make any sense," Frances said. "I worked with Mateo. He's a good detective. He wouldn't be so dumb as to get caught up in something like that."

Maya sighed, unfolded her arms, and crossed to sit next to Frances on the couch. She put a comforting arm around her. "Max said his sources are pretty solid."

"Max is serving time for corruption," Frances scoffed.

Maya couldn't deny her remark stung just a little bit. Max was, after all, her husband, at least at the moment, until the divorce was final. But Frances was right. He wasn't exactly an exemplary source, one to be trusted without question. He was looking to shave some time off his sentence, maybe testify in an upcoming case to speed up his parole hearing. There could be any number of reasons Max wanted to finger Mateo. But having been married to the man for fourteen years before his arrest, she could tell when he was being straight with her, and earlier that day, during their time in the prison visiting room, she felt he was being honest about what he knew. And Frances deserved to know.

"What else did he say?" Frances asked.

Maya shrugged. "Not much. But it sounds like the walls are closing in, and Mateo is seriously enmeshed in the whole mess."

Coach Vinnie suddenly appeared. "Maya, I didn't know you were here. I was in the bedroom watching the Red Sox kick some New York Yankee butt."

"Hi, Vinnie," Maya said quietly.

Vinnie immediately picked up on the cues. "Something wrong?"

Maya opened her mouth to speak, but Frances cut her off. "No, nothing. Just some girl talk."

"Anybody want a beer? I'm heading to the fridge," Vinnie said.

"I'd love one, but ask me again in about a week," Frances said, patting her belly.

"I'm fine, thanks," Maya said with a thin smile.

Vinnie shrugged and ambled off into the kitchen.

Frances turned and leaned into Maya as much as her body could manage and whispered, "I don't want him knowing what's going on. He worries enough about me as it is."

"Got it," Maya said. "But he's going to find out eventually. Everybody is."

"I know, but let him just get through the childbirth first, which is making him a nervous wreck, then we will deal with the rest of it."

Mateo was Vinnie's friend. And maybe there was a chance Vinnie was aware of what was going on in the department, but Maya highly doubted he was in the loop, despite the closeness between the two men.

Maya noticed Frances taking deep breaths and continuing to hold a hand on top of her swelled tummy.

"You're not finally going into labor, are you?"

Frances shook her head. "No, I always do this to calm myself down. Trust me, if I was going into labor, you'd know it from my screaming."

Maya worried as she stared at Frances, who was visibly shaken by this news. She closed her eyes and kept breathing deeply and exhaling until finally she had relaxed herself into a calmer state.

"I'm starting to feel guilty for telling you anything," Maya said.

Frances shook her head. "No, I needed to know."

Maya sat with her in silence. She reached out to take Frances's hand, but Frances gently pushed it away as her mind seemed to race about what she had just learned. She turned to Maya and was about to speak when Vinnie passed through with a bottle of beer. He winked at her and headed back into the bedroom. When he was gone, Frances finally spoke. "You're not going to get into the middle of this, are you, Maya?"

Maya scrunched up her face, confused. "What do you mean?"

"Whatever Mateo might be mixed up with, it's really not your job to try and be the big hero and take down the entire police department—"

Maya sat up straight. "I know that, Frances. I'm just relating to you what Max told me. Besides, it sounds like Internal Affairs is already on top of it."

Frances's face was pale, and she was starting to get worked up. "Good, because you shouldn't stick your nose into it, like you always do—"

"Frances, I know he's your friend, but why are you being so—?"

"You're not a cop anymore!"

Maya was thunderstruck by Frances's agitated tone as she struggled to stand up with little success. Finally, Maya popped to her feet and grabbed Frances by the hand, hauling her up from the couch.

"You . . . you better go now. I'm feeling a little nauseous," Frances sputtered.

"Can I get you anything?"

"Please, just go, Maya!"

Frances fled to the bathroom, slamming the door behind her.

Maya stood in the middle of the living room in a state of shock. She could hear the muted sound of the television in the bedroom broadcasting the Red Sox game. And she could faintly make out Frances vomiting in the bathroom. She wanted to go to her, hold her head, and pat her on the back and tell her everything would be fine, but she knew the last thing Frances wanted at the moment was for Maya to help her, or be anywhere near her, and that's what Maya found so intrinsically disturbing.

CHAPTER FORTY-FOUR

While driving home, Maya received a text from Vanessa letting her know that she was at Ryan's house studying for an upcoming test. She was decidedly vague about what subject, which set off Maya's alarm bells. It sounded more like another rushed excuse to cover up what they might actually be doing.

Maya's head was pounding, and she was still feeling jarred and bothered by Frances's reaction to her bombshell news about Detective Mateo Reyes. She pulled into a gas station to fill up her tank and get some much-needed coffee, hoping a shot of caffeine might make her headache go away.

Maya glanced at the digital numbers rising as the fuel pumped into her car, and couldn't believe how expensive gas was at over three dollars a gallon. She was already over her monthly budget. She tried to erase her money concerns from her mind and texted Vanessa back, informing her she was going to swing by the Wallage house and pick her up. She just needed an address.

Vanessa hemmed and hawed at first, trying to convince her that they were not done studying and Ryan could give her a lift home later, but Maya wasn't having any of it. She ordered her daughter to text the address now. After a couple more quick back-and-forths, Vanessa reluctantly sent her the address. Maya removed the nozzle from her tank and waited for her receipt to print out before getting back behind the wheel and following the GPS directions to the Wallage home.

When Maya pulled up out front, the size of the house took her breath away. Of course it made sense that Sandra lived in such an opulent home, but it was so far removed from her own circumstances that she couldn't help but have a stunned reaction. She got out of the car and walked up the path dividing the immaculately kept lawn to the front door where she rang the bell.

After a moment, Sandra opened the door with a surprised look on her face. "Maya! What are you doing here? How did you know—?"

"I'm sorry to bother you. Vanessa texted me your address. I just came by to pick her up."

"Please, come in, I'll make us some coffee."

"No, thanks, I just had some. I don't want to be up all night. I have trouble sleeping as it is," Maya said.

Maya tried to contain her astonishment at how beautifully decorated the house was. In what little spare time she had, sometimes she would flip through home and garden magazines, gazing at all the lovely homes that were so far out of her league and price range. They were fantasies, dream houses, like the ones she admired in the movies or on TV when she was a little girl.

Sandra led her into the living room, where Ryan and Vanessa sat closely together on the couch, their laptops side by side on the coffee table. They both had guilty looks on their faces, like the last thing they had been doing before she walked in was studying.

"It'll be your fault if we fail our test tomorrow because you made us quit studying together so early," Vanessa huffed.

"If you fail, then you didn't study enough in the first place. The test is tomorrow, so you should already have put in the time to prepare," Maya said flatly.

"Oh, she's good," Ryan joked.

Maya had to suppress a smile.

She liked this kid, even though she wasn't entirely comfortable about the way he looked at her daughter. Still, if Vanessa had to have a lovesick boyfriend following her around, Ryan seemed like a good choice.

"Can we have just a few more minutes to go over some more test prep questions? This exam counts for twenty percent of our final grade."

Maya sighed. "Fine."

"We can wait in the kitchen," Sandra said.

Maya eyed Vanessa suspiciously, signaling her to not take too long, and then she followed Sandra into the beautiful kitchen with expensive-looking stainless-steel appliances, an island in the middle like she had always wanted for her own kitchen, and a lovely table and chairs painted white with a classy print table cloth surrounded by accents, and best of all, an antique china cabinet. All of it pulled together so perfectly as if Martha Stewart had designed it herself.

"Are you sure you don't want any coffee?" Sandra asked.

"No, thank you," Maya said, her mind elsewhere.

"What's bothering you?" Sandra asked.

Maya snapped out of her thoughts. "What?"

"You seem to be a million miles away."

Sandra crossed to the counter and opened a cake tin. Inside was a delicious-looking cake. She cut two pieces and brought them over to the kitchen table on two dessert plates. "You may be able to say no to coffee, but try saying no to my lemon Bundt cake. Have a seat."

Maya was in Sandra's castle, so she did as she was told. Maya took the small silver fork Sandra held out to her and then she cut into the cake and took a bite. It practically melted in her mouth. "Delicious."

"Thanks. So are you going to talk to me?" Sandra said casually, popping a piece of cake into her mouth.

Maya couldn't help but notice how much more comfortable Sandra was getting the more she hung around her. In fact, she found it quite charming. Sandra considered herself a friend now.

Maya debated with herself about whether it was smart to bring Sandra up to speed on what she had heard from Max, but that only lasted a few seconds because, in her mind now, Sandra was no longer a peripheral figure in her life. They had been working together on the Maisie Portman case and their kids were dating. And since she couldn't discuss any of this with Frances apparently, and Sandra was so eager and willing to be her confidante, she decided to come clean and voice what she had just learned.

Sandra sat opposite her at the kitchen table, wide-eyed and gorging on the cake as Maya explained everything, getting up only once to pour herself a cup of black coffee after the timer on the coffeemaker interrupted Maya's complete rundown of information regarding Detective Mateo Reyes.

When she finished, Sandra sat quietly, churning everything over in her mind.

"I know it's a lot. I'm still overwhelmed thinking about it myself," Maya said, finishing her piece of cake.

Sandra suddenly startled her by pounding a fist down on the kitchen table. "I bet he covered up the crime scene!"

"What? What are you talking about?" Maya asked, totally confused.

"Maisie Portman! He was the first detective on the scene! When you saw those straight marks on Maisie's neck and tried to tell him about it, he completely dismissed you. I thought it was a sexist thing, like he didn't want a woman taking over his case, but maybe he just didn't want to hear it because he was determined to make Maisie's death look like a suicide!"

It was something Maya hadn't even thought about. The last thing in her mind was connecting the police corruption case with the Maisie Portman case. "But why?"

"Because Maisie was all about breaking major scandals on her Dirty Laundry website. Perhaps she somehow uncovered Mateo's involvement in the police department corruption case and was about to blow the whistle on him!" Sandra explained breathlessly before jumping to her feet and pacing around the kitchen, her mind exploding with thoughts fast and furious. "Yes! Maybe he found out what she was going to do, and he showed up at the school on the night of the PTA meeting and found her in her office, where he confronted her! He warned her to not publish her story, and when she refused, he strangled her, forged the suicide note, and then staged the hanging! When we found the body and called the police, he was already nearby and just happened to show up first on the scene!"

Maya stared at Sandra, slack-jawed. "How did you—?"

"I don't have a regular job, so I have plenty of time to watch a lot of detective shows."

Maya couldn't help but smile. "It's a very interesting theory, but there is one giant flaw in it."

Sandra frowned. "What?"

"All of Maisie's stories on the Dirty Laundry site were related to the high school. They were all about the teachers or students or administrative staff. As far as I know, Mateo has no connection to the school. He's not married to a teacher, and he's not a father, so he doesn't have any kids enrolled."

Sandra slumped over. "You're right. I didn't think about that."

But Sandra's off-the-cuff theory had sparked something inside Maya. In her gut, she knew Sandra was onto something. Mateo had shown up at the crime scene awfully quick the night they had discovered Maisie's body.

Maybe Sandra was partially right.

Maybe there was more to the story still to be found.

They had to dig deeper.

CHAPTER FORTY-FIVE

Oscar Dunford beamed from ear to ear when he saw Maya standing in the doorway with a pizza box. "How did you know I'd be working late?"

"You always work late," Maya said, smirking before entering the cramped office and setting the pizza down on his desk. She opened the box with a flourish. "Pepperoni and mushroom. Your favorite."

"You spoil me," Oscar said, his eyes dancing as Maya pulled a piece out and handed it to him. "I can't wait to hear the reason for this late-night romantic tryst."

"I need a favor," Maya said.

"Let me put on my big-surprise face."

"What's your take on Detective Reyes?"

"Mateo? He's okay. A little arrogant. A real macho type. Works out a lot. But he's never personally given me any trouble, so I don't have a problem with him."

"Corrupt?"

Oscar flinched slightly but recovered quickly and shrugged. "I don't know about that."

"You can't hide anything from me, Oscar. We know each other intimately."

"If that was true, I would have already knocked that pizza box off the top of my desk and had you sprawled out as I—"

"All right, you win. Thanks for that visual, which has now been permanently burned into my brain. Let's just agree we're really good friends. Good enough that I know when you're not being straight with me."

Oscar cleared his throat. "I've heard some things. . . ."

"What kind of things?"

"Rumors. But that's all they are. Rumors."

"Well, I heard Internal Affairs has been sniffing around here lately."

"Who told you that?"

"I still have a few sources."

She wasn't eager to tell him it was her incarcerated husband, who was the last person in the department to be sent up on corruption charges.

Oscar nodded as he took a bite of the pizza and talked with his mouth full. "Yeah, they've been here a few times interviewing people. But they haven't gotten to me yet. Doesn't matter though. I don't have anything useful to tell them."

"How's the pizza?"

"Not enough cheese. Luigi's never puts on enough cheese. But I won't hold that against you. So what can I do for you this fine evening since this obviously isn't a bona fide date?"

"Do you have access to Detective Reyes's case reports?"

"Is the pope Catholic?"

"I don't know, is he?"

"Now you're just playing with me. Of course he is. I think. Pope Francis is kind of a rebel, so who really knows?" Oscar tapped a few keys with his greasy fingers. "Which report do you want to look at?"

"Maisie Portman."

Within seconds, the official report was on Oscar's computer screen.

Maya read the file as Oscar scrolled down. One thing immediately jumped out to her. "Wait!"

Oscar, startled, stopped scrolling.

Maya pointed at a section of the file. "According to Detective Reyes, the crime scene investigators reported a V-shaped bruise on Maisie's neck, which was indicative of a self-hanging. That's a lie right there. I distinctly remember seeing a straight line bruise across her neck."

"That may be true, but he has crime scene photos to back him up. Look."

Oscar opened an attached photo with a close-up of Maisie's neck shortly after her body was discovered. The bruise was clearly in a V shape, which corroborated the report.

Maya studied the photo. "Is there any way he could have photoshopped this?"

"Sure, anything's possible, I guess. But why?"

Maya nudged Oscar out of his chair and took his place behind the desk, scrolling down farther. She stopped on another section, this one describing the suicide note. "It says here a handwriting expert confirmed that the suicide note was written by Maisie. But he doesn't give the name of the expert."

"Charlie Littlefield. He's the one we use for cases like this. Cool guy. We play paintball together a couple of times a year."

"Can you call him?"

"What for?"

"I want to confirm he did an analysis of the suicide note."

Oscar shrugged again and reached for his cell phone.

Maya continued reading the report as Oscar wandered out into the hall and chatted with his buddy Charlie. After a few minutes, Oscar ended the call and returned to hover over Maya.

"He was never called in for the Maisie Portman case," Oscar said.

"Which means unless there is another handwriting expert out there, Mateo is lying in his report."

Oscar reached for a large slice of pizza but Maya grabbed his wrist, stopping him.

"Oscar, is there any way you can get a hold of the original autopsy report?"

"Is the pope—?"

"Been there, done that. Just do it," Maya ordered as she stood up, allowing him to slide back into his chair and start typing.

"Don't eat that big slice. It has my name on it," Oscar said while tapping the keys on his computer.

Maya squeezed Oscar's shoulder. "It's all yours."

After a few seconds, Oscar pulled up another file, and his eyes widened. "Well, color me surprised."

Maya leaned in for a closer look. "What?"

"CSI reported a straight-line bruise on Maisie Portman's neck. There is no mention of any V-shape. Hold on."

Oscar opened an attached photo.

Maya gasped.

It was clear as day.

A straight-line bruise across Maisie Portman's neck.

"He doctored the photo," Maya whispered.

Oscar sat back in his chair. "Unbelievable."

Then, remembering the big slice of pizza awaiting him, Oscar reached over, grabbed it by the crust, folded it, and shoved half of it into his mouth.

"But I don't understand. Once homicide ruled the death a suicide, wouldn't the crime scene investigator have come out to refute the findings based on his own observations?" Maya asked.

"Not necessarily. Most of them just come in and do their job. Cops are in charge of closing the case. I'm sure there are inconsistencies all the time. They're usually already focused on the next case."

"Maybe, but there is also the possibility that the crime scene guy is corrupt too and has Mateo's back."

"I doubt it," Oscar argued. "If he was corrupt, he probably would've gotten rid of the original report. It's clear to me Mateo revised the report on his own. Once it is officially submitted, the crime scene investigators rarely ask to read a closed-case report."

"Sandra was right. Mateo wanted to ensure that Maisie Portman's death would be officially ruled a suicide. But why? What was the connection?"

"I'm not a detective here, Maya, I'm just the lovelorn tech guy, waiting for you to wake up one day and realize I am the man of your dreams, here right in front of you, all this time."

Maya cracked a smile. Then she reached down and kissed Oscar on the cheek. "I appreciate all you do for me."

She headed for the door.

"Wait, we haven't finished our first date. There are still five slices of pizza left."

"I'll be back. I'm going to check out the locker room."

"What for?"

"I'm going to try to find Mateo's locker."

"There must be seventy-five lockers there."

"You wouldn't happen to know which one belongs to him, do you?"

"I'm dying to resort to the 'pope is Catholic' line, but I don't want you to yell at me again."

"Let's go," Maya said.

Oscar stuffed the remaining crust into his mouth and followed her out.

The precinct was relatively empty except for a couple of desk officers working late and an officer manning the reception desk. Maya and Oscar quietly crossed the bullpen and went into the men's locker room. One officer was taking a shower but was out of their view. Maya knew that as long as she heard the water running, they would be safe.

Oscar pointed to a locker at the end of a row numbered sixty-five. "That's Reyes's locker." There was a padlock on it.

Maya turned to Oscar and folded her arms. "You know everything about hacking into a computer, what do you know about breaking into a locker?"

"I got this," Oscar said, racing out of the room and returning a few minutes later with a bolt cutter.

Maya arched an eyebrow. "Where did you get that?"

"The trunk of my car. You never know when you might need one," he answered matter-of-factly.

"I'd like to see what else you have in the trunk of your car," Maya said with a smile.

"Maybe when we're engaged," Oscar said. "In the meantime, I'll remain a man of mystery."

Suddenly the water in the shower stopped.

Maya grabbed Oscar by the shirtsleeve and pulled him around the corner just as they saw a glimpse of a man in a white towel round the corner, his feet padding on the tile floor as he left a small trail of water behind him. He twirled the lock on his own locker and opened it. Just as Maya peered around to see what he was doing, the officer, who was young and muscular, dropped his towel. Maya almost let out an audible gasp. She closed her eyes and turned away, thankful that she and Oscar had not busted open the lock on Mateo's locker because this guy had the one right next to it and surely would have noticed.

They waited for what seemed like an eternity for the officer to dress himself and then stand, staring at himself in the mirror, checking his nose hairs and spraying cologne on his thick neck. He obviously had a late date. Finally, when he was satisfied with how sexy he looked, he sauntered out of the locker room.

Maya and Oscar came out of hiding and had Mateo's locker opened within seconds.

Maya crinkled her nose as she sifted through sweaty T-shirts and jock straps until finally, buried beneath a pile of dirty gym clothes, she found a cell phone. She pulled it out.

"He left his phone here?" Oscar said, dumbfounded.

"Look at the protective case. It has a floral print. I'm

guessing, since Mateo is a macho guy, as you say, he wouldn't have such a feminine-looking cell phone case. This isn't his."

"Then whose is it?"

"It has to be Maisie's. He probably pocketed it at the crime scene."

Maya tapped the screen. The numbers and letters for the passcode popped up. Maya wracked her brain trying to come up with a password Maisie might plausibly use.

"Do you know her birthday?" Oscar asked.

Maya shook her head. "No."

She tried a few number combinations.

None worked.

"What's your password?" Oscar asked.

"VKVKVK," Maya said. "My daughter's initials three times."

"Maisie didn't have kids."

"I know that, Oscar, but you asked me! What's yours?"

"I don't want to say."

"Why not? I just told you mine, which I find very disturbing, because now you have access to my phone and you're a borderline stalker."

Oscar struggled a bit and then relented. "Okay, it's ODLVMK."

"Why wouldn't you want to tell me that?"

"Think about it."

"OD could be your initials."

Oscar nodded, embarrassed.

"LV?"

"Loves . . ." Oscar mumbled.

Maya thought about it some more. "MK . . . Oh my god, Oscar! Oscar Dunford loves Maya Kendrick?"

"You *made* me tell you!"

"I want you to change that as soon as we're done here."

"Did Maisie have a boyfriend?"

"Yes, a guy named Spencer Jennings. Try his initials three times."

It didn't work.

"We're never going to figure this out. It could be her grandmother or a cousin or her favorite pop star or just some random numbers strung together that make absolutely no sense. . . ."

"Was there someone else besides her boyfriend she might have thought about all the time?"

"No, she . . . ," Maya stopped. "Wait a minute. Her sister was secretly dating a married man, Maisie's boss, and Maisie wasn't happy about it at all. . . . I thought it was because she was so uptight and moralistic, but maybe . . . maybe she was secretly in love with him and that's the reason she didn't approve of her sister seeing him!"

Maya tried *John*, then *Hicks*, both to no avail.

Oscar watched her curiously. "The password has to be six numbers or letters."

Maya kept trying different variations, even MPLVJH, *Maisie Portman loves John Hicks*, like Oscar's password, but predictably she had no luck. Maybe it was Hicks's birthday, but Maya had no idea when he was born. Finally, she was about to give up when something popped into her head. When she and Sandra were leaving the Hicks house, she remembered Sandra mentioning that Maisie called him Johnny. It was worth a shot.

Maya typed in *Johnny*.

Six letters.

The home screen on the cell phone suddenly appeared.

Oscar clapped his hands. "You did it!"

Maya clicked on Maisie's texts and quickly began scrolling down them. There were dozens, if not hundreds of back-and-forth texts between Maisie and her sister, Chelsea, the same ones Sandra had found on Chelsea's phone in the hotel room. Maisie was threatening to expose Chelsea's affair with Principal Hicks on her website, and Chelsea kept begging her not to destroy his marriage, which she feared, rightfully so, might ruin her own relationship with him. Maisie was pigheaded and unyielding and refused to abide by her sister's pleas, mostly out of spite and jealousy. No wonder Chelsea was so single-minded in getting her hands on Maisie's phone when she had first hired Maya. She didn't want evidence of the affair leaking out if someone else came across their texts.

Further down, Maya saw a phone number associated with another series of texts.

Her heart sank.

Her stomach churned.

She suddenly felt like she was going to be physically ill.

There were six of them.

Each one more desperate than the last.

Please listen to reason, Maisie. Think about what you're doing.

Why won't you answer my texts? We need to talk about this!

You will ruin lives if you do this, Maisie.

I am warning you. Don't do anything you will regret.

If you go through with this, I will come after you.

This is my last warning. If you do this, you are a dead woman.

That was the last one.

And then nothing.

There was no name associated with the phone number from Maisie's list of contacts.

But it didn't matter.

Because Maya knew the number.

She had been calling it for years.

The number belonged to Frances Turner.

CHAPTER FORTY-SIX

Maya was in a fog as she drove back to her office from the police precinct. She had heartburn from the pepperoni and was feeling sick to her stomach, but not from the pizza. At a stoplight, she picked up her phone from the passenger's seat and texted Sandra. She didn't want to be alone right now and asked if Sandra would meet her at the office.

Sandra quickly replied that she would be happy to come to her and asked for fifteen minutes to finish feeding her sons dinner.

Fourteen minutes later, when Maya pulled up in front of the office building, she spotted Sandra's Audi already parked out front. The woman sure was prompt. Maya got out of the car, entered the building, and took the stairs up to the second floor where she found Sandra waiting for her outside the door.

"I got here as soon as I could," Sandra said breathlessly. "Your text struck me as ominous, like something was wrong."

"That's an understatement," Maya mumbled as she unlocked the door and ushered Sandra inside and closed the door behind them. "Have a seat."

"Did I do something wrong . . . again?" Sandra asked tentatively.

Maya couldn't help but smile as she crossed behind her desk. "No, Sandra, you're fine."

Sandra sat tentatively in the chair facing Maya's desk that was reserved for clients.

Maya didn't offer her coffee or water. She just plopped down and dropped her head in her hands.

Sandra slowly leaned forward. "Whatever it is, it must be really bad."

Maya nodded, her hands still pressed against her face. She took a deep breath, exhaled slowly, and then set her hands down on her desk. "It's Frances."

"Is she in labor? Did you just come from the hospital?" Sandra gasped, quickly sitting straight up in her chair. Worry lines suddenly appeared on her forehead. "Is she okay? Are there complications?"

"This has nothing to do with the pregnancy. It's something far more serious."

And with that, Maya started babbling about everything she had just learned.

The doctored police report.

Maisie Portman's cell phone in Detective Reyes's locker.

The threatening texts from Frances.

Sandra's expression went from curious to surprise to utter shock all within a matter of seconds.

When Maya finished, Sandra sat back in her chair, her head spinning. "Are you saying I was right? About Detective Reyes?"

Maya nodded solemnly. "Pretty much."

"And Frances was in on it?"

"Kind of looks that way."

It was hard saying it out loud.

Maya still couldn't get her head around the fact that Frances, her business partner, her best friend, who for years had had her back when they were police officers and when they opened their own shingle as private eyes, was a dirty cop too. Like Mateo. Like her husband, Max.

"I don't understand. How did Frances—?"

"When she left the department and came to work with me, I remember she was decidedly vague about the reason. She told me she was tired of answering to sexist male superiors, tired of hitting the glass ceiling every time she put in for a promotion. I remember thinking at the time that it didn't make sense to me. A lot of women advanced to sergeant and lieutenant. We even had a female captain at one point. The world's changed. I thought maybe that was just an excuse, that she really wanted to focus on her relationship with Vinnie, maybe have a kid, get a job where she could make her own schedule, that's what I let myself believe. . . ."

"But your gut was telling you something else?"

"It was just strange, how she left. It was such a quick decision and so out of the blue. She had worked so hard to rise up through the ranks and then she just threw it all away. I just had trouble buying it, and then, when she got pregnant earlier this year, I finally let go of my suspicions. I said to myself, 'See, you were wrong. Frances wants a family, and working with me will allow her to devote more time to that, no more night shifts, no more working holidays, I can pick up the slack when she's not here. . . .' But now I know I was right. I think she quit because she had gotten involved in the rampant corruption plaguing the department. I think the walls were starting to close in and she had to get out. . . . It was a self-preservation move."

"So why did Mateo stay? If the Internal Affairs division was getting close to breaking the corruption scandal wide-open, and he was feeling the heat too, wouldn't he have left as well?"

Maya shrugged. "Who knows? My best guess is arrogance. The guy thinks he's invincible and can probably weather any storm, which this is shaping up to be apparently, according to my husband, Max."

"But that still doesn't explain how any of this is connected to Maisie Portman supposedly hanging herself in her office? You said yourself there was no connection to the high school, and that Maisie only wrote stories on her website that were directly related to either a student or teacher."

"That's when I thought it was just Mateo. The minute I saw those texts from Frances on Maisie's phone, it all became very clear. . . . Vinnie, he's the connection."

"Wait, Coach Vinnie?"

Maya nodded. "Frances's boyfriend. The father of her baby."

Sandra gasped as the realization hit her like a freight train barreling toward the station with no hand brake. "Coach Vinnie!"

"That's right," Maya said, her head still clouded by the revelation of Frances's heartbreaking betrayal.

Sandra leaped to her feet. "Maisie must have found out what was happening at the department, maybe through a friend or contact who worked there, or in the Internal Affairs division, and she was about to drop the bomb because Frances was carrying Coach Vinnie's baby! That was her angle! I can see the headline now! 'Football Coach's Baby Mama Caught Up in Police Corruption Scandal!'"

"I used to get after Vanessa all the time for visiting the site to read all about the latest gossip at school, and I remember a few times when Dirty Laundry was dropping hints about a whopper of a story that was coming, and how it involved someone in the athletic department, and how some big secrets were about to bring down some very powerful people in Portland. But there was nothing specific, only that a huge bomb was going to go off in a few days."

"Frances must have picked up on the clues!"

"She used to complain that Vinnie would barely speak to her in the morning whenever she spent the night at his place because he was so preoccupied with finding out what dirty laundry was going to be aired on the site. He was addicted to it!"

"It must have been quite a shock when Maisie began dangling hints about a story involving someone in the athletic department!"

Maya still couldn't believe what she was saying even as all the pieces began falling into place. "Frances had to have put two and two together. She probably enlisted some tech guy to trace the IP address of the Dirty Laundry site to Maisie just like I did, and that's when she started sending her the threatening texts."

Maya turned on her desktop and clicked on the Dirty Laundry site, which was still active. She scrolled down to Maisie's posts about the brewing scandal she was about to expose. Maya's eyes widened. "According to this post that went up about a week before she died, she was going to reveal her latest scoop on September twenty-eighth. But she didn't. She waited."

"September twenty-eighth? I remember that day because it was the day of my first PTA meeting as president."

"Why did she stay silent?" Maya mused.

Sandra's face darkened. "She didn't."

"What?"

"She didn't stay silent. She went with a bigger story. My husband's sex scandal down in Washington!"

"I'm sorry . . . ," Maya said, shifting uncomfortably.

"Forget it. The whole world knows now. She probably decided to postpone her police-corruption story until all the fervor over my troubles died down, which gave Frances the time she needed to take care of the problem."

"Wait," Maya said, scooting her chair closer and fervently tapping on her keyboard.

Sandra circled around the desk and hovered over her shoulder.

Maya brought her calendar up on the screen. "That's the day we found Maisie hanging in her office. Look down there. It reads, *Frances, doctor's appointment*. She took the whole afternoon off, and I didn't see her until the next morning. I thought it was strange she had a doctor's appointment, because she had just had her ultrasound a few days before and everything checked out fine. I asked her if anything was wrong when she called and told me she was on her way to the doctor and she said no, that it was just a routine appointment. I remember thinking how awfully close it was to her last appointment."

"She was lying," Sandra said quietly.

"We can certainly check with her doctor to find out, but I'm guessing that you're right."

Sandra was starting to get excited. "Then if she *was* lying, she has no alibi. She could have gone to Maisie Portman's office, killed her, and then staged the whole suicide and—" Sandra abruptly stopped talking as she saw the revolted look on Maya's face. "I'm sorry . . ."

Maya collected herself and shifted into detective mode. "No, we need to figure this out. The fact she's my best friend is irrelevant."

Sandra heard her words, but Maya's body language didn't seem to agree. The truth was killing her, and she had every reason to feel overwhelmed, disgusted, and betrayed.

Maya stood up, her mind meticulously tracking the probable course of events in her mind. "Frances was eight months pregnant and Maisie was an able-bodied woman. Doesn't seem natural that Frances could overpower her."

"But as a police officer, Frances surely would have been trained in how to subdue someone, right?"

Maya nodded. "Yes. But all the training in the world doesn't prepare you for being a mere few weeks from giving birth. I'm having trouble buying Frances could single-handedly kill Maisie and stage the suicide, like lifting her up on the chair to tie a rope around her neck."

"Maybe she had help. Maybe Mateo did all the heavy

lifting. That's why he was the first on the scene when we called nine-one-one!"

"He was her coconspirator. He had just as much to lose if the truth got out. I'm betting he was the one who strangled Maisie and then the two of them staged the crime scene to look like a suicide together."

Suddenly they heard a thump coming from outside the office.

Sandra turned to go outside and check it out, but Maya sprang from behind her desk and intercepted her. "No, Sandra. You stay right here."

Sandra nodded nervously, and then Maya stepped gingerly over to the door and opened it as softly as she could. The door was old and creaky, so her efforts were for naught. She cautiously poked her head out into the darkened, shadowy hallway. There was nothing there. Glancing back and holding up a hand for Sandra to stay put, she edged her whole body out into the hallway and looked around. She instinctively reached into her bag for her handgun, and raising it up in front of her, she made her way down the hall, around the corner to the old service elevator, to make sure there was no one lurking in a corner somewhere. Satisfied the coast was clear, she doubled back the other way, passing the office and creeping down to the other end of the hall and finding nothing. Since it was well after eight in the evening, no one else seemed to be working in the office building. She reholstered her gun and walked back to her office.

The moment she entered she knew something was wrong.

Sandra was not where she had left her.

"Sandra?"

She stepped farther inside and suddenly the door slammed shut behind her, startling her. She spun around to see Sandra wedged up against the wall behind the door, a man's hand clamped firmly over her mouth, a gun pressed against her right temple.

As he pushed Sandra forward, his face fell into the light.

It was Detective Mateo Reyes.

CHAPTER FORTY-SEVEN

Maya tried her best to stay calm and stone-faced. She didn't want to give the slightest indication to Mateo that he had sent shivers down her spine and a healthy dose of fear through her heart.

Sandra's eyes were popped open, and she was shaking as she struggled in his strong grip. He took his hand away from her mouth and shoved her toward Maya, who caught her as she stumbled to keep her from falling to the floor.

"What do you want, Mateo?"

He smirked as he pointed the gun at both of them. "What do I *want*? You don't think I heard everything you two were saying in here? I was right outside the door listening! I came by the station earlier tonight to catch up on some paperwork and spied you and that goober Oscar rifling through my locker. I've been following you ever since. I think you know what I want. I want you two out of my hair!"

Maya could feel Sandra's manicured nails cutting into her arm because she was squeezing so tight. Maya knew she had to keep calm so Sandra would not fall apart.

Mateo's eyes narrowed as he formulated some kind of plan in his head, and then he gestured toward the door with his gun. "Come on, let's go."

Maya took Sandra by the hand and led her out the door. She was still shaking. Mateo followed behind them and prodded them to move faster by poking Maya in the back with the barrel of his gun as they made their way down the hall. They took the elevator to the first floor and headed out the door.

Once outside, Mateo nodded toward a gray van parked across the street. "Over there. Move it."

Maya knew once they were in that van, the chances of them surviving would drop precipitously, but they had no choice. Mateo had the upper hand at the moment.

He pushed Sandra toward the driver's side door. "You. You're driving."

Sandra froze and stared at the van. "Is it an automatic or stick shift? I can't drive a stick shift. I tried to learn once, but I ended up stripping the gears of my father's Jeep Wrangler when I was sixteen."

Maya felt sorry for Sandra. She was a bundle of nerves, but there was nothing she could do for her with a gun pressed into the small of her back.

"You're fine! Just get in!" Mateo spit out.

Sandra opened the door and climbed behind the wheel.

Mateo led Maya around to the back. "Open it."

Maya pulled the back doors of the van open, and before she could see what was in there, Mateo roughly lifted her up and gave her a violent shove, sending her hurtling across the hard metal floor inside. She banged her head against the wall of the van. Mateo jumped in, slammed the doors shut, while keeping the gun trained on her the whole time. There was a rolled-up tarp, some duct tape, and a shovel piled in the corner. None of those items made her feel any better.

Mateo shouted up front to Sandra as he tossed her the ignition key. "Drive."

"Where are we going?"

"I'll tell you where to go. Just head for the Ninety-Five."

They were going to get on the freeway.

Where was he taking them?

Maya feared he would exit onto a country road toward some wooded area where he could easily dispose of them.

Sandra turned the ignition key, and the van roared to life. She pulled away from the curb and drove down the street, turning toward the highway on-ramp.

Mateo bent down and picked up the roll of duct tape. He kept his gun pointed at Maya as he used his teeth to tear open a piece of tape and then with one hand wrapped it tightly around her ankles. He did the same with her wrists. Once she was securely bound, he finally lowered the gun.

"Keep quiet or I'll tape your mouth shut too," he spit out.

Maya didn't say a word.

Confident she would no longer be a problem, he focused on Sandra, who had just pulled the van onto the 95 freeway heading north.

"Keep going until you get to Exit Sixty-Three."

Maya knew that was the exit for Gray and New Gloucester. He would probably have her take Maine 115 west, to the Sebago Lakes region via North Windham, where there were plenty of rural roads and thick woods, the perfect area to dump two bodies late at night. It was getting foggy, and at one point Sandra had to use the wipers to remove the heavy mist settling on the windshield.

Maya tried reaching for the gun holstered on her leg but it was difficult with her hands and feet bound, but she tried anyway. However, in her desperate effort to retrieve her weapon, she made too much noise and attracted Mateo's attention so she was forced to stop when he turned around and stared at her suspiciously. She waited until his back was turned to her again before she tried something else. She studied the contents of the van. The tarp. The shovel. Nothing useful. Then she remembered her car keys in her pocket. They were much easier to get her hands on than her gun, so she shoved a hand in her pants pocket, stretching her fingers as far as they could go until her middle finger was touching the key ring. She managed to drag the keys toward her until she was able to get a firm hold on them. Then, slowly, so they wouldn't jangle, she removed them from her pocket and then used one of the keys to saw through the tape around her ankles. She was about halfway through when Mateo turned around to check up on her again. She stopped suddenly, covering the keys with her hand. His cop brain instinctively knew she was up to something, but he couldn't figure out what it was yet.

"Exit Sixty-Three is just up ahead," Sandra said dismally, almost resigned to their fate.

Mateo swiveled back around to make sure she was following his driving instructions, and Maya got back to work at cutting loose her bonds. She felt the van turning onto the exit ramp. Time was running out. She was just about all the way through the tape when Mateo suddenly spun around and saw what she was doing. He angrily aimed his gun at her.

As Maya pulled her legs apart, snapping the tape free, she screamed, "Sandra, crank the wheel!"

Sandra didn't even hesitate. With all her might, she jerked the steering wheel to the right, and the van violently swerved. Mateo immediately lost his balance and went crashing into the side of the van. In an instant, with her hands still taped up, Maya flopped down on her back and lashed out with a scissor kick, one foot smashing into Mateo's face and the other nailing the hand that was holding the gun. Mateo automatically reached up with both hands to protect his face, and the gun clattered to the metal floor of the van.

Mateo quickly realized what Maya was doing, and with blood running from his busted nose and his eyes wild with fury, he made a lunge for the gun, but Maya was already on her feet and used her body like a battering ram, plowing into him, and they both smashed into the back of the driver's seat. Sandra screamed.

"Sandra, pull over!"

The van screeched to a stop.

Maya was at a disadvantage with her hands still tied, and Mateo knew it. He wrestled her to the floor and wrapped his big fleshy hands around her neck and started squeezing. Maya fought to breathe, but spotted the gun lying on the floor just a few inches from them.

Sandra unhooked her seat belt and turned around to see what was happening. Maya desperately tried to signal toward the gun with her eyes, which were just about to roll up in her head as Mateo choked the life out of her.

Sandra was frozen in fear, not picking up on Maya's last-ditch effort before succumbing and slipping into unconsciousness.

Finally, as if a miracle had been bestowed upon them, Sandra spotted the gun lying on the floor near her. She gasped and made a grab for it. She stood up and aimed it at the back of Mateo's head.

"Stop it, Mateo, or I'll shoot!"

He loosened his grip on Maya's neck.

Maya, relieved, turned over on her side and began coughing.

Mateo slowly stood up and turned to Sandra, whose hand was visibly shaking as she held the gun on him. He sneered. "What are you going to do, shoot me?"

Sandra nodded.

"Have you ever held a gun before, Sandra?"

She shook her head.

"I can see that. It's one thing to see it on TV, but it's an entirely different thing to fire one in real life."

Sandra tried maintaining a poker face, but her emotions from this whole ordeal were getting the best of her and tears began welling up in her eyes.

"I don't think you have the guts to actually kill me, what do you think, Sandra?"

She didn't answer him. She just kept trying to unsteadily keep the heavy gun pointed at him, but it was getting harder, and the tears were now streaming down her cheeks.

"You know what I think, Sandra? I think you're not going to shoot me," Mateo sneered.

Sandra finally lowered the gun, defeated. "You're right," she cried, staring down at the floor of the van. But before Mateo had a chance to snatch the gun from her possession, Sandra raised her eyes back up at him. "But she will."

Mateo looked at her confused, and then Maya pressed the barrel of her own gun against the back of his neck and whispered, "With pleasure."

Sandra had bought her just enough time to unholster her own gun from her thigh, which proved to be much easier now that her legs were free.

Mateo slowly raised his hands up in the air and Maya ordered him to get on the floor as Sandra used the duct tape to secure his hands and feet and for good measure, she slapped a thick piece of tape across his mouth so they wouldn't have to hear him talk anymore. Once that was done, Maya kept watch as Sandra got back behind the wheel.

"Are we going to the police?" Sandra asked.

"Not yet. We have to make a house call first."

Within minutes they were back on the 95 freeway, heading south, and were soon rolling slowly down a residential street to an apartment building where Sandra managed to find a parking spot right out front.

Maya jumped out of the back of the van and called to Sandra, "Keep an eye on him. I won't be long."

Sandra nodded, getting more comfortable holding a gun, which she kept aimed right at Mateo's head, who was slumped over on the floor, knowing what was ahead for him.

Maya took the stairs up to the second floor and steeled herself as she stopped in front of a unit and rapped loudly on the door.

A few seconds later, Frances opened it.

"Maya, what are you doing here so late?"

"Were you expecting Mateo?"

"Mateo? What are you talking about?"

"It's over, Frances. I know everything."

There was a moment's hesitation as Frances considered her next move, but it only took another glance at Maya's hardened face, the disappointment and feeling of betrayal in her blazing eyes, for Frances to believe it truly was over. She grabbed her belly, and Maya thought she was going to fake labor pains in order to gain some last-minute sympathy, but she didn't. She just held on to her pregnant belly and looked down, ashamed of herself.

"Where is he?" Frances whispered.

"Down in the van. Sandra's watching him. He tried to kill us."

Frances gasped and looked back up. "What?"

"He was trying to take care of loose ends. Like you did with poor Maisie Portman."

"I never wanted any of this to ever touch you, Maya, I swear. Mateo promised he wouldn't hurt you."

"He lied," Maya said coldly.

At that moment, a woman appeared at Maya's side. She was rather stern-looking, in her midforties. She wasn't wearing a uniform, but she still gave off the air of a police officer. "This is Sally Jordan from Internal Affairs. Have you two met yet?"

Sally didn't offer her hand or greet her with a smile. She just pulled out a pair of handcuffs.

"I called Sally on the way over here and let her know what was going on. She's here to take you in."

Frances didn't argue. She simply opened the door to let them both inside.

"Give me a minute to change before we go, would you, please?" Frances quietly asked.

Sally nodded and replied gruffly, "Make it quick."

Suddenly Coach Vinnie ambled in from the bedroom. "We got any more Bud Lights in the fridge, babe?" He stopped at the sight of Maya and the strange nonresponsive woman next to her. "Hey, Maya, you're just in time. Bottom of the seventh. Red Sox up by two."

"We can't stay, Vinnie," Maya said softly.

Vinnie looked around, his eyes settling on his shattered girlfriend, who was barely managing to hold it together at this point. "Frances, is something wrong?"

Maya knew then that Coach Vinnie had been in the dark this whole time about his fiancée's criminal misdeeds.

And she hated to have to be the one to break the news to him as IA officer Sally Ross escorted Frances into the bedroom to get her changed and to make sure she didn't try to climb out a window to flee down the fire escape.

CHAPTER FORTY-EIGHT

The United flight from Portland to Washington, DC, was predictably delayed, taking off almost ninety minutes past its scheduled departure time due to a vague maintenance issue. Once Sandra was buckled into her first-class seat and the small commuter jet was finally airborne and heading south to the nation's capital, she wondered if this rash decision had been the right one. She had been up all night, unable to sleep, but by morning, after getting the boys off to school, she had decided it was the right time to do this. She cleared her calendar, booked the flight at the last minute on her laptop, and then, without packing an overnight bag, she got in her car and drove straight to the airport.

When the plane landed just after noon, she walked straight outside to the taxi line, and within minutes was riding in the back of a yellow cab zipping along Interstate

66 east, listening to her driver drone on about the latest band of protesters outside the White House clogging up traffic on Pennsylvania Avenue. Forty minutes later, she was dropped off in front of the Russell Senate Office Building on Constitution Avenue. After alerting security that she was there to see her husband, the junior U.S. senator from the state of Maine, she waited in the magnificent rotunda area, watching the hustle and bustle of press, lobbyists, pages, and politicians conducting business and interviews on what appeared to be a particularly busy day.

Finally, after almost fifteen minutes, Sandra spotted the smug smile of her husband's aide Preston Lambert approaching.

"Mrs. Wallage," he said brightly. "To what do we owe this pleasure?"

She knew what he really wanted to say was, *What the hell are you doing here?* But he was too smart to let his real feelings come into the light.

"I need to speak with Stephen," she said coldly.

He was a little thrown off guard by her abrupt demeanor but worked hard to cover with a breezy air of jocularity. "Does Stephen know you're in town, because I swear I heard him mention you were home in Portland this morning?"

"I just arrived."

"I see," he said, trying to read her face and figure out just what this was all about.

Preston led her into the elevator, and on the short ride up to the office, he tried his hand at some small talk. "I heard the police made an arrest in that nasty business involving the vice principal's death at the high school up there."

"Yes, they did," Sandra answered politely, but in a clipped tone.

Finally realizing he was failing miserably at turning on the charm for his boss's wife, Preston gave up, and they walked the rest of the way down the hall in silence after getting off the elevator.

Once they were inside the reception area of Stephen's senate office, Preston absentmindedly adjusted his tie. "Can I get you some coffee?"

Sandra shook her head. "No, thank you."

"He's just wrapping up a meeting. He shouldn't be too long," Preston said, still a little discombobulated by Sandra's surprise appearance in DC.

"Hello, Mrs. Wallage," said a cute, young African American girl in her early twenties from behind a desk. It was another aide, Suzanne. This one she liked, so she offered a warm smile.

"Nice to see you again, Suzanne. I love that blouse."

"Thank you! I got it on sale at Nordstrom Rack! They have the best stuff!"

Preston grimaced that Sandra seemed more pleased to see a lowly assistant. It would be so much easier for him if he possessed a genuine personality like Suzanne.

After ten more minutes, the door to Stephen's office opened and he escorted out a gorgeous woman in her thirties, confident, immaculately dressed in a perfectly tailored business suit. He had a hand resting on her lower back.

"Get me whatever information you can on the drug trials before the vote," he said as she turned and shook his hand.

"Will do, Stephen, I appreciate you seeing me on such short notice," the woman said.

Stephen, who had obviously been alerted to his wife's arrival by Preston, led the woman over to Sandra. "Darling, this is Deborah Crowley from the Commonwealth Fund. This is my wife, Sandra."

The woman grabbed Sandra's hand and pumped it. "I've heard so much about you."

Sandra went right into politician's wife mode. "It's a pleasure to meet you, Ms. Crowley. I love the work that you people do."

There was a slight awkward pause after they got the pleasantries out of the way as Stephen stared at her, still trying to figure out what she was doing here, like his irritating aide, Preston. Once the daily schedule was set, no one in the office liked any disruptions or distractions. Except Suzanne, who seemed honestly happy to see Sandra.

Once Deborah Crowley was gone, Stephen took Sandra into his arms, planted a kiss on her cheek, and then whisked her into his office, stopping only to say to Suzanne, "Hold my calls."

He shut the door behind them. "Why didn't you tell me you were making a trip down here?"

"Because I just decided to come this morning."

"Did you drop your luggage off at the apartment first?"

"I'm not staying. I've booked a return flight later this afternoon. I want to be back by the time the boys come home for dinner tonight."

"I see," he said warily.

They both sat down on the couch.

Stephen studied her face. "So what is it? Is it something serious?"

His eyes flicked away as if he was struggling with how to act, not sure what was coming next, or if he was prepared to hear it.

Sandra took a deep breath and exhaled. "I think we should separate."

The color drained from Stephen's face.

She couldn't tell if it was because she wanted a separation or because he suddenly feared the political fallout of a separation.

"Why?"

"*Why?* Stephen, you know why."

"If this is about that false rumor on that muckraking website—"

"It's not just about that. This has been a long time coming. I'm not saying we should officially file papers or anything like that, I just need a breather, that's all. I've been thinking about a lot of things lately, and it feels right to just take a break."

"For how long?"

"I don't know."

His mind raced. He despised not being in control, and right now he was not in control. He reached out to take her hand, but she demurred and moved it away.

"Wow . . . ," he said, stunned she had so obviously rebuffed him. "So the fact that I want to work on our marriage and try to fix whatever it is that's broken, that doesn't matter to you right now?"

"I just need time."

He knew he wasn't going to get anywhere with her, at least not now. So he conceded defeat and just nodded his head. "Okay . . . I guess I'll stay at the apartment here until you figure out what you need to figure out."

"Thank you for understanding."

His phone buzzed. It was a text. "Preston is going crazy not knowing what's going on in here. He's trying to get me to my next appointment."

"Well, I would hate to make Preston's life more difficult, so I'm going to go now."

Sandra stood up.

Stephen sat on the couch a moment longer, still reeling
from Sandra's sudden and unexpected announcement.
But then he hauled himself up and looked into Sandra's
eyes. He had a knowing, guilty look on his face, like he
was painfully aware why all of this was happening. Sandra gave him a wan smile and then turned and left the office.

"Goodbye, Suzanne," she said as she brusquely passed
a confused-looking Preston and walked out the door.

"'Bye, Mrs. Wallage!" Suzanne called after her.

As she marched down the hall toward the elevator, she
faintly heard Preston exclaim, "What was all that about?"

She had a few hours to kill before her flight, so she
took a taxi to the Lincoln Memorial. It was her favorite
monument in all of Washington. Whenever she was in
town, she loved to sit on the steps, just under the watchful
eye of Honest Abe, and behold all the landmarks. She
wondered if perhaps she had been too rash in her decision. The last few weeks had profoundly changed her; her
friendship with Maya had opened her eyes to a whole
new world she had yet to explore. But did that mean she
had to upend her marriage in order to do that?

Her instinct was telling her this had been the right call.

But she always could be counted on to second-guess
herself.

However, after a quick lunch alone and some retail
therapy at Nordstrom Rack, when she was back in a taxi
on her way to Washington Dulles and her flight home to
Maine, her phone lit up with a *Washington Post* breaking-

news headline. "U.S. Senator Admits to Using Taxpayer Money to Hush Up Sexual Harrassment Claim."

Sandra stared at the headline.

She didn't have to open her phone and read the whole story.

She had already pored over all the details on the Dirty Laundry website, which first broke the story that now a major newspaper was finally confirming.

She stared out the window knowing that, yes, she had made the right call.

CHAPTER FORTY-NINE

When Maya asked Coach Vinnie to dinner, she had tried to talk him into meeting her at a nice, fine-dining establishment in the Old Port, but he had politely declined, opting for a hidden corner booth in a loud, cheap diner near his home that boasted tasty burgers and salty fries, but above all, a modicum of privacy. It was true Coach Vinnie was a no-frills kind of guy to begin with, who didn't like having to wear a button-up shirt to eat, but most important to him these days was that he didn't want to risk the stares of the locals, who would undoubtedly give him pitying looks, or even worse, come up to him and tell him he was in their thoughts and prayers, or if there was anything they could do to make his life a little easier, to please let them know. Vinnie didn't want anything from these people, especially their pity.

After Frances's arrest, the police had quickly concluded

that Vinnie had been an innocent party. Frances had jumped through a lot of hoops to keep it that way. She knew the man she loved was dedicated to his job at the school and in many ways being a football coach defined who he was, and he worshipped the opportunity to make a living doing what he loved most. Maya knew a part of why Frances went to such desperate lengths to put a lid on the scandal that was threatening to boil over wasn't simply due to self-preservation. She was also protecting her partner from suffering because of her own actions.

Vinnie fundamentally knew this, but that didn't make adjusting to life without Frances any easier. He vowed to stand by her during her trial, but Maya was already seeing cracks in this commitment as the allegations and charges came so startlingly into focus after her arrest. Vinnie publicly maintained his support, but she had heard through a few mutual friends that he was stunned by the breadth of crimes Frances and Mateo had been involved with, and he was starting to distance himself. However, because of the fact that they were about to be parents together, he knew that would inexplicably keep their lives entwined forever.

When she first arrived to find him already pounding down a strawberry milkshake at the diner, she wasn't sure if she should hug him or just shake his hand, but mercifully he stood up and hugged her first. She sat down opposite him in the cherry-red booth and picked up a menu. There was some awkward small talk about the team's recent winning streak followed by a polite inquiry about Vanessa and how she had been doing, but once a generous amount of comfort food had been ordered off the plastic menu, Maya got right down to business.

"How have you been holding up?"

Vinnie chugged the rest of his shake and set the large glass down on the table and shrugged. "Rotten."

"I'm sure it's been tough."

"I miss her. That woman I'm reading about in the *Portland Press Herald* every day is not the woman I've been dating for the past three years."

"I know . . . I've been struggling with the same thing. We worked so closely together. I keep asking myself, 'How could I not know what she was doing?'"

"When she was at home, she was so playful and sweet and so excited to be a mother and . . . then to find out she was capable of murder . . ." Vinnie sighed. "I'll never understand it."

"Have you gone to see her?"

Vinnie nodded. He was a tough, resilient man, not one to outwardly display any kind of emotion, but all of this was just too much for him, and he couldn't stop himself from crying. He quickly tried to wipe away the tears streaming down his cheeks with his hammy fist. "I had to. We have a lot to talk about, a lot of decisions to make."

Maya was afraid to ask, but she had to know. It had been first and foremost in her mind as all of this unfolded. "What's going to happen with the baby?"

"I'm taking her. I'm going to raise her," he said, a smile slowly creeping open as he thought about his soon-to-be newborn. It was probably the first time he had smiled in a while.

"*Her?* I thought she was having a boy."

"Doctor misread the ultrasound. What she thought indicated a boy was just a shadow," he chuckled. "You know what? I kinda wanted a girl all along."

"Congratulations."

"My parents live in Brunswick. They'll take her when

I'm at work. They're obviously upset about Frances, but they're excited to be grandparents and a big part of the baby's life. She'll be raised right and be well loved."

"I have no doubt," Maya said, reaching over and squeezing his hand.

She went to pull her hand away, but Vinnie grabbed it and desperately held it. He wasn't ready to let go. He needed a friend. They sat there, clutching each other, in silence, until the waitress appeared with their burgers and fries. Maya took a bite of her bacon cheeseburger, swallowed, and then looked at Vinnie. "I'd like to go see Frances."

Vinnie held his double burger in front of his mouth. He was chewing, his mouth closed, as ketchup dripped down over his chubby fingers. He stared past her and didn't answer her question at first, but then dropped his burger on the plate, wiped his hands with his napkin, and said softly, "She's not ready, Maya."

Maya nodded. "Okay . . ."

"I told her it might be a good idea to talk to you, maybe you can help her in some way, maybe be a character witness at her trial and testify about the Frances who was your friend and coworker, not this monster who was so corrupt and . . ." Vinnie stopped himself and pressed the palms of his hands down on the table and fixed his eyes on Maya. "She's too guilt-ridden right now about all she's done. She told me she just can't face you. . . . Maybe with a little time . . ."

"Well, I'll be here when she's ready."

Now it was Maya's turn to get emotional.

Like Vinnie, she too was having trouble reconciling the Frances who was about to go on trial for corruption and murder and the Frances who was her closest girlfriend, the girlfriend who worried about her emotional well-being after her husband went to prison, the god-mother to Vanessa, the Dolly Levi always on the lookout for a man to fix Maya up with when she became single again. That Frances, her BFF, was the one who she was desperately going to miss seeing every day, and her heart was broken over it.

CHAPTER FIFTY

Sandra knew the boys would take the news of the separation hard, but at the same time, they were resilient
and strong and would adjust to the change. By now, the
news of their father's scandal had cycled through two
whole news days and was now receding into the dustbin
of history along with all the misdeeds of countless other
politicians. It had been rough at school weathering the
taunts of students, but remarkably the press focused
solely on hounding Senator Wallage and not his two vul-
nerable teenage sons. For that, Sandra was grateful. Jack
put on a brave face when Stephen called, chitchatting
with his father amiably, ignoring the proverbial elephant
in the room. Ryan, on the other hand, was a bit harder on
his dad, questioning his judgment and integrity, and to
Stephen's credit, his father stayed on the phone and took

it like a man, promising his son he would try and do better.

Sandra knew he asked about her every time he called the house because she could hear the boys filling him in with what she was up to, how despite the surge of support, Sandra had ultimately decided to resign as the PTA president. She didn't want to be a distraction, or in any way become the focal point when it should always be about the well-being and education of the students. And although Principal Hicks remained in his position, his reputation had been severely diminished when the truth about his affair with Chelsea Portman came to light via some intrepid local reporters. His wife, Alice, left him and Chelsea ultimately dumped him. His job at the school was the only thing he had left to cling to, so he was holding on to it with all his might, despite the rumors that the school board was actively looking for a replacement to start next fall.

Sandra puttered in the kitchen, where her homemade Bolognese sauce bubbled in a pot on the stove as she boiled water in another to cook some fettuccini she had just made in her old-fashioned Italian-made pasta machine. She checked the wall clock. Her dinner guests were five minutes late. She opened a bottle of cabernet to let it breathe and set about whisking her own Italian vinaigrette dressing in a ceramic bowl for the salad that was chilling in the refrigerator.

The doorbell rang.

She heard Jack on the phone in the living room. "Dad, I've got to go. Okay, I'll tell her." After he hung up, he called into the kitchen. "Dad sends his love."

She couldn't help but smile.

That man was never going to give up.

"Get the door, will you, please?" Sandra called back.

As she picked up a small spoon to taste the dressing, she heard Jack open the door and greet their guests.

"Ryan, your pookie sweetie honey is here!" Jack yelled up the stairs.

She heard Vanessa laugh as Ryan pounded down the steps to greet her, probably ignoring his brother because he was too busy trying to steal a kiss.

"Is your mother in the kitchen?" she heard Maya ask.

"Yeah," Jack said. "Go on in. I'll be in the living room watching TV with the volume really loud so I don't have to hear these two suck face."

Maya appeared in the kitchen. "Sure smells good."

"It's nothing really. Just a simple pasta and sauce. It's my go-to-meal when I get home too late to whip up something fancier."

"Busy day?"

"Still dealing with the fallout. I thought I'd have a lot more free time after I resigned as PTA president, but it turns out Al Pacino was right in that Godfather movie. Every time I try to get out, they pull me back in!"

Maya chuckled. "And I thought the politics in Washington were bad enough." But then she caught herself. "Oh God, I'm sorry, I shouldn't have brought that up."

"It's fine. Really," Sandra said, pouring some wine into two glasses and handing one to Maya. "Stephen and I are talking . . . occasionally . . . at least when I forget to check the caller ID and just pick up the phone."

Maya grinned. "That's something."

"And how are you? How's business?" Sandra knew not to ask specifically about Frances. Vanessa had told her that her mother was still struggling and still hurting, so Sandra kept it vague so as not to tear the Band-Aid off the wound.

Maya sighed. "Fine. Until this week. Remarkably I just got two cases. Nothing too earth-shattering. An identity theft and another suspected infidelity case."

"You'll never go broke chasing after cheating spouses," Sandra said with a smile.

"Let's toast to that," Maya said, raising her glass of wine.

They clinked glasses and each took a sip.

"That's good," Maya said.

"I'm glad you like it. I have two more bottles. I hope you came here in an Uber."

"No, but as luck would have it, Vanessa has an impeccable driving record, at least for the four whole months she's had her license."

Sandra set her wine down on the counter and stirred the Bolognese sauce with a ladle.

They gossiped some more about the goings-on at school, and they were on their second glass of cabernet when Sandra started to suspect Maya was dancing around something she wanted to talk about. Sure enough, by the time Sandra reached for the bottle to refill Maya's glass that she hadn't even finished drinking yet, Maya had apparently worked up the nerve to finally come out with it.

"I was wondering . . ."

"Yes?"

It looked like she might lose her nerve.

"Maya, what is it?"

"I wasn't going to ask you about this tonight, but maybe it's the wine loosening me up."

"Well, keep drinking then. You've got me intrigued now."

"It's just that . . . these last few days I've been thinking a lot about you and me, and even though I hate to admit it, I miss you hanging around."

"Yes, I'll marry you. Just as soon as I get through divorcing Stephen, but only if the kids approve."

Maya laughed. "You know where I'm going with this."

"Yes, but I want to hear you say it."

"I need your help."

"God, I've been waiting so long for this!"

"Hold on. It's not like I'm offering you a full partnership or anything. . . ."

"I understand."

"It's just part-time for now, and the pay is *really* low. . . ."

"That's fine. Stephen's still paying all the bills."

"Good, because I may even have to defer your paycheck for a while, at least until I can catch up financially and get the business back in the black."

"I certainly can help with drumming up more business."

"So you'll do it?"

Sandra paused. "You know what? I'll have to think about it."

"Really?"

"Of course not! I'll do it!"

Maya shook her head. "I totally knew you would jump at this."

Sandra raised her wineglass. "Let's toast to our new partnership."

Maya pulled back her glass. "You didn't hear me. This is not a partnership. I'm the boss. You work for me."

"I heard you," Sandra said as she smiled and walked out of the kitchen. "Dinner's ready! Hey, guys, guess what? Maya asked me to join her private investigation firm! We're going to be partners!"